The Plantation Affair

By

Gregory Jonathan Scott

ISBN: 0991467434
ISBN-13: 978-0-9914674-3-3

DEDICATION

To Scott, as always, I love you and will never, ever hide that I do.
Now let's hold hands in public. Tomorrow we kiss.

To my comical and caring father William (Willy), who is my true
number one fan and has been ever since I can remember. His
enthusiasm and support with everything I've set out to do and
accomplished has been cherished and will always be held dear.
I hear you bragging about me from here, even to the people you
just met. I love that about you and it tells me you really care.
Thank you for letting me be me, dad. I love you for that, more
than you know.

To all those who have a difficult time understanding me, us, him,
her and them.

ACKNOWLEDGMENTS

Everybody who has been instrumental in the production of this project.

Chapter 1

In Logan's opinion, the morning sun broke horizon way before he thought it should have. He wasn't quite ready for its brilliance to invade his cozy dormancy just yet. In truth he was still sleepy from the restless stint he had last night. His mind was battling with his own personal problems, which made it difficult for him to fall asleep straightaway, as well as stay asleep.

The stray cat perched in front of his face all night long looking for attention didn't help the situation much either. Off and on throughout Logan's sleepless night, the weird cat groomed the hair on his head as if it thought he was in need of a bath. It's how they do it. Lickety, lick, lick, lick. Enough to drive anybody batty. The cat's tongue was loaded with tiny razor like daggers, so scarring irritation was inflicted with every lick when the tongue scraped across his scalp.

Logan was a couple hours shy of a good night's rest and his immobile body was telling him he should still be sleeping. The light outside the window seemed brighter than ever and was giving him a message that was far from saying 'go back to bed.'

Today being no different from any other morning, Logan's

eyes flickered erratically at the same time the rooster crowed to welcome in daybreak. By the looks of things, it was going to be another clear day aside from the dismal shadow that was normally brought on daily by the other servants working and living at the Royal Manor.

Georgia had many monstrous homes in the hills called plantations and because the house Logan tends to was one of the grandest in the village, he branded the owners as the Royal Family. Something quirky he came up with because coincidentally their last name is Royal and it seemed fitting to give them the significant title.

The other domestics that worked the big house on the hill are all rather unkind to Logan for some reason or another and he's not really clear as to why. He always figured that it was because his flesh tone was much lighter than theirs and that he should be picking cotton and addressing the boss as *Massah* a little differently than them. He never really gave much thought to it being any reason other than his caramel color, nor did he ever understand why there should be any difference. The year was eighteen eighty-three, so it seemed that this should no longer be a concern.

How much longer will this nonsense go on?

Logan didn't get it. The President abolished slavery years ago, but people still tried to get away with chaining the black family to the tree out back and whipping them if they didn't obey a direct order.

He lay blinking away the new days light in a rustic carriage house hayloft while waiting for the rap on the door that told him it was time to get up and begin his responsibilities the way a master's slave normally did. He was no slave or owned by anybody mind you, those days are gone thank God, but the situation he was in surely made him feel like one.

He worked very hard and didn't receive enough reward to compensate for the amount of work he actually did. He really didn't have reason to complain. Logan had food on the table and a roof over his head, as well as chickens and goats to call his friends. He loved them. Loved them all. They were more like his direct family than any person he knew.

3

He was placed at the Manor by a fluky draw, which started with his Mother.

Logan's small family existed of only his mother and him. His father, who he never really remembered, was blacker than black, the kind that was hunted by the Ku Klux Klan back in the day. His father's blessed soul went off to battle only a few years after Logan was born and never came back according to what his mother told him. Of course he believed her, she was his mother. It was a time just after slavery was abolished and black men were sent off to war as front runners in a fight for freedom. It didn't quite pan out as making much sense, 'we set you free to fight a battle so that we can be free'.

We, meaning them.

Logan mentioned his mother in past tense, because until recently she took care of him the best she could, with consideration of their state of affairs at the Plantation. All was good up until the day she was trampled to death by a runaway horse carriage startled by a white bandit that stole food from a corner merchant one sunny afternoon just over a year ago.

His mother was crossing the street with an apron full of fresh vegetables and fruits for the royal family when it happened. She never saw it coming. Within the split second she turned her head toward the thief as he ran by, she went down. Produce scattered across the cobblestone roadway as the carriage knocked her to the ground and dragged her a few hundred feet to her reported place of death.

That day was the worst day of Logan's life and it took many days after in order for him to get over his sudden loss. He'd always been bothered by how his life changed due to somebody else's selfish sin. This didn't make a bit of sense to him and neither did his other burden.

Logan didn't know if he would ever understand why God took his parents away from him at such a young age, but perhaps he knew Logan was going to be fine on his own. He was in this place for a reason and right now only God knows why and Logan was meant to figure it out as he went along with life.

Logan had always been grateful to the Royal family for letting him stay after his mother's untimely demise in the cross roads of Townsend Square, but every day he still wished for a better life for himself.

Because the family struck him as royal people, he secretly addressed them more formally as King Dante, Queen Priscilla and their only son, Prince Deklan. More quirky titles he engaged on the people he worked for.

Even though Logan's mother had skin as white as snow and it was rare for white flesh to be servants, the Royal family still hired her as an employee and assigned her to work in the kitchen to prepare the meals that were served to the royal table. She was the best cook on earth as far as Logan was concerned and it was evident by how strong he grew up to be. He wouldn't say that he was a gorgeous creature by any means, but his reflection in any looking glass gave back a strong square jaw line, full rose colored lips, a narrow nose from his mother's side and gray-green eyes that shimmered when presented with only a hint of gracious light. He was what many people referred to as a combo pack, because his parents were from opposite sides of the color spectrum. One white and one black. His mother always said he was as striking as his father and the smile on his face let her know that he was happy to hear that. She named him Logan, after his father. His father's name was actually Anglo. Yes – oddly different, however a twist on letter arrangement gave him the name he favors.

Logan's parents were introduced to one another during their short time of employment at the manor. His mother batted an eye and his father chased after it. He was the grounds keeper while his mother fed the family.

During his parents spare time, Logan was surly conceived somewhere on this very land. They were never married, so not only is he a combo pack, it also makes him a bastard in many people's eyes. Tag him a mutt. A decent looking mixed up mutt if that makes any sense.

Thanks mom. Thanks Dad.

Sure enough the knock on the door came without obstruction, along with a nasty tempered kitchen servant hollering for his so-called long awaited breakfast ingredients. At the same time making certain Logan didn't have a good start to his day.

Why?

Logan got up wearing the same cinder tarnished clothes he had on yesterday, splashed his face with cool water from the tin basin on the cabinet next to his bed and headed over to the step stairs that took him to the ground level.

He slept in the carriage house behind the Manor with the animals, not only because he had no other choice, but because he actually liked it. As he mentioned before, he loved these animals. Logan enjoyed the chickens and goats that he shared a home with. They didn't yell, talk back or judge him as he was. As long as he fed them, they loved him unconditionally.

Too bad the human race didn't think this way. The world would be a much better place for everybody if they did.

Living with the animals he considered his pets, really made it easier to take care of them every day. They became his friends and seemed to understand him more than the average human being did. They didn't care that he was a man of two colors, or that he was different than other lads his age. What other boys found stimulating about life, he did not. He went his own way and gushed over things they didn't seem interested in.

The chickens beneath his feet squabbled and scattered as if he purposely tried to step on them. "Hush your noise," Logan said and hopped back onto the first step just in case they were right about him trying to flatten them with his great big foot.

Also begging for breakfast, a few bleeps piped from the goats as well. Everybody was hungry and so was he.

Being optimistic that today was going to be a better day than yesterday, Logan danced with a whistle around to the backside of the carriage house where the storage shed was and lifted two sacks of grain over each shoulder. Huffing, he carried them back to the carriage house to fill the troughs with feed for the flightless birds. They clucked and pecked at him as a way to speed up the feeding process. Logan was doing his best considering he was holding the forty pound bag with one hand while the other was holding hungry animals at bay until he was done.

In the meantime, Logan was rump busted a few times by his gruff little goat friends. They were hungry too, but he insisted that they needed to wait their turn in line. "Hang on fellas, you're next," he assured them. "Straw and wheat is on the way."

After feeding the goats and then letting the cows out to pasture, he collected eggs from the hen house and then carried them to the kitchen along with large buckets of wheat flour he pulverized the day before. His arms were full and as usual the load was heavy and unbalanced.

Logan never looked into the windows of the house because he found it to be disrespectful and on the verge of being meddlesome. He kept to himself mostly when it came to the human race. He considered himself a loner, but the animals were his passion anyway and they never showed any excessive contempt nor did they ask questions regarding his private affairs. As far as he knew, the royal family had no idea that he even existed or even took part in keeping their kitchen stocked with food.

Before he had a chance to tap his toe against the kitchen door to announce his arrival, the door burst open and a big fat black woman whose name he didn't know pushed through the doorway and yelled out to him that he was thirty seconds late. He presumed she wanted everybody inside to hear her yelling by the tone and the blast of her enormous voice. Logan apologized to her as he always did and carried the food products to the huge stone counter along the backside of the room.

Before Logan turned around, potato sacks of meat fats and buckets full of food scraps were thrown into his arms. Slop of waste products circled the bucket, sloshed across the front of his shirt and tumbled down his trousers. An everyday occurrence acted out by the servants who disliked him without reason. He came to the conclusion that they dumped on him purposely. Every day he silently asked himself why.

On Logan's way out the door, somebody from behind forced him outside with a kick to his rear end. He stumbled down the steps and fell face first into the bucket of slop and spoiling meat fats. He lay there a minute while the servants laughed at him from the open doorway. He didn't look back. He refused. There was no way he was going to give them any satisfaction of humiliating him in broad daylight.

7

Standing up with a smile on his face, Logan thought of how much more the animals were going to take to him when he showed up wearing slop. More love for him as they cleaned him up with happy chops.

"Silly fool," somebody cackled as the door slammed shut, followed by the sound of the horizontal lock bar dropping into place in order to keep him out unless invited.

Logan leaned over and picked up as much of everything as he could from the ground and carried it to the slop house for the pigs to eat. They cherished him even more when he showed up with food. In the distance he could see them running toward him as he walked their way. They knew what he had and couldn't wait to get it.

After visiting and feeding pigs, he went back to the carriage house where he felt more at ease. The animals greeted him with enthusiasm exactly the way he knew they would. He patted their heads and hugged them while he removed his dirty clothes and tossed them to the ground on top of a pile of straw. A few of the goats trotted over and laid down on them, rolling a few times to gather his scent and grab a few licks of the clinging scraps.

Logan quickly ran down to the river to clean up and then returned to the barnyard to gather vegetables, fruits and grains for the evening's dinner. It was a repeat performance as it was in the morning, but hopefully not as messy. The garbage was always a morning chore so getting slopped in the evening was an event he didn't usually have to be concerned about. The bottom of a boot to his bum was an encounter reserved for his sunny wake up call.

The last thing Logan did before bedtime was clean out the soot from the kitchen stoves while he refreshed them with dry wood and a few chunky coals for the next day's kitchen routines.

Soot spotted him here and there like it normally did, but before heading to bed, he patted himself down to rid as much of the dust as he could. He said goodnight to the animals, climbed the step stairs to the loft and turned in for what he hoped to be a good night's rest.

Chapter 2

"Look at your son Priscilla," Dante made sure his queen of the manor was seeing what he saw. Overlooking the grand hall down below from where they were standing, they watched their young son wander somberly from one end to the other. His hands clasped behind his back, watching his own feet shuffle across the floor.

"What do you mean, Dante?" Priscilla asked while she looked down at her only child.

"Does he look lonely to you?" Instead of answering her, Dante asked another question.

"Hmm." She expressed with no words, just pursed her lips and tugged at the string of jewels around her narrow neck.

"It's time for him to find someone. A companion. Settle into his roll at taking my place. I don't want to be doing this forever you know. I need to settle in myself, perhaps retire. Go fishing. Paint a picture. I don't know, but Deklan needs to take over so I can enjoy the time I have left. I've done my time." Dante gestured to his wife that it was time for Deklan to take over the family business. Get more involved with the Almonds.

"I agree," Ms. Priscilla replied with the usual short answer. She pressed her poofed up skirt with her hands and then brought them together at the front of her jeweled waist.

Dante reminded Priscilla that their son Deklan had a birthday coming soon and that a large assembly of the town's people would be a perfect way to introduce a young lady to their son.

"That's a nice idea," She bleeped and kept her answer short once again.

"Okay then. Decided. We'll find him someone to marry on his twenty fourth birthday." Dante turned to a servant standing nearby and requested that he go fetch their son and tell him to meet the both of them in the dining hall library on the first floor.

Like a nervous weasel about to be chased, the servant scurried away to find Deklan and bring him back to his parents who would be waiting in the library as mentioned.

~~~~ * ~~~~

The dimly lit library looked more dusty than usual, so both Dante and Priscilla chose not to take a seat anywhere until it was properly cleaned.

Deklan entered the large wood trimmed room alone and quietly closed the double doors behind him. Dust billowed from above his head and fell to the floor around him like snowflakes did in winter. "It's time for a dust broom don't you think, father?" He suggested, extending a hand over his head like a canopy to block the dusty flakes that were falling on him. He stepped closer to his parents and asked what the reason was for this unscheduled engagement.

As usual his father spoke while his mother stood quietly nearby. "My son," his father started. "We think you should start thinking about settling down with someone and get more involved in the family business."

"What are you saying?" Deklan replied. "Are you planning on going somewhere soon? Are you alright?"

Ms. Priscilla stepped forward. "No, no my dear, Deklan. We just want you to be prepared when the time does come. Have you thought much about a companion?"

"You mean marriage? Well, I, well," He stuttered. "Unh, No, not really." It seemed a bit soon for a decision like this and the question of a marriage came at him much too fast. He was not prepared for this nor had he given much thought about it. He had dismissed the idea mostly because the companion he would prefer may not be considered a suitable match for what his parents were expecting to represent the leader of the company. His face went white and the space between his eyebrows went screwy, muddling his handsome features.

Priscilla glanced at Dante with a confused expression over her brow and then gazed back at Deklan for a better answer.

Interrupting the strange silence, Deklan's father spoke on the verge of a whisper, "Son. It is only a matter of time that we will be passing this company on to you and bequeathing all this to our only child. It's important that you're ready to take over the responsibilities as a leader and that you have someone at your side to enjoy it with."

"I am sorry father, but I am not ready," Deklan proclaimed. "I don't even know anybody that I find suitable. I'm sorry. I am not ready for this." His anger rose.

"You do not have to make up your mind overnight," His father added. "Your birthday is in a few days, so our thoughts were to arrange a formal event on that night and invite highly regarded town's people over to celebrate with us. Perhaps during this affair you will come across a suitable bride or at least become acquainted with somebody you may find fitting to join you in holy matrimony."

Being a bit aggressive, Deklan raised his voice, "Father, Please. I don't want a bride or companion or whatever you want to call it right now. I have plenty of time to find a sidekick, but now is not good."

"Deklan, please." His mother stepped in, holding out her hand as if to comfort her agitated child.

Sr. Dante chortled, "What do you know about when a good time is? You're young and we are wise and this is the right time."

"Okay, Okay." Deklan rushed to the libraries exit and turned back with his hand gripping the iron handle. "Do what you must. Order me a princess, but I cannot promise this engagement will be what you plan or expect." He swung the heavy door open and stormed away.

"Okay, that went well." Dante scratched his head, commenting. "We will proceed as planned. He'll come around, I am sure of it. We know what's best for him." He pounded a pointy finger on the table he stood next to.

~~~~ * ~~~~

With disregard to the conversation Deklan had with his parents, he angrily treaded down the corridor and out to the horse stables. He hopped on his favorite steed, Chadwick and rode him from the stable into the woods at lightning speed. He needed to get away from what just took place. He needed to think on his own. Deklan was feeling more alone than he ever had before and wanted time to himself in order to figure his way out from the dreadful heartache he was enduring. He rode until he reached an open field overcrowded with cloves where he brought Chadwick to a stop and hopped off. The scent of the pungent weeds helped him relax. It was like a sedative.

His eyes became heavy as he quietly lay next to Chadwick on the ground. He dozed off while wrestling with his wandering thoughts of marriage to an unknown lady bride he knew for sure he didn't want.

How was he going to make it through something like this if it didn't feel the least bit natural to him?

Chapter 3

Dusk had made its appearance and the moon above helped Logan find his way through the darkness a little easier than if it was not there at all. Its slim crescent sliver cast only a small amount of light, so making out what was in front of him was no simple task. There wasn't much light coming from it to illuminate his pathway, but he managed to find his way with a few hit and misses.

He had a good idea where he was at, but still felt disoriented when he turned his head or became distracted in any way.

The field felt dry beneath his feet and he figured it was due to receiving little to no rain in the past few weeks. A deluge would certainly be nice. It would help bring down the high heat from the sun as well as feed the crops with the moisture they desperately needed to survive.

He skimmed the ground in front of him, looking for any clovers that would grant him some Irish luck. So many clovers in the field yet there never seemed to be a stem that bestowed any leaves of four. He would take a wild guess and say that no luck was planned to present itself to him anytime soon.

Heading eastward, Logan detected movement on the ground ahead of him. He was startled by his trifling imagination of a wild animal that would ravage him until he bled. He froze while thinking it would probably be best to run from whatever wild beast was waiting in the brush.

It moved again. He lost his breath. Standing nearly motionless, he moved his foot backwards in order to back step the same paces that got him where he stood.

Logan let out a sigh of relief as soon as he heard a cluck and a scratch at dry leaves across the ground. "Dirty bird," he grumbled, immediately trying to corral the chicken that should be in her coop getting ready to lay tomorrow mornings eggs.

"Betty Lu," He said, not really knowing if that was her name, but he called her that anyway. "You should not be out here, now scram." He waved his arms out in front of him so she would take off running in the direction he wanted her to go. Back home where she belonged.

While weaving side to side, hopeful at keeping the bird from running in the wrong direction, Logan's bare feet started stinging from the dry weeds laid out across the ground.

The chicken took off running and so did he. He was sure he looked ridiculous chasing her down the hill while clapping his hands at her, but it was the only way he could keep her moving. It was either that or he was going to have to pick her up and carry her home. Chickens were reckless and they smelled like barnyard poop. His decision to let her run while he followed close behind was a wise one.

Up the hill and behind him, he heard a horse running. Its pounding hooves against the ground were getting louder as it approached. Logan reacted fast by lunging to the left so that he could step out of the way from the runaway horse. "Betty Lu!" Afraid for her well being too, he hollered. "Get out of the way!"

The galloping horse whinnied when it met up with the feather flapping bird and the rider immediately tugged hard on the reigns the second he realized there was a chicken in his pathway. Stopping sharp as if there was a wall in front of him, the horse reared up and its rider rolled backward across the horse's hind side and landed on the ground. The light from the moon showed eerie through the rising dust around the horses feet. The sight was frightening in respect to the characteristics of a horrific animal attack on All-Hallows night.

Logan's male instincts to protect kicked in and he quickly took a dive toward the rider to pull him out from under the frantically stomping horse. He held him tightly in a steely lock, arms wrapped around him like a bear hug. Gravity took over and down the hillside they went.

At the same time Deklan and Logan rolled down hill, the chicken fled and the horse did too. Strangely enough, as if what just took place did not, the horse instantly encountered its calm and took to grazing about one hundred paces away.

When the pulling force of gravity finally gave in and let them be, they both abruptly rolled to a stop about halfway down the hill. They ended up lying face to face, with Logan positioned comfortably on the bottom, huffing from the weight of the man on top of him, grunting a little from the loss of breath.

Being that it was dark outside made it troublesome for either of them to identify who the other person was. There was a charge between Logan's legs and he felt the rider's hard ridge growing firmer as it pressed against his groin. They lay still for several seconds before the man on horseback realized what just happened. The look on his handsome face showed a sure sign that he'd been knocked a little stunned.

The man grew quiet, very quiet and Logan could feel his warm breath on his cheek. The horseman shifted ever so slightly before snapping out of his dazed state of mind. Shuddering as if startled, the horse rider quickly pushed himself off of Logan and hobbled on one leg as if he hurt his foot. "Excuse me," he bleeped.

A mention of moonbeam fell just right across the man's face and Logan gasped when he recognized him to be Deklan from the Manor. Logan's stomach went sour and then instantly knotted up, quickly shifting his gaze and forcing himself to stop staring.

As Deklan stood up, he pounded himself down to remove the soil that was clinging to his clothing. "It's not very wise to be roaming out in these fields all alone so late at night you know." His deep crisp voice said as if concerned.

Logan sat up straight and then stood too, abstaining from

looking him square in the eyes. "Yes sir," he replied with his head down as if being scolded by a parent. Not that it mattered or was really any of his business, but he went into detail as to why he was out in the field all alone in the first place. "I was chasing my chicken, sir." Smirking after he said it because it sounded comical.

Deklan snickered too, covering his mouth with his hand that hid his grin. "Did you see where your chicken ran off too?"

Like a shy boy, Logan tucked his thumbs behind his suspenders, "No sir, but I believe she took off into the woods. She will find her way home I'm sure."

Lowering a brow, "Please call me Deklan. Addressing me as sir is too formal and it sounds strange to be called that."

Logan nodded and lowered his head further as if Deklan was truly royalty and duty called to respect him with a bow. Logan knew him, but could tell that Deklan had no idea who he was, or knew that Logan worked at the Manor where he lived.

Sneaking a glance at Deklan while he was looking up at the moon, Logan could see he was focused on something other than what he was doing at the moment. His blank stare told him that. "Are you okay?" Logan asked him in case he was injured from his fall off the horse.

Deklan looked himself over, shook out his arms, "I'm good. Thanks for asking." He smiled. "Are you good?"

Logan smiled back. "I'm fine."

"It's pretty dark out here. You going to find your way home okay?" He kindly asked, once again sounding concerned.

Logan told him he was alright and that the chicken would lead the way.

Deklan laughed. "Okay. Have a good night." He then walked over to his grazing horse and mounted it like a champion rider. The horse trotted away, leaving Logan behind with a distant wink.

On his way back to the carriage house where he lived, Logan mused over how polite Deklan was. It actually surprised him. Being that his family was wealthy and established, Logan was expecting a different tone and attitude from him.

Logan found Betty Lu in the woods where he thought she'd

be, picked her up and carried her the rest of the way home.

She clucked and squabbled a bit while in his arms, possibly out of anger for being off the ground and not in control of her footsteps. He couldn't really tell.

Chapter 4

Back at the big house, the butler of the Manor, Sir Wattsworth carried out Senior Dante's requests pertaining to the celebration. He corralled the domestic workers in the house for a meeting, anointing them to assist with the impending arrangements.

Sir Wattsworth pulled the families business registration log from a dusty shelf that Dante had stored in the Manors library. To start with, he thought the log would help him identify some of the town's people who would make the best choices as attendee's. He generated the long list of guests while the servants followed through with other tasks related to the birthday event scheduled for Deklan.

The list of admirable companions that Wattsworth put together consisted of many different sorts, from the very wealthy to the near poor pauper. All of whom were actually able to marry Deklan and were near his own age. The list was quite long and consisted of both male and female guests. From this roster, he figured there was likely to be someone that would be suitable for Deklan.

The next morning arrived quickly for Wattsworth and the

demands of the day were already resting heavily on his shoulders. For starters, he intensely scuffled to be sure the invitations for the chosen guests were being taken care of and would be distributed straightaway.

In the main hall and by second hand orders from Wattsworth, selected servants were filling several woven sacks with the invitations and organizing them based on region of the villages.

Outside, messengers were standing by who would deliver the folded invites to each of the selected homes.

The commotion of loading the messenger wagons with sacks of parcel outside the palace caught Logan's attention so he stopped what he was doing to take a look at what was going on. At first he could only think that excess trash was being removed from the premises, but wondered why he was not involved with it or why it wasn't being tossed on him.

He stood quietly with the goats and chickens while he continued emptying their kernels of dry corn and weedy wheat stalks into their feeding troughs.

It appeared to Logan that it was starting to settle down a bit at the Manor as he witnessed the wagons pull away and travel out into the lane to take the sacks to wherever they needed to go.

Deciding to mind his own business, Logan finished up with the animals' breakfast before running out back to get what was needed for the royal family's morning meal.

Logan's arms were full as he once again tapped his toe against the big wooden door to the kitchen entrance. The door blew open the same way it did the day before and he was quickly pulled in by his elbow and then shoved even further by a hand at his backside.

On his way out, Logan tried to avoid getting messed up again by another kick to the britches, so he propelled himself quickly through the doorway only to clumsily catch his toe on the threshold at his feet. Causing humiliation to himself without help from anyone else, he tripped down the steps and onto the ground. He heard them laughing behind him as he went down, face first in dirt and slop.

This time the outcome was different from all the others. In

front of Logan, pressed against his cheek lay a paper note with writing scrawled across one side. He figured it was from the sacks of trash he saw being removed by the carriage wagons earlier that day. When he stood up, the paper piece peeled away from his check and feather floated to the ground, landing softly with the words face up and clearly in view. Logan didn't want to be intrusive by looking at what didn't pertain to him, but he couldn't seem to help himself. His eyes just wouldn't look away.

He tipped his head a bit to align his vision more evenly with the writing on the letter and saw that it was referencing something about a birthday event in the next few days and what he could tell, it was for the lad of the house, Deklan. A specific time was not mentioned, only that it will be at dusk. Logan knew he wasn't invited, as they – the help – never were. The times set aside for celebration were usually reserved for the servants to work, hired to serve the family and guests and then clean up after the events had ended.

Sarcastically speaking, it's a wonderful life.

Logan first looked casually over his shoulder to see if anybody else was nearby before he went down on his hands and knees to pick up the waste he gallantly spilled across the ground. The last thing he reached for was the small note and as he did, another big-footed boot came in contact with his rear end.

What the heck and why?

Hollering came with the foot as he glided forward a few feet before stopping. Logan's arms stretched out ahead of him to catch his fall. He looked back over his shoulder again to see a tall thin black man that looked more skeleton like than human reaching for the letter on the ground that was now behind Logan near his feet.

"This doesn't belong to you, little bug," the skinny man screeched. "As if there was any chance somebody like you would even be invited to a special event like this one. You don't mix with these people any more than we do and you never will. Now get back to work before I send the dogs after you." He picked the letter up, glanced at it and then folded it into his apron pocket.

Logan stood and dusted himself off, gathered the garbage and headed back to the swine shed to feed the pigs.

Logan hummed to keep from being sad and at the same

time was thinking how nice it would be if he was asked to join the birthday party for Prince Deklan. He wiped the thought from his mind, because the way he saw it, that was not going to happen. Those people didn't even know his name, nor even knew he was living behind the plantation in the carriage house.

He went on feeding the animals and then expired to the river to take his morning bath. The water felt more refreshing today than it did any other day for some reason. Maybe because he was covered with hot dirt this time or perhaps because his head was boiling with anger toward the people that kicked him down every morning. Who knew? It felt more exhilarating than it usually did.

Logan floundered in the water a bit longer than he normally did, letting the river flow over him to wash away his anxiety. He didn't usually hang out like this, but felt it was time he took advantage of a good thing.

While lying face up like a stick built water raft, he watched the birds twitter in the trees above him. The two were so happy being together that it made him think of one day finding a close friend of his own who he could enjoy being with. He knew the animals were considered his first choice of friendship, but human interaction of the friendly kind could be all right as well.

Logan lost track of time during his few moments of isolation and the obnoxious noise that snapped him out of his daze was distant yelling coming from the kitchens doorway. He sprang skyward quickly because he knew the blasting voice was meant for him. His arms chopped at water in a drastic attempt to propel himself toward the riverbank as fast as he could make himself go. As a result, water was splashing all over the place, which made it seem like rain coming down all around him. He could hardly see a thing in front of him, so panic took over while his solitude quickly diminished.

Hopping into his dirty shirt and trousers, he raced as fast as I could back to the barn to gather the eggs and wheat flour as he should have already done. Not counting, he only hoped that he grabbed enough of what was needed for the day.

Logan took off to the kitchen fast, barefoot and smelling like sludge. The fat black woman yelling in the doorway saw him coming and somewhat stepped aside to let him through. As he squeezed by, her enormous stomach grew bigger as she breathed and the great big orb banged into him. He bounced off of it and shot to the back of the room like he was a steel ball fired from a heated cannon. Apprehensively he let out a laugh as he stumbled, because it struck him as being funny, but contained himself professionally. All he wanted to do was to leave the things he came in with and get out of the kitchen straightaway.

On his way out, Logan hesitated. He was in such a hysterical rush that it slipped his mind he had already made one breakfast trip that morning. Nothing was said as he left the kitchen, not even a glance by anybody working the grill. They must have been too focused on what needed to be done for the upcoming event to notice he was in and out for the second time that morning.

Logan stood outside the door for a spell to make sure nobody came at him with raging fists that pointed out his thoughtless mistake and to remind him of what it was he was supposed to be doing in the kitchen. Refraining from running like he wanted to, he checked the basket to the left of the kitchen window to see if there were any special instructions that he needed to take care of. Nothing was there, so that gave him the idea that perhaps the hollering from the big fat woman was not meant for him.

Whistling a made up song, Logan drifted back to the carriage house to continue with his already scheduled chores. The same ones he took care of yesterday and the same ones the day before that, and the same ones he will take care of tomorrow.

While he busied himself with work, he started thinking about the celebration that was being arranged and imagined Deklan inviting him to it. It was a long shot for even thinking it, but a lad can have his dreams.

Once word got out that Deklan was on the block to be married, all the young ladies turned wickedly giddy and stupidly competitive.

Their radical behavior was an effort to help boost their chances at being the chosen princess of The Royal Manor.

Chaos broke out in the town square as the hysterical ladies

shopped for the most exquisite merchandise that would highlight their assets to the son of the royal empire. Gold and silver brocades, shimmering silks and other various fabrics of discriminating taste were being purchased like never before. It was outrageous.

Heirloom Jewels were getting polished. Facial paint was heavily applied in manner that would hide the unsightly blemishes so not to deflect the decision of being the chosen one.

Dusty hairpieces were piled as high as they could go with respect in keeping the fair maiden's from tipping over. Curly locks were pulled down over the cheekbones to show off a more slimming facial expression.

Decorating the human body with handmade materials was a ritual performed by most ladies so that they could reel in the attention of their potential suitor. Instead of looking appealing, most of the time they looked more like All-Hallows costume artists.

Arguments between consumers occurred at the merchants counter.

All the rivalry broke out as if Deklan was choosing his prize by appearance alone.

It was certainly going to be a night to remember. One Logan wished he would not be missing.

Chapter 5

The day was busy for Logan, being that he had to make sure the kitchen was fully stocked with all the items to fulfill the needs of the staff, family and guests. It was a chore. Tedious and repetitive.

The times he had to himself were only at night it seemed, so into the dark he ran again. Logan was craving apples and pears for some reason and decided to get out of bed and head to the clover field to pick some fresh fruit.

The slivered moon was wider than last night, however it was still rather dark again, but a bit brighter than last. This made it necessary to carefully watch his step as he tiptoed up and over the hill. There was just enough light from the moon to light his way and this time he surely needed to watch for horses, clucking chickens and monstrous creatures of the night. He was not taking any chances at getting attacked or trampled this time, by runaway horses and scary chickens.

There was a slight breeze that felt good against his bare chest and made fruit tree climbing a little more bearable during the heat wave laced with humidity.

Logan collected fruit from the trees many times before, so finding them in the darkness wasn't too difficult. He finally reached them and decided to hit the pear tree first. It was his favorite of the two crunchy fruits.

He propped the ladder against the pear tree that he left in the field for the day to day pickings and climbed up into the tree to grab his evening snack.

Finding a sturdy branch, he sat comfortably as he bit into the freshly picked fruit. The sensation met his desire as expected and his eyes closed while he savored its flavor. It was crunchy and sweet. Just the way he liked them. With each bite, he hummed.

He turned his back against the trunk of the tree and dangled one leg over the branch he was sitting on, looking out across the clover field and enjoying the peace he was feeling.

"Not again," He said, talking to himself. "Who is this coming over the hill now?" He wanted solitude not a party.

Wait. It was him. Deklan.

Out of all the trees in the field, Deklan chose to stop his horse next to the one Logan was sitting in.

Incredible.

Logan stopped chewing, afraid that Deklan would hear him up in the tree. He sat motionless in order to prevent his movements from giving away his secret location. Logan watched Deklan quietly as he dismounted his horse and led the huge animal under the pear tree to munch on a few fallen fruits. Logan slowed his breathing and sat even more still. "Oh Sweet surrender." He hummed.

A few pears fell from the tree and hit the ground with a timid thud. Deklan looked up and then back down at where the fruit landed. Logan's heart started pounding and he felt the rhythm burst in his ears. The booming was so loud and he was sure Deklan could hear it too.

Deklan reached for the fruit, polished it on the front of his shirt and took a bite. He hummed the same way Logan did with each savory bite. He knew a good thing when he tasted it, Logan could tell. They were a lot alike in that respect.

Logan's dark skin blended well with the dark tree, thank

God. To be safe and keep himself hidden well, he closed his eyes and mouth to keep the moons light from reflecting off my glossy white planes.

A dead giveaway for a black man in the dark, for sure.

After Deklan finished his pear, he mounted his horse and walked him out from under the tree, leaning into his mane in order to prevent a tree branch from pulling his hair. He had fine-looking hair. It was a little unkempt, but looked good, or maybe just windblown, dark blond and tipped his shoulders in feathered wisps.

Logan sighed and took a small breath, bringing in much needed fresh air that he was lacking from trying to stay silent.

Deklan turned his horse around and faced the tree.

Logan's breathing when shallow again and he froze.

By the look on Deklan's face Logan could tell he heard him.

"Holy Bollocks!" Logan buzzed.

There was no getting out of this one so Logan figured it best to just get out of the tree and face his invader.

"Who's there?" Deklan shouted. His horse recoiled from the sudden noise and began to canter and stomp his hooves against the ground. Deklan reached to his side as if he was going for a weapon. A dagger perhaps.

Logan sat frozen. He couldn't move. 'Bollocks!' He hissed again.

"Come out." Deklan insisted, grabbing the blade attached to his belt.

Without hesitating, Logan climbed down and stood in the shadows of the pear tree. "Hello again," He meekly said without giving his name or letting Deklan see his face. He stepped into the moonlight, held his hands in plain sight so Deklan could see that he meant no harm or was carrying any injurious weapon.

"It's you." Deklan removed his hand from the blade and looked down at Logan. "I had a suspicion it was you. Why is it that I always run into you out here at night time?"

Logan placed his thumbs behind his suspenders as he always did and pushed his broad bare chest forward. "I could ask you the same thing."

"Yes, but I asked the question first." Deklan's horse seemed antsy and acted as though it wanted to get moving.

"Night time is peaceful to me and it's much cooler than during the day." Logan was distracted by the sound of a cricket at his feet, prompting him to look down. "What about you?" He asked.

Deklan answered short, "The same. What you said. Except that I was expecting to be alone."

Logan was intrigued by the huge horse in front of him. He's seen him before, but never up close. He stepped closer to the horse and held out a hand. "May I?" He asked.

Deklan nodded. "So you found the best fruit tree in the forest too, did you? This is my favorite."

"It's a good one. My preference as well." Logan stroked the bridge of the horse's rubbery nose and by its reaction, seemed to enjoy Logan's touch. The horse made snorting noises and bobbed his head up and down as if praising Logan's generous petting. He sensed Logan was an animal lover by the way he caressed him. In return, his big nose nudged Logan's shoulder to show he trusted him and begged him not to stop.

"No shoes or shirt?" Deklan scanned the front of Logan. "Do you have a home or do you live out here in the woods?"

Logan laughed. "Oh no. I have a home, which I should be getting back to before I am missed." It wasn't his immediate family he was talking about, but the animals he considered to be. Deklan didn't need to know this, so he didn't tell him otherwise.

"You need a ride?" Deklan asked, pulling back on the reigns.

Hesitating at first, "Uh, sure," Logan replied, stepping back and to the side of the big Clydesdale. His thinking was not to let Deklan take him all the way home, but someplace nearby. Hope he understood.

Deklan reached down to grab hold of Logan's right hand. With a hefty tug, Deklan lifted him up and over the horse's rump where he landed into the empty space at his backside. Deklan scooted forward a little to make room for Logan in the saddle seat behind him. The saddle rise in the back forced Logan to slide toward him, which pressed his bare chest tightly against Deklan's back. He smelled fresh, like sharp spices and lavender. It was an interesting combination for a man, however Logan found it to be a good one. Logan wanted to lay his cheek in his hair that draped like silk over the back of Deklan's broad shoulders, but refrained and still took in the aroma of the gentle man in front of him.

"Ready? Hang on." Deklan turned the horse around and headed up the hill.

The sudden commotion jostled Logan's balance and he responded by wrapping his arms securely around Deklan's waist, locking his fingers together across his belt buckle. "Whoa," he said. "Sorry." Logan loosened his grip.

"Whoa? Why?" Deklan laughed and quickly placed his hand over Logan's to hold them in place. "No. Don't be sorry. I told you to hang on. Chadwick can be a bit antsy. At times he rides a little rough."

Logan inhaled, followed by an exhale, leaving his hands right where he first placed them.

Omigawd his hair smelled good.

Deklan snapped the reigns. "Where to?"

"Straight ahead," Logan said. "You're going in the right direction."

They rode for about five to ten minutes before seeing the Manor up ahead. Logan stayed quiet the whole time and thought it strange that Deklan didn't ask his name or anything about him. Not to go against what he was thinking, but he didn't ask Deklan anything either.

Deklan slowed the Clydesdale with a tug to the reigns. "Hey!" He called to Logan. "The Manor is up ahead, where do I drop you off?"

Logan acted like he wasn't paying attention to where he was, "OH!" He perked up. "You can let me go here. I can walk the rest of the way."

"Don't be silly. Where to?" Deklan insisted.

Logan thought that Deklan was inconspicuously trying to figuring him out. He reluctantly let go of Deklan's waist by slowly pulling his hands loose and then sat up straight behind him.

"Right here is good. Really."

"Really?" He stammered.

"Yes Really. You can drop me off right here." Logan was about to hop off while the horse was still moving, but before he had a chance, Deklan tugged Chadwick to a stop first.

"Oka-ay." Deklan's voice went singsong as he twisted in the saddle to face Logan at his backside. "We have reached your stop." He reached his hand to Logan's to help him down. Deklan held it tight and long.

It seemed quite a ways to the ground, so the help Deklan gave was very much appreciated. Logan's bare feet hit the dirt before Deklan let go. His touch was warm and Logan could tell his soul was too. He liked Deklan.

"I guess this is where you get off?" Deklan worked the horse around until he was facing Logan on the ground. He squinted as if he was trying to get a good look at Logan's face and lock his image into his memory.

Logan looked away as if he sensed something over his right shoulder. Nothing was there, he just didn't feel comfortable with Deklan knowing who he was just yet or that he maintained the kitchen vittles for him and his family.

Is that strange?

Logan waved to Deklan. "I guess I'll see you around." His thumbs met his suspenders at his chest and then slid downward to his waist. His thumbs locked behind the fasteners the way he liked it and he felt secure. Logan's signature stance and he looked good when he did it.

Deklan smiled, looking directly at Logan's caramel colored chest as it projected forward with strength and pride. He saluted him and then squeezed Chadwick with the heels of his boots. "Giddy-up." He cracked his cheek a few times to tell the horse to get moving.

Logan stood where he was and watched him leave. The prince of night rode out of sight.

Deklan's long hair flipped softly in the breeze as he turned back and saluted again.

Logan waved, turned around and whistled the entire way

back to the carriage house. He had a silly-happy-feeling inside, which was good. It was a first for him. Good human interaction felt nice.

When Logan opened the door, a chicken pecked his toe and a goat bleeped at him with scorn.

Chapter 6

There was still what seemed to be a lot of bustling going on at the Manor. Logan saw several carriage wagons filled with party effects being delivered to the house. He could tell it was going to be a lively night by the way the staff was working in and outside of the mansion. They looked like nervous ants milling for food.

Logan had to laugh.

In the massive backyard there were two enormous canvas rooftop covers going up. One placed on each side of the lengthy pool, which ran from the rear of the house to the furthest point of the yard. The pool was enormous and he wondered what anybody would ever do with a pool that size. Logan figured the tents were meant to keep everybody shaded as well as stock all the food that was on the menu to be served.

Butler Wattsworth was in charge of it all, which left him scrambling around, pointing and giving orders out to everybody on the grounds.

By the looks of things, Logan was probably the only one not invited to help out. He saw everybody from the kitchen he knew and a few that he had seen from time to time around the manor.

He presumed the skinny black man from the kitchen was right, he didn't belong with these people and probably never will.

No big deal really, Logan was truly content with his life he was given and most of the time was happy just being left alone. He understood himself to be a loner. He had everything he needed to survive and probably more than most other people did.

Logan kept wondering what it would be like if he was invited to the birthday celebration and how things would go if he ran into Deklan. Deklan was so pleasant the past few times they ran into one another and it made him think a close friendship could come of it. In a good way, Logan's stomach whirled just thinking about it because he knew how he felt, but was not too sure if Deklan was feeling the same way he did. The horseback ride the other night certainly made him wonder a few things about Deklan and himself. The thought left Logan smiling, which then led to a full out grin.

On the upside, Logan was close enough to see the birthday event where he would be sitting, so in all actuality he considered himself to technically be part of the party. He wouldn't actually be dancing with the prince, but if he could hear the music and witness the laughter, he was there.

While sitting in the window next to his bed on the second floor watching all the commotion down below, Logan saw a door open up at the south side of the manor that never gets used. It surprised him to see it open up.

Another surprise turned up when he saw who came out of the door. His face lit up when he saw it was Deklan. To Logan, Deklan looked like he was escaping from whatever was going on inside.

Deklan quickly sidestepped along the manor with his back against the wall as if he was trying not to be seen. He crept craftily to the corner of the house before taking off with a crouched gallop to the trees where Logan had been running into him lately.

It was difficult for Logan to just sit still and not stare at Deklan's strong physic. He liked the way he looked and the way his hair flipped away from his face as he ran. He thought about following Deklan wherever he was going but decided against it in order to keep his admiration for him a secret.

Or should he go?

Maybe the reason Deklan was headed back into the woods was to see if he would run into Logan again.

That would be grand.

Logan figured it was best to stay where he was at so Deklan could be alone to carry out whatever he needed to do on his own. He was sneaking away for a purpose, Logan presumed, so if he was hanging in the shadows, it would only intrude on Deklan's need for wanting to be by himself.

Deklan soon disappeared under the heavy foliage of the forest and it irritated Logan a bit that he didn't know what was on his mind and why he was making a run for the woods.

Repressing the urge to jump out the window, Logan sat back at last, pleased with himself that he chose not to go out and chase his dream. He fidgeted before pulling himself away from the plank wood window sill.

Lying in bed with his arms propping his head forward off the pillow, Logan couldn't get Deklan off his mind. For many reasons, Logan continued to think about that handsome man. He shifted while doing a quick study of his face that had been implanted in his memory from the few times they stood close enough to see each other.

What was wrong with Logan?

Logan rolled over and stared out the window while listening to the noise outside.

Time was passing slowly for Logan, but if he had something to do, perhaps it would be moving a little faster.

Logan heard shouting in the distance. It was Butler Wattsworth giving out more orders. Unlike himself, time for the staff must be moving too quickly and they had only a single day to get it all done. The next day was Deklan's twenty fourth birthday, so everything had to be ready by then. Time was ticking.

Someplace out in the woods, Deklan was wandering alone, just the way he wanted it. He needed time on his own from the way it looked when Logan saw him sneaking off, most likely to do some thinking, no doubt.

Suddenly clouds covered the sky and defeated the sun in an

instant. It turned dark almost immediately and rain came down hard. It was nice because there's been no rain for days. It was needed badly and it cooled the warm air fast. Although good for the grounds, the rain was a massive intrusion for Wattsworth and his team.

Logan laughed when he saw everybody outside run for shelter under the great big tents.

While Deklan ran, there was a question that played over and over again in his head, but he had no answer for it at the time. One thing he knew was that he needed to run away.

Deklan came to a narrow creek and clumsily jumped to the other side. His foot landed on a mossy rock and he slipped into the water. He grumbled as the water filled his shoe and he scrambled as quickly as he could to remove it from the creeks embrace before it pulled the rest of him in.

He took off again, running the edge of the bank, ducking beneath tree branches that seemed as though they were reaching out to grab him.

What was he running from? There was nobody chasing him nor was he in any danger.

Blocking rain from his eyes, Deklan ran for cover and stooped under the fullest tree he could find. He grimaced and groaned, disturbed that he was out there in the first place. The situation was totally a bad one and it was purely his own fault, but it was mind satisfying to get away from all the talk about finding a female bride he wasn't interested in having.

Fortunately for him he ended up beneath an apple tree. He was hungry and bored, so the tree he landed under made for a perfect match.

Deklan reached up and plucked a bright red one from the twig that dangled above his head, scrubbed it against his wet shirt and took a horse sized bite, nearly chopping it in half. His face went screwy by the apples tartness. It was sour, which coincidentally matched his streaming thoughts.

He peered through the wet trees and watched the rain fall even harder. It found him too and soaked him through and through.

Deklan started to move out from under the apple tree and as soon as he did he slowed down. At that moment he made a decision. He was going to turn around, go back home and face his qualms. It was probably a good idea anyway.

Why not just be unhappy instead of both miserably wet and unhappy.

Deklan slogged through misty woods, wet brush, sticky ground cover and snapping tree branches. He shivered as the air got colder and he felt the freezing rain run down his back. He sneezed, blinked and then wiped the water from his eyes as best he could.

He finally spotted lights up ahead and was able to make out that they were definitely coming from the Manor. Completely hesitant about taking another step, he settled under another tree and let the rain take over his surroundings and soak him even more. He didn't care. Somehow getting saturated seemed better than being flooded by marriage proposals at home. He wanted to stay right where he was. Wet, miserable and troubled.

Deklan looked good wet. At least he did to Logan.

Despairing times called for desperate actions so Deklan stayed put and shivered. He slumped down beneath another tree, sitting with his back against rough bark. He closed his eyes to an apparent doze and without reason, scalding tears took over his eyes.

The clouds moved across the sky fast and the sun quickly vanquished the rain, making Deklan somehow feel as if he was just saved. He met up with Chadwick in the barn, hopped on him bareback and took off running up into the open fields. The late evening sun warmed him and he was feeling some relief from being wet.

While Deklan was out gallivanting with Chadwick, the celebration setup broke into full swing once again. The miserable rain intruded on the Manor for what was thankfully a short time, but was over, so the setup had to go on.

Never enough time, it seemed. Never enough time.

Butler Wattsworth clutched his parchment sheets, checking them twice to be sure nothing was missed. As far as he could tell, everything was going as planned and getting done.

Deklan didn't seem to notice but the sun began to set. His eyes had adjusted to the darkness and before he knew it he was running Chadwick into the night.

Soon the shadows all around them went long until they blended together and covered the ground in total blackness. By this, Deklan decided it was time to end the ride and call it a night.

Chapter 7

The evening came for Logan too, so he decided to take his swim a bit farther down the river. It was late and he thankfully had nowhere to be or anybody to tend to.

Thank God.

Other than small noises that may have been birds, crickets or even creepy bugs, the night was rather quiet. This made Logan believe that he and the fishes were the only ones swimming in the river at the time.

Logan removed every piece of clothing he had on, which of course left him completely nude and appeared blue in the surging sliver moonlight. In the daylight his skin was light caramel, but at night time when the moon was out, he turned a shimmering shade of blue.

Funny how that works.

Being naked stimulated him, even though the water felt chilling when he first got in. He sank down on his hands and knees in the shallow water and started crawling across the rocky riverbed until his head and shoulders were the only part of him that were exposed to the outside elements. When he paddled his feet, each kick bumped his bare bottom upward into the fresh air too. It made him laugh each time the cool air spanked his exposed flesh.

Logan crawled along the river a while, dragging his feet behind him until he came to an area even shallower than the waters he came from. He stopped at a place that permitted him to roll over and lay with his backside to the bedrock, leaving his entire front side exposed to the open air. He was a free spirit at that moment and it certainly felt good, no doubt. He wasn't sure if it was the cool breeze racing across his exposed body that made him tremble with exhilaration or because certain areas that were normally covered up were getting blown for the very first time by the cool night wind.

Even though Logan was alone and it was dark, he felt compelled to cover himself up. He reached for the largest water lily he could find and laid it neatly over the abnormally large extension below his waist.

With his arms outstretched to his sides and his feet floating on the surface of the water, he floundered silently while listening to creatures of the night noisily communicate with one another.

It was extremely peaceful, that it came easy for him to relax. It happened. He was content.

~~~~ * ~~~~

Trudging through the undergrowth, ignoring the snapping twigs and squishing mush beneath his feet, Deklan found a pair of trousers folded in the hollow of a tree up side the river. It seemed a little strange to him finding clothes out in the woods at this time of night, but figured somebody may have forgotten them or was still nearby taking an evening swim in the river. Bare footed imprints on the ground looked to be freshly set so the latter of his two presumptions gave the impression as being the more sound choice.

Today was a wet one, raining off and on all day. The clouds looked as though they were not planning to leave any time soon. Thankfully there hadn't been too much rainfall so a good chance still stood that there would be a foot trail to follow. Slogging through the forest while tugging at Chadwick's reins was not his idea of fun, but it was easier than trying to direct him from horseback through and around prickly bushes and broken tree limbs.

The prints on the ground pivoted into the river straightaway, making believe whoever trousers were hidden in the tree had gone for a swim.

His original plan was to escape from the Manor to mull over his thoughts in silence, which the nighttime strolls always allowed him to just that. This time he wanted to make time for himself without his parents drilling him about getting married.

Enough already.

Even though Deklan wanted to be alone with his thoughts, his curiosity pricked his desire to keep going and find out whose clothes were stuffed in the hollow of that tree. It helped get his mind off home anyway.

He hopped back on Chadwick and cantered along the mushy bank while he looked into the river every few steps. If there was anybody taking a midnight swim, he was hoping to see who it was. The darkness took possession of the woods, which made it rather difficult to see much of anything, but the reflection of the moon across the water's surface was the only evidence of movement out there.

The soft ground underneath Chadwick's hooves left his footsteps quiet as he walked. Anybody swimming in the water or even nearby would be surprised by this horse's subtle arrival.

Together Chadwick and Deklan crept forward.

~~~~ * ~~~~

While Logan was lying in the river face to the sky, he couldn't get his mind off Deklan. He was striking on all aspects of a human being and the fact that he was so kind made his beauty even more pleasing.

Deklan had an aristocratic face, square chin, strong angular jaw line that was lightly shadowed with dark facial hair. His light complexion absorbed the glistening light beams from the moon that reflected off his flesh like shimmering diamonds. His bright blue eyes that were fringed with long lashes dazzled like polished sapphires behind loose strands of long dark blonde hair that fell free from the short ponytail tied at the back of his head.

Deklan felt strong and solid from what Logan could tell during the brief encounter they had while rolling together down the hillside. Logan remembered getting a glimpse of his chest and how it was dusted with hair that resembled wisps of feathers. His attraction to a man with chest hair almost outranked a beautiful face. Logan knew it sounded crazy, but he did like his men to be masculine and a hairy chest added to that. Deklan carried himself in a way that displayed a virile quality, so naturally he had all the perks that Logan liked.

Whoa. What? Surprise.

Logan shook his head after catching sight of Deklan towering above him on horseback. It scared him and he screamed while splashing water haphazardly during his wild bout to stand up. He looked like a crooked stork as he attempted to cover himself up with his clumsy hands, but his exaggerated male organ didn't allow any sort of success at concealing what protruded so grandly between his legs. There was a lot there and it always seemed to get in his way.

Astonished at what he saw, Deklan stared. His mouth dropped wide open as if he just saw the sun come out at nighttime. He caught himself staring and quickly blinked. "Hey." He broke contact with Logan's oversized crotch and then looked him in the face. "You will catch a chill if you run around in the night like that."

To subdue his humiliation, Logan never made eye contact with Deklan. All he let him see was the topside of his scalp, keeping it that way purposely. Not only was Logan embarrassed because he stood completely naked in front of Deklan, but he really didn't want him to put a face to a caramel colored stork with a significantly sized male organ that made him appear to be deformed. He was hoping Deklan didn't recognize him from the night before. He told Deklan that he was right about catching a chill before he turned away from him and his horse. His feet started walking along the riverbank on their own which took him back to the same place where he left his trousers. Logan couldn't wait to get back to his pants to avoid further mortification for being nude in front of a horse and an attractive man.

Deklan silently followed Logan on horseback. Feeling awkward, Logan wasn't quite sure what to do with himself, walk without saying anything or strike up a conversation – in the nude. He was horrified. With his bare bottom facing Deklan, he had the feeling that he was watching it flex with every step he took. All Logan wanted to do is get dressed.

Logan finally heard Deklan's voice behind him. "Aren't you the one I ran into a couple nights ago in the clover field?"

Logan wanted to run. For real. "Unh – Yes."

"This is a pleasant surprise." Deklan was smiling and he couldn't take his eyes away from Logan's rear end. He thought it was cute and he liked the color.

In Logan's head, he was not sure what Deklan was referring to. Did he like what he was seeing from behind or was he actually being cordial?

"I have to admit, this is not the view I was expecting to see tonight, but it's okay." Deklan said as if he heard Logan's thoughts.

Logan wondered again, 'What was he referring to?'

Chapter 8

There were only a few hours to finish what needed to be taken care of at the Manor and it was evident that Wattsworth was running on spurts of steam. Nightfall was minutes from making its appearance and soon there would be wagons pulling up to the house with potential brides for Deklan.

Logan didn't have Deklan quite figured out yet, but he was almost close to certain a bride was not part of his plan. It's just a feeling he had.

Noticing that dusk was breaking and the sun was melting into the horizon, Logan saw the lighted torches alongside the walkway of the plantation's entryway begin to glow a little brighter. Against the darkening sky, the lanterns burned beautifully and became more vivid as time passed by.

Logan quietly hummed a made up song to myself as he glanced up at the candlelight's flickering in the small windows scattered along the backside of the manor's walls. He could see a few images waver behind the light while the individuals rummaged around to get ready for the fancy night.

He took to the river again as he did earlier in the day and

floundered until his dreams seemed real. Logan was happy and thought if his fantasy actually came to life, he wanted to be clean and fresh.

The night was peaceful even though the sound of crickets and frogs voiced their opinions to each other as to who could croak the loudest. He floated on the surface of the water just listening. It was tranquil really and bid him to want to stay there forever.

Logan dried himself off with a cotton cloth he made out of an old dress skirt of his mothers. It worked perfectly for occasions such as this one. He covered himself with the cloth and crept back to the carriage house as if he was sneaking.

He pointed himself to the candlelight he left burning in his bedside window. Even though the river flowed close by his yard out back, the candle was a sure way of finding his way back home a little easier.

Before going inside, Logan looked out across the grounds and watched all the horse drawn carriages lined up at the front entry of the Manor. It was an amazing vision to see how many people were actually going to be filling the plantation hall. Too bad he was sitting on the outside overlooking the splendid event. Like the kitchen servant said, he didn't belong there and would never mingle with such people.

Logan sighed and went inside his little dilapidated barn style house that he shared with the chickens and goats.

He had just finished putting on his nightshirt when he heard rustling outside his door and then a gentle rap against its frame with what sounded to be from a wooden stick. "Who could that be at this time of evening?" He asked a chicken standing next to him. He thought it might be someone from the kitchen staff come to tell him he forgot something, so he rushed to answer it before he heard yelling through the wood panels.

Pushing a chicken out of his pathway with his foot, he went to the door and peeked through an open crack. He saw a silhouette of a man his size standing there.

Puzzled by who it was, Logan hesitated a minute before making the decision to open the door. A second gentle rap that sounded much like that wooden stick he heard a moment ago tapped against the boards again. Wood against wood reverberated a high pitched echo inside the carriage house. The chickens ran and the goats backed into a corner at the rear.

Logan was not one to be frightened, so he graciously opened up the door to see who it was.

In front of Logan stood a skinny man who he had never seen before, nor did he have any idea why he was at his door. The man was about Logan's height, maybe a little shorter by an inch or two. He was thin or at least the pinstriped pants and jacket he was wearing made him appear thinner than he looked to be. He appeared to be from a place outside the village Logan lived in by the clothing he was wearing. Logan had never seen such attire on a man before, which made him question where he came from. The skinny man looked strange to him and it made Logan a bit leery as to if it was wise to invite him in.

Logan said good evening to him and asked if he had lost his way. After he mentioned that, he told him the birthday celebration he figured he was here to attend was across the way at the Manor and he needed to go to the front entry if he planned not to miss out on the spectacular event. Logan pointed across the grounds where the man needed to be.

The skinny man looked over his shoulder where Logan was pointing and then turned back to say he was not in the area for a party, but to see him.

A little taken back, Logan pursed his lips as if he was about to say 'What?' and then forced his brows together in the middle until his forehead wrinkled. All he said next was, 'Huh?"

The man repeated but added his name this time. "Logan, I'm here to see you. I have a gift from your father that is ready to pass on to you."

The man sounded so formal when he spoke.

Logan stood there with a blank stare and just looked at him. Speechless. "Huh?" he said again. He looked at the man stupidly again, wondering who he was and how he knew his name.

"May I come in before the chickens decide to run free," he brightly asked.

Fumbling for words and the handle on the door, Logan

waved for him to come inside. "Yeah – Unh, sure sir. Come in".

They looked at each other for a few moments, realizing that there was a bit of a resemblance between the two of them. They both blinked to clear their heads and then went on observing the other.

A chicken clucked and the scratchy silence was broken.

"I don't have much to offer sir, but you are welcome to a cup of water and an apple," Logan nervously said. "Would you like that, mister?"

"No thank you, Logan. I don't have much time," he replied, fussing with the large tattered box he brought with him that was tucked under his arm. He laid it on a rickety table to the right of the door. "This is for you, from your father." He tapped its mushy lid.

Logan was not sure what was going on, but it was truly an event that he considered out of the ordinary.

First an unknown stranger walked up to his door and tapped on it. The clothes he was wearing didn't seem to be from the current time. He looked a bit like Logan in the face except his skin tone was white and Logan's was black or more so caramel due to his interracial parents. Aside from the man being much paler than Logan, they could probably be considered twins if his build were more muscular than it was.

He looked at Logan. "Logan, it's time to believe."

With that being said, Logan's curiosity spiraled downward because he really didn't have any idea what was going on. It appeared somewhat mystical. Something seemed warped and he started wondering if he drowned out back in the river and this was all part of passing on. He pinched himself to be sure. It hurt. When the chicken pecked his bare toe, that hurt too. He was very much alive.

What was really happening? It was all very strange.

The man in the pinstripe suit asked Logan to sit down at the table next to the box he carried in with him.

Logan did what he asked and waited for the man to divulge to him the reason for his unexpected visit.

The man laid a hand on the box top and took a deep breath

before speaking.

Clutching the seat of his chair, Logan first glanced at the box and then looked up at the man touching it and he saw what seemed to be a mirror in front of him that reflected images of white people when looked into. His head was hurting, but wasn't sure that the pain was even real. None of what was happening seemed real. Logan at this point found it outlandish to ask the man's name, so he nicknamed him the mirror man instead. The name suited him because it was as if Logan was looking at his own reflection, only the man's skin tone was much paler.

Logan noticed a glow around the mirror man's face and wondered if it was coming from the candle light up stairs or the mystery man was actually shining.

Eloquently he spoke, "This old box I have for you is from your father. He wanted me to give it to you on a night that was going to be significant. A night you will always remember."

A chill sped down Logan's back, and just like that, the joy he felt in the river earlier had disappeared. For some reason, he had a feeling the man was going to tell him what he already was aware of. But the thing Logan didn't know was what on earth was in that tattered old box and how it was related to what the mirror man was going to say to him.

Should any of this be believed? It seemed farfetched and more like a fairytale.

Logan was not certain of when it started, but he noticed his neck muscles tightened.

The mirror man softly rubbed the box top in a loose fashion and continued to tell Logan why he was in his kitchen. "This may seem a bit extreme, so I would like you to stay seated, if you please. Think of me as your godfather, kind of like a fairy, but without wings."

Logan swallowed hard and tried to get control. It all seemed crazy. He knew there was really no reason to ask his name because it just seemed absurd to do so. What he just heard didn't quite make any sense. There's no such thing as fairies.

Did death really play out in the river out back?

"Tonight you are going to meet somebody amazingly special." The mirror man ran his hand across the box top and then stopped at the edge as if he was planning to open it up.

The mirror man carried on, speaking in such a ceremonial manner that Logan could hardly understand him. "I am your sentinel for the evening, but only for tonight. As you can see, I am a clear resemblance of your father's image, an extension of his inner spirit, which is meant to ease your acceptance of me. Nobody other than you can see or hear me. I am here to guide you to the biddings of your heart. You have grown up to be the man your father expected and he wishes for you to be happy. I come to help you during a time that won't be easy for you or your selected soul mate. In this box I pass on to you the confidence to seek and keep your harmonized soul. You will know who it is almost immediately and the relationship will be recognized this evening. Don the contents of this box to the celebration tonight, but know that it can only be with you this one time and only until midnight."

Why does everything end at midnight? Crazy rule.

Logan swallowed hard again. This time his throat felt dryer than before. The sensation of ingesting a pinecone was evident. It hurt like the dickens, even more when he gulped a second time. "But wait—," he stuttered. "But this isn't how you think. I can't exhibit love in a public place the way it feels natural to me or would like to. I can't take this box or anything inside it. This won't work." Logan stammered and drifted away. His voice lowered, "This won't work."

The mirror man placed his finger in front of his own lips as a signal to shush Logan. "Hush, Logan. It's alright. Your father and I know everything about you. Unfortunately this isn't going to be an easy journey, but it will work out."

The mirror man walked around Logan's backside and began to massage his tensing shoulders. "Your father's spirit created me to direct you to your soul mate. You must put on these clothes and I will then take you to the celebration by horse and carriage."

"But - ," Logan started.

"No buts. You must believe," He interrupted. "Open the box. Hurry. We do not have time to waste."

"But how will I know I have met my soul mate?" Logan asked.

"You'll know. Just believe. Now hurry."

Doubtful at first, Logan hesitantly released the grip he had on the chair he was sitting in and stood up. Slowly he grabbed both sides of the tattered box and lifted. There was a sudden odor of mildew that quickly vanquished as soon as the cover cleared the box bottom. He propped the lid against the leg of his chair while he waited for the air in front of him to clear. He wasn't waiting for the bad smell to dissipate, but the glistening smoke that appeared above the contents of the box. It was almost magical. Borderline beautiful. Mystical even.

Logan's discontentment dissolved and he started to relax as if the magic dust coming from the box was a comfort serum. He was mesmerized and didn't notice anything going on around him.

At the time Logan didn't realize the mirror man stepped away from his shoulders, but as the magic fog settled, he soon saw the image of his father standing in front of him on the other side of the table. He saw his angel. His guardian, or what the mirror man referred to as, his Fairy.

Logan stood quietly while he looked down into the tattered box and saw the most spectacular bundle of fabric he had ever seen in his life.

"Go ahead, take hold of it." Smiling, the mirror man whispered. "It is yours for the evening. It will bring you good fortune."

Reaching in, Logan lifted the brilliant gown as if it would disintegrate by his touch. He carefully removed it from its ragged home. First he held what looked to be a blouse of pure white silk, tailored with rich gold thread. The front placket had two double-breasted rows of silver and gold buttons running from bottom to top. It had a large wide collar that stood high and firm with a bow like scarf tied around the neck. The double layered cuffs on the long sleeved shirt were fastened together with two silver and gold links. Like he thought earlier, the blouse was brilliant and he didn't feel worthy enough to be wearing something so stunning.

"It's yours Logan. Put it on." Logan's father's voice rang from the mirror man. It was a different tone than before. It had to be him.

Afraid that he would ruin its beauty, Logan held back a few

minutes before continuing. Anxiously, but carefully, he removed his nightshirt and put on the silk blouse. The fit was perfection. How did they know?

The mirror man helped Logan button it up and then neatly tied the bow-tie around his neck.

The next item to come out of the box that was tucked beneath the shirt was shin length trousers. Logan reached for them and carefully put them on. They were also constructed of fine white silk but heavier than the blouse. The panel across the front was also double laced with a row of silver and gold buttons embellishing each hip. He carefully fastened the panel in place on each side. He couldn't see himself in any reflection, but could tell he was stunning. He could feel it.

Seeing the look on the mirror man's face told Logan he was doing fine.

"Dashing," said the fairy. "Keep going. There's more." He pointed.

Logan reached into the box again and pulled out a lightweight pale auburn coat that looked as though it would reach just above his knees. He ran his finger along the gold stitching that lined the lapel and then circled the rims of each gold button that were reflecting sparks of light around the room. The leather belt was wide and stiff and it had a large square framed buckle that was mostly made of silver. A rope of gold trim accented the edges and completely glazed the backside.

Logan's personal fairy helped him put the coat on while he buckled the belt. They left the coat open in the middle to allow the shirt and trousers beneath the lightweight coat to remain visible.

There was another item of clothing inside the box as if the bottom of it was never ending. But before Logan took hold of the next item, the mirror man removed a heavy silver necklace from around his own neck that he had tucked down the front of his pinstriped jacket. He took it off and transferred it to Logan's. It hung graciously against his chest with the emerald laced Fleur-De-Lis pendant resting in front of his heart. The green stones were Logan's favorite and they made him feel attractive.

The mirror man steadily stepped backward and motioned for Logan to retrieve the final article of clothing from the box.

Inside he discovered a frosted vanilla cloak edged in short white fur that may have been mink or angora. Logan wasn't quite sure what it was, but it was beautiful all the same. When placed over his shoulders, it seemed to have broadened his stature by about ten or more inches. He felt masculine and striking all at the same time. If he were to wed, this would certainly be his garment of choice.

The mirror man handed him stocking covers for his feet and then removed the shoes he was wearing. Logan didn't notice before, but the footwear the fairy had on were made-up of tanned vanilla leather and fastened with bold silver buckles that matched the belt Logan already had fixed around his waist. He handed the shoes to Logan and told him they were for his to wear. Once more the fit was perfect.

"What about you?" Logan asked while he adjusted his feet into the comfortable shoes he just gave him.

"Don't worry about me, I am always prepared." The fairy's feet were magically covered in chocolate brown slippers with a gold threaded Fleur-De-Lis emblem embroidered on the topside vamp.

"Where did those come from?" Logan stared with doubt that all the mystical events that were going on around him were actually happening.

Where was he? Was Logan dreaming? Was he dead? Was he in fairytale land or someplace of the like?

Logan wanted to see what he looked like, but there was no looking glass or reflective surface of any kind nearby for him to gaze into.

Tugging at his finger, the mirror man spun a white gold ring over his knuckle and took it off. "One more item to add a polished touch to your ensemble." He held up the jewelry piece that he removed from his finger. "Take this ring and together with the necklace around your neck will keep you and your soul mate safe and protected."

Logan held out his left hand and the mirror man slipped the ring onto Logan's finger. It fit nicely as if it belonged there. He gripped the medallion and held his fist tightly against his chest. A deluge of emotion surfaced and Logan's eyes began to water a little. It was a heavy moment and he could feel an endearing soul closing in on his.

"I know you're not able to see what I see, but understand when I tell you this. You look amazing and your true love will know who you are when you walk into the room." The mirror man opened up his arms and wrapped them around Logan's shoulders. Hugging him.

"Thank you for seeing what I don't." He hugged back.

"Time to go." Stepping away from Logan and gripping both hands to his shoulders at full arm's length, the mirror man then swung his left hand toward the door, opening up a pathway for Logan to follow. "Your carriage awaits you."

At first Logan thought a carriage was not needed because he could walk to the Manor in just a few long strides, but the idea of a horse drawn basket delivering him to the doorstep of the Prince's palace was another magical moment that he just could not leave out of this evening's fairy tale.

When Logan stepped up to the open carriage, he caught a glimpse of his reflection in a puddle on the ground. It wasn't very clear but he stopped to gaze anyway and took a peek at what the mirror man saw. He was right, Logan was truly striking and to see himself like he did gave him the confidence he needed to enter the mansions front door where he had never been invited through before. Even though his self-reliance rose, his nerves were still a little on the edge and his insides went touchy.

The mirror man opened up the side door to the carriage so Logan could step in without gripping the handle himself. Within moments of closing the door, the carriage started moving and he was on his way to the plantations doorstep to supposedly meet his mate.

Chapter 9

Commotion was stirring inside the radiant Manor. The village people were filing in like army of ants channeling their food to the colonies nest. The line started from the carriage parkway outside, continued on up the step-way to the entry and flowed down the staircase on the inside. It looked to be a slow moving line that didn't seem to be going anywhere very fast. The line appeared to be at a standstill.

The general society were all being greeted by some of the servant's on entry and acknowledged once again by more servants when they reached the bottom of the mahogany staircase that took them into a massive lobby. Beyond that, everybody flowed into the grand hall at the main manor's center point.

Known to make their appearance after everyone arrived, the royal family kept themselves out of sight in the beginning.

A picture of subtle purity was all that came to mind. The young maidens yet to be broken in were hopeful to be the prince's one choice. They came to the event looking puffed up and overdressed. The ladies could hardly move or breathe in there cheeky ball gowns.

The grand hall started out cold, but the increasing bodies being loaded into the room were letting off a heat source that would keep everybody warm if not on the verge of burning up.

The downside to a full room of people is that the smell of flower pedals and corn pummeled starch were emanating everywhere. Because of this, it made breathing in the much needed cleaner air nearly nonexistent on the inside.

All the starchy powders were intended to disguise the bad odors coming from the women as their pasty bodies beneath all the fabulous layers began to heat up there private parts and release their much unwanted feminine vapors.

God help us. Everyone.

All the ladies carried fans to keep themselves cool or to hide their true gluttonous smile from the prince.

The dark of the night was creeping in fast and it appeared that everybody had already arrived. The stairway was now empty except for a few single men perched against the stair rail waiting to snag any unwanted stray that the wealthy Deklan found too unsettling to marry.

Sir Butler Wattsworth separated himself from the hall and took to the master wing to inform Dante that all the guests had arrived and it was a good time for the family to join the event without further delay.

The music mellowed, letting everybody know that the guests of honor were on their way in. It was formal and almost imperial like.

All the milling within the great room came to a standstill and focus was now on the entry at the back of the room. Everybody waited quietly as if the President of the United States was about to make his appearance.

Scattered whispers as well as bashful giggles from the excited young ladies in waiting were heard. Insatiable parents shoved their child to the front so that the young groom to be could get a better look at his future bride. Poofs of odor absorbing powders bellowed from the ladies skirts as mothers gave their spoiled daughters a push into the open spaces.

It was a despicable display to see parents prostituting their child in exchange for wealth.

The quartet finally started playing as the main family entered the room. The Hall opened up as if Moses just parted the sea. The people moved to the outer edges of the room that left an open space in the center as a way to allow Deklan and his parents to make their way to the head table at the end of the Grand Hall. They greeted almost everyone on their way through. None of whom Deklan found appealing enough to catch his eye. He bowed his head and repeated good evening to everybody he passed. Keeping his hands clasped tightly behind his back, he kept walking a straight and narrow line.

The music tinkled in the hall and was becoming more and more droning as time went on. It seemed to be the same racketeering noise that just kept repeating. If it wasn't the same song, the ticky, ticky, ticky of the harp and plucky stringed instruments certainly all sounded the same.

From all the twirling on the dance floor, Deklan was feeling sick as well as getting sore feet. He no longer wanted to be forced to mingle with all the ladies he truly wasn't interested in. He was wearing out fast and there wasn't a single soul in the room that he even found to be a good match for himself. The evening was turning out to be a disappointment and he had a feeling it was going to regress downward unless a miracle walked through the front door and knocked him on the head. He was certain of what he wanted and he knew it wasn't there.

Throughout the evening, Deklan cordially danced with every available maiden at the party. Fat ones, skinny ones, even ones with feminine hygiene issues that had him holding his breath nearly half the night. He wanted to die. He wanted to leave.

Chapter 10

Logan was doing okay with the whole situation that was transpiring in front of him, but when the door to the carriage opened up again calling invitation to exit, reality punched him and it all became real. His nerves went back to lurching inside him and he started to feel sickly. He thought he even turned a light shade of green. He was close to being in ruin.

Outside the carriage door, the mirror man was standing there waiting. He gave Logan a few more bits of advice as he lent his hand to help him out.

The stairway in front of them turned out to be more massive than Logan thought it was going to be, but he made his way up them anyways. When his foot reached the third step, he turned around to see the mirror man off and discovered that he was already gone. As if by magic, the carriage, the horse and the fairy had disappeared. They were nowhere. Logan suddenly felt alone again and sensed as though he stepped deeper into a dream.

In order to bring comfort to himself, he reached for the necklace and held it with the same hand that possessed the silver ring. He proceeded up the grand stairway as the mirror man had intended him to do.

The pit of Logan's stomach was going through bouts of somersaults with every step he took toward the fancy event up ahead. He didn't have any inkling as to whom he was destined to meet inside or if he was going to find his soul mate at all. Logan had been told he was, but who really knew for sure. He looked up into the thin traces of light between the double doors while he climbed the magical stairway.

The closer he got to the entry way, the easier it was for him to hear what was going on inside. He mostly heard the resonance of a four string quartet and the reverberating clatter of a harpsichord. He could tell that sound anywhere. Sometimes it tarnished his eardrums if played badly or reached a certain high pitched key. It was not one of his favorite instruments and Logan could most certainly do without the noisemaker.

Behind the stifling music that was being played, he also heard a lot of voices muttering no-nonsense jabber. All of which demonstrated to be untruthful tales tangled with imitation smiles as a way of getting what they wanted and probably didn't deserve.

What seemed like more than a mile up a rocky hillside, Logan finally reached the top of the stairway. In front of him stood two massive French doors that were left slightly ajar at the center seam. From between them came a soft yellow light that painted his entire being gold. Somehow it felt warm and seemed to touch his soul with glistening grace.

At that instant, Logan knew he was at the right place at the right time and should enter as if he was initially invited by scribbles on a parchment letter page. Much like the one he found outside the kitchen door in the dirt that adhered itself to his face. Maybe that was for him, but never made it to his door. Whatever the case may be, he was where he was supposed to be and that piece of paper may have been the initial nudge he needed to set him on his way.

Logan stood a minute before entering. What ticked as only a few short moments felt like a stalling eternity. He was unsure of what the outcome would be on the other side of those doors so it left him feeling a little skittish.

Courage eventually built up inside him after he inhaled

deeply. There he held his breath, took a step forward and slipped through the opening between the two large doors with the pretty yellow glow. He blew out the air that was stuck in his lungs before lack of fresher oxygen made him pass out.

When he stepped into brighter light at the top of the stairs, he looked down and noticed a few heads turn toward him and stare. The halo of light he could feel ricocheting all around him made him feel like an angel standing before them.

Soon after, whispering streamed around the room in a rush and immediately set the rest of the heads in motion to look his way. Breathy gasps and pointing fingers came with whispering, 'Who is that? Where did he come from? And why is he here?'

Logan brought no child with him to push in front of the prince and he clearly wasn't a female. He could tell by expressions that most of the crowd thought he didn't belong there and should go back to where he came from. It was almost as though they were threatened by his staggering existence.

He gripped the pendant with his ringed finger. "Father, give me strength," he whispered to his dad as well as the lord above.

Leaving the eventful ballroom was not going to happen. Logan was sent to this place for a reason and by what his guidance Fairy told him, he was going to find his true mate and lifelong companion under this very roof.

Logan was frightened by the selection that was compiled in front of him. With that, his heart was definitely not about to say yes just yet. He continued to stand still while looking beyond the powdery mist that was taking over the large room.

Down below he could see many female faces that were wrestling behind clouds of what he presumed to be starchy powders with added floral fragrances. The lacey fans they held were without a doubt waving away the cloud so they could see what was in front of them or used to blow away the many floral odors that were combined into one bad smell.

Logan spotted Deklan's mother and father lean into one another at the opposite end of the room. Deklan's father pointed a finger Logan's way, which made him think that the man was asking who he was.

In front of the podium where the Royal's were sitting,

Logan saw Deklan awkwardly dancing at full arm's length with a pale white fleshy red headed girl who showed off a split-toothed grin. Logan could tell she was not for Deklan by the exaggerated body language and the distance he placed between the two of them. Deklan was cordial and politeness was why he put himself through the miss fitted partnership that would only last for a spell.

Logan has seen Deklan close up before, but this time he was fantastically stunning. Logan could tell this easily as his pupils dilated while trying to keep focus on the handsome prince. It was known that the irises go through bouts of stress when one spots another being they are attracted to. Logan's went crazy when he saw Deklan and widened instantly. Logan's heart pounded wildly beneath his ribcage, on the verge of losing rhythm and for a moment thought he would lose consciousness. Deklan looked much different than he did during their other encounters, and Logan was sure he would look different to Deklan too. Logan always saw him wearing heavily woven britches and a loosely fitted linen shirt. This time he was polished in brides-groom white, with embellishments of gold and silver, much like his own.

Was this who Logan was supposed to meet? Could he be his soul mate? Impossible, but he hoped. They were from two different worlds. How could an exquisite young man like Deklan find affection in a pauper chap like Logan? The whole idea just didn't make sense. He hoped even harder.

While Logan slowly descended down the stairs, he kept his eyes on the striking prince. As he stepped downward, everybody else in the ballroom became lost in a murky blur.

Suddenly Deklan noticed Logan on the stairs and his dance steps slowed to a mere stumble. His eyes widened in the same way Logan's did when he first spotted him take a few more steps to the main floor. Deklan's connection with the pale-faced red head broke and she appeared to drift away.

Deklan stopped abruptly and faced Logan, forgetting the chunky girl he was paired with.

Logan's feet left the final step while their eye contact remained fixed on each other.

Logan looked away quickly and so did Deklan. Both lads

focused hard on the floor in front of them before speculation circled the room that the two of them were attracted to each other.

It was amazing.

A more permanent distraction mounted when the next fair maiden waiting in line ran to Deklan and forced his hand to dance with her. She pulled him close, twisted one of his arms around her waist and vice gripped his other hand with link-locked fingers. Deklan seemed out of touch with his new partner for the evident reason that he stayed connected to Logan at the foot of the stairway.

Logan held back his white toothy grin with a slight sideways smirk, letting Deklan know that he secured his connection to his heart.

Just then, his dance shut down. Prince Deklan, as Logan liked to call him, let go of the chubby girl and walked his way. Their eyes met again and stayed fixed. As Deklan strolled toward Logan, the kerosene lamps behind him seemed to lower to a dimmer burn.

The grand hall went quiet along with dropping jaws and hand covered whispers. What took place in the room was not expected and the notion that the entire town was witnessing it put Logan a little bit on edge. He was not prepared for a public display, however by no means was he going to let him slip away.

This was his moment and all the hoping was coming true.

Another half grin from Logan was passed on to Deklan before he turned and moved over toward the wine table to swallow himself some much needed confidence. Looking over the piled fruit in the center of the table, Logan finally reached for a metal goblet. Just as he did, a virile white-gloved hand covered his. It was him. It was the Prince.

Could this be the mate to Logan's internal soul?

"Let me get that for you," Logan heard him say, quiet like a whisper. Deklan's deep voice rang beyond sensual that it gave Logan burning chills.

What did his fairy know that he didn't and what took so long for it to transpire?

Logan dissolved as Deklan's warm breath graced his ear

and the heat of his body so close to Logan's sent a terrifying love sick signal through his bones. He was frightened and felt secure with him there all at the same time.

"Sure. Okay. Yes – Please." Logan bowed to him, looking ridiculous and clumsy as he did. It was his first reaction. What else was he supposed to do? He was new to meeting a prince and was terrified with such an attractive man standing only a few inches from his side. Deklan was exactly his sort and by the way Deklan was acting, Logan was pretty certain that he was Deklan's sort too.

Logan wasn't sure if Deklan was smiling or laughing at him. He knew his greeting was awkward, but it was a good attempt considering what was going on, so he bet on the smile.

Smiling and looking directly into Logan's eyes the entire time, Deklan skillfully reached for the carafe of red wine and with his hand still locked over Logan's, poured it into the goblet they were both holding.

"You know my name I'm sure. What is yours?" Deklan's deep voice soothed his nerves.

Logan was finding it hard to believe Deklan didn't recognize him from the river or the night he took him home on horseback. Did Logan's fairy godfather alter his looks or cast some strange spell on the handsome prince?

Deklan released his grasp slowly and Logan took the goblet from him, letting their fingers slip gently free from each other's. "Thanks," Logan said. "I mean – Unh – er – Logan. My name is Logan," he stupidly stammered.

That time Deklan's true laughter surfaced. It was okay though, because Logan faltered with words and his reply came across as being comical as if he told him his name was Thanks or Unh. Induced by embarrassment, he was sure his face changed to bright red.

Logan felt oddly warm and decided he needed some fresh air. He fanned himself with his goblet free hand while turning toward an open door located at the side of the great room that looked as though it led outside. He turned back. "Can you follow me outdoors or do you need to stay in here with your invited guests?"

Still holding on to the carafe of wine, Deklan snatched another goblet from the fruit table for himself. "These people are known by my father and will be fine without me. Besides this birthday party has already served its purpose, because I've found what I was looking for. Lead the way. I will be right behind you." He looked at Logan with misty eyes as if he were trying to see his soul.

Logan smiled, or actually grinned – wide. He was pining hard.

The two lads walked out the side door to a well-tailored courtyard. Green topiary and floral arrangements were scattered everywhere and the air was much fresher than the dusty odor that was taking over the inside.

Following a stone path, they walked side-by-side until they reached the pond in the middle of the lawn. Sporadically placed on all sides were marble benches for observation and meditation. Instead of taking one close by, they strode to the far side of the water pool and chose a seat there. It was perfectly secluded, and in the darkness nobody would be able to define that it was the two of them sitting together.

They carried on with blotchy chatter, trying not to lose connection with the other. They mainly spoke of what they liked and disliked. The usual conversation when two people meet for the very first time.

Even though Logan gave up a lot of details about himself, he did however withhold his secret that he worked at the Manor and spent his days and nights just outside the kitchen door. Logan stayed quiet about that because he didn't want Deklan to know he was poor and that he bathed in the river out back. The dazzling clothes Logan had on were misleading and gave the wrong impression regarding his actual character. He wasn't certain if it would change Deklan's decision to stay or go if he knew who Logan really was. Logan kept it to himself, at least for the time being anyway.

Deklan was charming in the way Logan thought a prince would be and he seemed to show signs of wanting to be more than just simple friends. Logan could tell by the way Deklan smiled, the way he purposely leaned into his personal space and the way he sneakily pressed his knee and shoulder against his while sitting next to him on the bench. Call it a hunch, but Logan could feel his attraction inching in on him. The connection was sincere and above all he could tell it was heartfelt.

Deklan pressed himself tighter against Logan's shoulder, and surprisingly he whispered, "Why don't we dance?" He stood up and reached for his hand. "Come, it will be fun."

Daring was what it would be.

Logan looked up at Deklan and made an excuse to avoid leaving his seat. "But there's no music. I'm not a good dancer without music."

Deklan flipped his hand in a come hither manner. "Come on. Rise up. You don't need music to dance with me. I'll lead you to the stars and back."

"I do need it. I hardly have any rhythm with music," Logan confessed, getting more nervous as time moved by.

"Come. Dance with me." Deklan waved his hand at Logan again, signaling for him to rise.

Logan rose and followed his direction, hoping there was nobody watching who would find offence with two men holding one another or found it right to spear them dead.

Considering there was no music playing in the background, Logan discovered that he wasn't doing too badly.

Deklan held Logan the same way he did to him on their horseback ride a few days ago, with a tight grip and very close. Something about dancing with Deklan helped Logan maintain steady footwork. Logan's rhythm remained intact and it appeared as if he knew what he was doing. Deklan was good at leading and Logan was happy to follow.

Deklan pulled Logan tighter against his strong body, feeling his heartbeat when he met Logan's chest. They swayed with their cheeks less than an inch from each other's and Logan nearly dissolved when Deklan whispered in his ear.

"You see, you have excellent rhythm. Might I be wrong, but this could work out well for the both of us." Deklan took a chance and took a few steps forward, insinuating how much fun two men could have together.

Logan grinned and backed away. Actually, he thought he panicked. He smiled at Deklan in a quirky manner and sat back down on the bench where he probably should have stayed in the first place. Nervously, Logan lifted the goblet of wine for the much needed support he left behind earlier, hopeful he didn't appear desperate for grabbing a fermented beverage so quickly.

Aside from all the small talk, Deklan made a comment that Logan had unusual eyes for a man with his skin tone. He also mentioned that his eyes were what he first noticed when he saw him for the first time all alone on the stairway. They captivated him instantly and caused the uncontrolled reaction Logan had on him.

Deklan took the goblet from Logan's grasp and set it down on the bench beside them. "Can I kiss you?" He politely asked, holding his hand.

Logan didn't expect Deklan's request and at the same time thought he was taking huge strides at getting closer. His face went long as Deklan moved in. Logan didn't answer at first, but then stuttered, "I – I'm sorry, I've never kissed another man before." He backed up a bit and then closed his eyes.

Deklan moved with him and drew himself close enough so that Logan could feel Deklan's breath on his skin. He shuddered the moment Deklan kissed him. Deklan's mouth closed over Logan's and it felt gentle and flawless.

The perfect kiss lasted for more than a single spin on a timepiece before Deklan moved away, nipping Logan's bottom lip as he did. "That wasn't so bad now was it?" Deklan spoke close to a whisper, still holding Logan's hand and caressing it with his thumb.

Once more, Logan's face went long, but with certain traces of a slanted smile. He said nothing and didn't have to. Deklan knew his answer before he asked it.

Deklan blinked, leaned forward and pressed his lips to Logan's again. They felt softer and comforting this time.

Logan was stirring inside and could sense their souls uniting. They have found one another by the blessing of his father and the mysterious mirror man. They directed him to where he was, knowing who he was and who was waiting for him.

"I have much I would like to tell you, but I cannot stay long," Logan confessed.

"Will I see you again after tonight?" Deklan's grip on his hands went tighter.

Logan hesitated with his answer and pulled his hands away. "I would like that very much, but I am not sure it's a good idea."

"Why would you say that?" Deklan went cold.

Logan looked down to hide his eyes. "You and I are not what is expected and I don't think this will be as easy for either of us the way you seem to think. Many people believe that this is going against human nature. What about your parents? What will they say and think? We will have to hide behind darkness in order to see each other. Trust me. I have seen what happens to the meek and unique. For god sake, it will be even worse for us being that you are white and English and I am a man of black flesh. How do you think that will look to the majority of the people in the village and those within the plantation? A dog may love a fish, but how will they live?"

"Hog wash, I say." Deklan stood up, turning away from Logan while talking to the sky. "They cannot expect me to marry a maiden if it will not make me happy. That is against *my* nature. It will not work. You are what I have been looking for and they need to understand that." He turned back toward Logan and took both hands in his again, knelt down in front of him and said with a quieter voice, "I cannot go back in that lonely house without you with me. I just can't."

Gripping Deklan's hands tighter, Logan couldn't seem to let go. "This will be a struggle with life. For you *and* for me. How can we be happy with that?"

"How can we be happy without that?" Deklan confessed.

The bell tower rang in the distance which gave warning that midnight had approached. Logan looked up toward the reverberating ring and remembered what the mirror man told him. He will lose the magic at midnight and for all he knew, Deklan went with it. "I am sorry, my prince, I have to go."

"No, you can't." Deklan squeezed his hands tighter. "You can't go. I won't let you."

The bell continued ringing and Logan felt a strange sensation saturating the space around him. "Tonight was the happiest night of my life, Deklan, but I must go now." He struggled to pull his hands from Deklan's grasp. His grip was tight, but he managed to pull free. The entire moment took place in what felt like slow motion as Logan began to slip away. He had to leave. He didn't want to risk being seen as the silhouette he was before meeting the mirror man.

Deklan began to sadden silently to himself and he bowed his head to the ground as he bumped into sorrow, "Noooooo." He then whispered, "don't go."

Logan turned away and ran through the darkness of night until he reached the stone wall at the edge of the garden. He climbed over it and jumped to the ground on the other side. He felt a sharp tug on the cloak he was wearing and noticed that a small piece of it was clinging to the spiky irons lining the topside of the stocky wall. As quickly as he saw it there, it vanished. Copper embers flickered and rose to the sky where it once was.

Back at the fish pond where Logan left him, Deklan dropped to his knees and dealt with sadness. As he did, he noticed the silver ring that Logan was wearing in his hand. The grip he had on Logan was so strong that when he pulled free, the ring had slipped from his finger. Deklan squeezed it tightly hoping that in some way it would bring Logan back to him. He stood and faced the empty space in front of him and softly muttered, "When will I see you again, Logan?"

Just as the mirror man said, the brilliant clothing on Logan's back began to fizzle and disappear as he ran away from Deklan's grasp. He lit up like a burning torch with glowering embers circling him, which rose to the sky to take refuge someplace in the spirit world where they may have come from. He looked like he was part of a glimmering fire, but in a flash, it vanished too and he was running back home barefoot and naked. Everything that just happened seemed almost dreamlike. Logan collided with anxiety, but kept on running.

He quickly burst into the carriage house, closed the door and climbed the stairs into bed. His heart was aching – Badly. His nose was stopped up, making it hard for him to breathe and his eyes went blurry from a deluge of tears. Logan was actually crying – tearing up. He was not able to keep his emotions in line.

What was happening? He was stronger than that.

When Logan left for the party earlier that evening, he was expecting it to be a happier time. Not like it was, painful and uncertain.

Why did this have to be so complicated?

He prayed for Deklan's happiness and wished like mad that it was not the last time he was going to see him. He _is_ his soul mate. He felt that when he was near him and knew for sure Deklan was who his Fairy Godfather told him he would meet. He went on weeping alone until he drifted off to sleep. As he floated away into another part of dreamland, he held the only treasure from the night in my grasp. The emerald necklace that the mirror man gave him was still with him. Logan wasn't sure how everything else he had on vanished into thin air, but the necklace did not. The clothing, the shoes, the mirror man – All gone. He looked at his hand and even the ring had disappeared. All of it except the necklace.

Why?

He held the stone in his hand and wished.

Has anybody ever died from loneliness and sorrow?

Chapter 11

Deklan was feeling sad and hollow the day after his birthday. He was supposed to feel better than what he did. Birthdays were meant to be happy occasions. His heart ached like he never knew it could.

Pressing a fisted hand to his chest, he held it there as if it were going to change the way he was feeling. The emptiness inside was overpowering him and the ring in his grasp only enhanced the sadness he felt since it reminded him of how happy he was the night before with Logan in his arms.

The prince was missing Logan and his heart was breaking.

"Why run away, Logan?" Deklan hummed as he placed the ring on his finger as two strong ranch hands escorted him by the arms down the corridor to meet with his Father and Mother in the dusty library. He knew this was not good by the way he was being dragged so harshly against his will.

This is not the dark ages. People aren't dragged to the dungeon anymore.

The outburst from his father came at him like a fired musket as soon as he was pushed through the library doorway.

"How could you make a spectacle of us like you did?" His father selfishly thought of himself and how this would reflect on him and the family. "You have disgraced us and our name. Do you know what you have done?"

Deklan stood motionless in front of his parents, not really knowing how to respond to his father's unsettling rage. He spun the ring around his middle finger and reflected back on last night. "I am not sure what to say to you, *DAD*. I have tried to tell the both of you for a very long time that I am not at all attracted to any female, ugly or beautiful, but you would not see or hear me. This is not my fault that it came out this way, but one thing I know for certain, I have found what I have been looking for last night and if you cannot let me be me, then I don't belong here. I connected with this gentleman in a way you will never know and I plan to find him and bring him home. There, I've said it. May I go now?"

"No you may not go now." Deklan's father stood up with a pointing finger. "This is not up for discussion and you are not making the decision. This is what you are going to do." He glanced at Deklan's mother for a brief moment as if he was looking for her to agree and then grabbed one of his fingers with each demand spewed out. "For starters, One— you will not see that *black* boy from last night ever again, whoever he is." He clearly stated with a racial slur. "Two— you will marry the lassie of our pleasing, and it will be soon to avoid further hostility against the Family. Three— you will stay close to home until the wedding so we can keep an eye on you. And don't give it a second thought that I won't lock your door. And four— you will apologize to your mother for making her cry and giving her the worst night of her life."

Deklan interposed quickly, "I do not agree with any of this and I think you are making a mistake bigger than you can understand. You plan to destroy people's lives because of your own selfish reasons. Why? You will first be taking away the chance for some lass to find her real true love so that this arrangement suits your needs. This will also be wasting her life and mine on a false marriage so that this small town can see that your only child is not in love with another lad. You will be making my life an unhappy one for deciding this for me. How do you see that this will be beneficial for anybody? Can't you see what you are doing?" Deklan lowered his head and sighed.

His mother stayed quiet but was sobbing while Sir Dante carried out his demands to their son. "You have no vote here. This is MY kingdom and I will run it the way I see that it should. You are getting married as we say, to whom we tell you to and it will be within the week. This affection for another lad of yours must end today. The sooner the better. For your sake and ours. NOW you may go."

"Really? This is how it will be?" Deklan was sickened with his father's idea of the perfect life for him. It wasn't in his favor and he knew it, but in favor and for the reputation of the Royal Almond monarchy. Deklan tripped backward as Wattsworth and the two hefty ranch hands dragged him away. The heels of his boots left black marks as they skidded across the slate floor. "You have just made me a prisoner in my own home, DAD," he hollered. His voice echoed loudly down the empty hall.

The servants tossed Deklan in his room like it was a prison cell. He fell to his knees and stayed there as the heavy doors behind him slammed shut. Weeping, he twisted the ring around his finger again. The touch of the ring was the only connection to the other half of his soul and it helped him feel less alone when holding it. His heart was really breaking and there was nobody there to help him heal.

Chapter 12

The only part of Logan's existence that Deklan had to hold on to was the ring that he unintentionally removed from his finger the other night. He held it close while he gazed out the large window from his room. The floor to ceiling drapes wavered as the breeze from the open window pushed against them. The flapping fabric on either side of him mimicked large wings and he looked like an angel. He was beautiful even during sadness. His boyish but masculine charm caused havoc on Logan's heart.

Bringing death to misery crossed Deklan's mind with thoughts of jumping out the window to the ground, but why give anybody the satisfaction of putting an end to his plantation love affair so quickly and easily because it was what they wanted.

Logan could actually see Deklan sitting in the window and it appeared he was looking right at Logan. Logan saw Deklan's face and could tell there was a problem and figured it had something to do with him and Deklan's parents.

While Logan watched him, Deklan briefly turned away and then back again. The thought in Logan's mind was that Deklan was wishing for his parents to enter and reconsider their approval of him being in love with another lad.

It was truly heartbreaking to see him like this. Logan started to turn sour toward Deklan's parents for putting him in that situation and for not letting him have the chance to love the person he was meant to love. They were taking a precious gift from their son and they had no idea how much they were breaking him down.

Logan sat in his window as Deklan sat in his. They were both connected to each other more than ever before as if the space between them had erected an imaginary tether.

Out of the blue and to Logan's surprise he felt a tug on my trousers around his ankle. He looked down and saw one of his goat buddies chewing his cuff. He was so engrossed in Deklan across the way that he had no idea how long the goat was eating his hemline. He swatted him away with the back of his hand and pulled his foot up and under his rump in order to hold it safely from the fabric eating varmint. It felt soggy underneath him as it started to saturate the seat of his pants.

When Logan turned back to face the outdoors, he was certain that Deklan looked straight into his window and glared right through him as if trying to figure out who he was. Logan quickly rolled back onto the bed, ducking below the sill so that Deklan didn't see him watching from a distance. The fuss of a chicken resting on Logan's pillow let him know that he almost flattened it during his rushed escape. It clucked and squabbled over the banister, flapping her wings all the way to the ground level.

"Oh bollocks." Logan almost crushed Betty Lu.

To Logan, Deklan seemed to be a prisoner in his own home. He could see it by the expression on his face and clearly noticed it in his actions. He was sulking and Logan was probably the only one who really knew why. Unfortunately he couldn't run to Deklan and comfort his soul mate.

Logan noticed that Deklan turned away from the window and faced the center of his room. There was commotion on the inside, but he couldn't see what was going on from where he was sitting down below in the carriage house. When Deklan turned back around, Logan saw that he placed the ring on the sill and blindly tucked it secretly into the corner at the ledge. He stood with his back to the ring as if guarding it from whoever was in there with him.

Whatever it was, it happened so quickly.

Without a warning call or even a knock, the door to Deklan's room burst open and slammed into the wall behind it.

Startled by the upsetting crash, Deklan quickly pushed the ring deeper into hiding. When he turned around, he noticed two servants standing in his room with his father and mother beside them. He stared at the four of them without any words spilling from his mouth, wondering what the reason was for their untimely intrusion. He backed against the window sill to block them from seeing the ring he tucked away in hiding.

His father scowled at him for what seemed like two full minutes before blurting out the reason for his angered entrance. "It is set, Deklan. Your wedding in being planned and we are sending the carriage to bring back the young lady we have chosen for you."

"WHAT?" Deklan shouted. "Have you all lost your minds? This isn't a dominion, it's a family home." He growled.

"This is the best decision for you and you know it." His father yelled back full of rage. "You will not embarrass us any further, you hear me?"

Deklan glared at his father and then over at his mother. "So this is what it's about? You are more worried about yourselves than you are about me. I understand."

"That is preposterous." His mother gasped.

"It is true." Deklan looked at her and then away, shuffling his feet across the floor to place as much space between them as possible. He didn't even want to be in the same room with them. "You two are afraid of what everybody is going to think about you and your precious family. Or are you more worried about your business?"

"For the most part we are concerned about you. And sure, we are considering the business as well." Dante motioned.

"Mostly me?" Deklan's eyebrow rose. "Sure you are."

"Don't be a spoiled brat, Deklan. Your mother and I have made this company into what it is today, so it's in your best interest to hear us out and not ruin it for you or anybody else." Sir Dante moved closer to Deklan to make sure he heard him yelling.

Crossing his arms tightly at his chest, Deklan leaned backward as a way to alleviate the loud noise bellowing from his father's wind pipe. He stood motionless after that and started to think of a way out of the mess he was in.

Why should Deklan be a part of destroying three people's lives? His life, Logan's life, and the poor Lass that will never know true love because of the disorder his father was making. It was unspeakable.

"Say something." His father demanded, grabbing Deklan's arm to loosen the hold he had on himself. He shook him.

"What do you want me to say? That I agree?" He dropped his arms so that his father would release the grip he had on him. He didn't want to be touched, especially by his unreasonable father. "Well I don't. It's senseless and I won't go through with it."

The temperature in the room felt like it rose fifty degrees as his father's head was looming in on a fire fed explosion. His mother covered her mouth as if she was about to vomit and crossed her other arm over her aching stomach to stop the onset of rumbling pain.

"Don't you dare talk to your mother and me with such contempt. You will be getting married. To a *girl*. And that is the end of this discussion." Dante turned away, grabbed Priscilla and dragged her out of Deklan's room like he had her on a leash.

By the look on his mother's face, Deklan was certain everything that was going on was being orchestrated by his father. She was showing signs of concern for him more than how this was all going to affect the family business. It seemed as though she could care less about living if Deklan was in a bad place. Call it the bond between a mother and her son. It would not be broken and there was always a tether that connected their hearts.

Deklan watched her leave at the same time feeling distraught by his father's selfish reasons. He slammed the door shut as soon as the last foot crossed the threshold, nearly removing the shoes from the last person that left the room.

Chapter 13

Another interruption announced itself by what sounded to be a more civilized tap on Deklan's door than the last abrupt intrusion. "What now?" He thought.

Instead of propping the chair under the door handle to block people out, he decided to open it up to see who it was. Majorly surprised. "Jeddah? What are you doing here?"

Jeddah was a friend of Deklan's who used to work as part of the maintenance crew at the manor. Deklan always had a brotherly regard for him, but unlike himself, Jeddah wasn't interested in love affairs with other lads. They have been friends for several years until Deklan's father let him go as a way to prevent his only son from carrying out his secret mindset toward a dark colored servant boy.

"How did you get in the house?" Deklan stepped back to open up a pathway for Jeddah to enter.

"I know all the secret doorways of this house. Remember I used to maintain and oil half the hinges around here." Jeddah smiled as he walked through the bedroom door, hugging Deklan on his way by.

"This is a pleasant surprise, but what brings you back here?" Deklan kept asking questions as he backed out of Jeddah's strong embrace.

Jeddah kept his voice low. "I heard people speaking out of line in the village as to what transpired at an event that took place here the other night. I wasn't surprised by their mention of you taking interest in a well-dressed lad instead of an elegant Lassie, but I was a bit troubled by what was being said outside your presence and thought you may need somebody on your side."

Deklan fidgeted. "You're not bothered with it?"

"No. Why should I be?" Jeddah answered with a question. His face went sharp.

"I just figured"—Deklan hesitated—"well, figured since everybody else was either trying to crucify me or make me change into someone I'm not, I imagined you were here to do the same."

"I would never do that to my friend and there's no reason to make any kind of a change." Jeddah reached out to him and gave him a tighter hug than before and then whispered in Deklan's ear, "You can't change what is supposed to be, my friend. You are the way you are for a reason and that is that."

Deklan's eyes began to swell as the hug reassured and soothed his snarled nerves. "Thank you, Jeddah. I needed this. Very much so."

They both took a seat in front of the fireplace on the south wall and exchanged stories of what has been going on in their lives over the past few years.

Deklan had a simple life, but lately a trying one. His frustrations mostly pertaining to recent events, whereas Jeddah had been traveling the river bank on a self-built floatation raft, fetching his own food from the wild while keeping clear of the white folk who still thought slavery was permissible.

For a short time now, Jeddah had been working off and on at a plantation just north of town. He was not much for staying in one place for too long, which made the whole idea of a permanent job cleaning other people's water closets again to be a bit off-putting to him. He was a free spirit and enjoyed his freedom as a river rat more than a household maintenance fellow. He is currently on the job but would soon be back to the riverbanks where he could be his own man, bonding with nature the way he enjoys it most.

Deklan told Jeddah about the night of his birthday. He started with how he fought off all the lassies that came at him in a manner that was off-putting to him and the way he came across his beautiful prince by way of a magical entrance.

He finished his story by explaining that the chap he met had mysteriously disappeared into darkness and his feeling was that he would never see him again. It was almost dreamlike the way the evening transpired with the only signs of it being real was the ring that fell into his hand.

Deklan got up and crossed to the window sill where he left the ring. It let out a faint chime as he lifted it from the stone landing. He looked at it and then placed it into the palm of his hand. "With this ring, I will find him and bring him home," he said, holding out his hand to show Jeddah the unique ring and to prove that his story was real.

"Then you need to find him," Jeddah bluntly said after hearing the sting in Deklan's voice. "I'll help you."

"That would mean a lot to me, Jeddah," Deklan replied. "I would like to get started straightaway, because my parents are already organizing my wedding and are planning to have me married by the end of the week."

"Then let's get started as quickly as tomorrow morning," Jeddah agreed. "Nice ring. It looks rare." He pointed at it just as Deklan slipped it on his middle finger.

With that being said, Deklan spun an idea in his head while twisting the ring around his finger. His plan was to search the village to find the man that the ring belonged to. It had to fit somebody and he was going to slip it on every finger until he found the person that once wore it. The chap that sealed the hole in his heart.

Chapter 14

Morning came and Logan slept in even though the rooster crowed at the crack of dawn and a stray cat was sitting only a few inches from his face waiting for him to serve breakfast. What all the animals in the house wanted and he didn't was to get up and start the day.

An animal's life was simple. Their main objective to make the day complete was to eat, sleep and poop. The circle of thought went on all day and every day for them. A life that had no interferences or inhibitions. Animals had a profound way of living. To them, life goes on with or without them and they didn't seem to have any phobias about how their neighbor lived their life. If everybody thought like an animal, the world just may be a much better place.

Logan's bed felt extra cozy, which made it ten times more difficult to get up and get the day started than it did the day before. Even though it was only a few minutes past his usual time to rise and shine, to him it still seemed comforting to just lie quietly in the realm of his feathery bed-wrap. Oh the life. If only he could stay.

He pushed the cat away with a gentle swish of his hand so

he could open up a space to swing his legs off the side of the bed and sit up. He needed to be up and ready before the kitchen help tooted their vocal horns with tones of vengeance.

Only moments after Logan became alert and conscious, his mind traveled back in time to the night he was a prince of a prince. Oh what a feeling. He knew someday he would share Deklan's warm bed instead of sleeping in the hayloft with chickens, goats and a stray kitty cat.

Logan bounced down the stairs, singing merrily with happy memories of a treasured night gone by. He swung the door open to begin his daily routine when he saw his prince on the grounds with another gentleman like himself. As he blinked away the sun that was digging at his eyes, he did a double take to make sure he was seeing what he thought he saw.

Did he miss something or was he seeing things that were not there?

His heart missed a few beats and he thought he stopped breathing for about a minute or even two.

Did Deklan think that person was Logan or was it just new help joining the manor?

Logan stepped backward and closed the door. He instantly turned to sadness and his musical voice willowed below silence. He was being silly, but couldn't help hold back his wandering thoughts.

He avidly seized possession of a man that was not really his, but all that transpired the other night made him believe Deklan was. He connected with him immediately on that magical night. The mirror man was right when he said he would know his soul mate. Logan could feel it and he knew Deklan did too. What Logan didn't understand was why Deklan was with that other black lad?

Logan went back outside, made his way to the chicken coop and grabbed the eggs he was expected to bring to the kitchen every morning. His regular routine proceeded as usual and he tried not to look at Deklan and his new acquaintance while he quickly slipped around the back side of the carriage house. It broke his heart to see him with another man and he scurried away so he didn't catch him watching.

When Logan reached the chicken coop, he turned back briefly and saw that the two gents were still standing at the front entrance, waiting or talking about something. He stood watching for a minute or two more. Secretly. Like he was spying. A flash of light beamed sharply from Deklan's finger and spiked Logan's left eye. He couldn't look away as if the ray was drawing him in. Logan blinked away the spots that had just been burned into his retina at the same time a horse carriage appeared beside them and they both got in.

What was going on and where were they off to?

"Oh bollocks." Logan hoped Deklan didn't think that lad was him.

Logan was normally a gentle being, but that day a heightened streak of upset surfaced and he inadvertently gripped an egg too tightly and squashed it in his grasp. He shook away the goop as best he could and wiped the rest of the sticky glop on his trousers.

Smart.

That morning Logan forced himself to finish his daily chores in half the time it normally took him so that he could rush out to the clover field to see if the two of them were headed that way. It was where he and Deklan continued running into one another, so he thought it was most certain Deklan was going to be taking the man there for a stroll or a morning picnic. Whatever it was, Logan wanted to be there to make sure his soul mate was not kissing the wrong chap.

He was obsessing over Deklan and he hardly knew him. The few times they met in the fields and at the river were splendid, but the night of the birthday event sealed the treaty and surely Logan was Deklan's favorite gift of the evening.

The suit Logan wore that night disguised the real person he was and deep down he wished he never wore it, but if he hadn't, perhaps the night would have turned out differently. The problem? Deklan may never really know it was Logan.

The bad scenario played over and over in Logan's mind. The night of the party and today as he watched him fawn after this black lad that should be him. His stomach groaned and it made an ugly noise.

Was it due to unsettled nerves or because Logan hadn't eaten anything since yesterday afternoon? Possibly both.

Logan couldn't wait any longer. He spun around and ran as fast as I could to the clover field, found himself at his favorite tree and climbed it. He sat on a branch and waited for the two of them to show up.

It felt like hours, but was only creeping in on one. It was obvious that they were not planning a picnic in the clover field or taking time out of their morning to pick apples and pears.

Maybe he was wrong.

Logan huffed and lay back against the trunk of the tree, plucked the nearest pear and started munching on it. The pear was a good one and comforted him during his time of need. The growling in his stomach stopped, but the ache in his chest did not.

Chapter 15

Jeddah and Deklan pulled away from the manor on their journey through town to find the man that was the other half to Deklan's soul.

Logan was the one he was connected to, not any of the ladies that pushed themselves on him at the birthday celebration and not even Jeddah, his longtime friend. Logan was being silly for thinking that the two of them were having a secret affair, but he didn't know.

When a heart knows what it wants, there is no stopping the way it feels.

During Deklan's search, their first stop was a quiet place outside of town. It was secluded away from everything, which made it seem like a winning choice for his soul mate to be hiding in because it appeared out of nowhere the same way Logan did that night. The home was interesting and he couldn't remember seeing it before.

The weather beaten house was pretty much rundown with faded clapboard siding that desperately needed a fresh coat of coloring and a rooftop that truly required repair. By the looks of the dry curling roof tiles that reduced in size over the years, it was certain to be leaking all the way through to the inside when it rained.

Their carriage stopped in front of the dilapidated old house where both Deklan and Jeddah got out. They crept up to the front door, stepping around overgrown weeds and swatting at fly's and bumble bees on their way.

Deklan glanced over at Jeddah with a face drowning in apprehension, deep down hoping that the love of his life was not living in the place in front of them.

A fat black man came to the door with a wooly shirt and suspenders that held up his great big pants. He detained them the same way Logan does, thumbs tucked behind the buckles at the waistline.

"Hello Sir," Deklan announced, fingers crossed with hopes that he was at the wrong place and the ring holder was not tucked away someplace inside.

Choking out a pipe smoker's hello, followed by 'what do you want,' the large round man tightly held the rickety door so that it didn't blow away with the gentle breeze.

"Gracious greetings, sir," Jeddah spoke first. "Hope we are not disturbing you, but we are seeking out a friend of ours that may be in the neighborhood. Do you live here alone?"

"No one here 'sept me," the big man answered with what sounded to be a limited education. "'Tis strange that yer friend didn't tell you where he was goin'."

Deklan stepped forward and added. "He left in a bit of a hurry, sir. Sorry to bother you and we will be taking up no more of your time."

"No problem." The big man smiled. His grapy grin glowed brightly in the dingy doorway. "Good luck to ya fella's in findin' yer li'l friend." He let the door go and the spring attached to the hinge snapped it back in place with a wobbly bang.

Deklan and Jeddah quickly stepped out of the way to avoid being swept inside the house by the swinging door.

"Thank you, sir." Jeddah nodded, backing up a few more steps.

Back in the carriage, Deklan snapped the reigns to get the horse moving toward town. "Hope we don't run into many more like that," he muttered.

"Prepare yourself. I'm sure there will be a few." Jeddah nudged Deklan. "Look there. Pull over." He pointed at another house tucked away on a wooded lot. This one looked as though it was not in as much need of repair as the last one, but still begged for a little tender love and care.

"This looks quaint." Deklan cast a cautious eye over Jeddah's shoulder and toward the gray house.

The place was in decent shape other than the dust forming on the trim and the leaf stained rooftop. At least the drive to the front door was maintained a little better than the previous one, which helped make it a solid choice as the pathway to the home.

They stepped up to the front door and knocked.

Nobody came. They knocked again.

Jeddah cupped his hands around his eyes and pressed them up tightly to the window. It was his meek attempt at peeking inside to see who or what was coming to the door.

Still nobody. They knocked again. This time harder.

After the third knock, they decided to turn away believing that nobody was home.

The door knob rattled.

Deklan turned back first, followed by Jeddah.

Anticipation started Deklan's heart pounding from a strong feeling that this was the home of his enchanted mate gone lost.

They waited for the door to open. When it did, a young man stood in front of them. Tall. Dark. A little tattered, but that made him uniquely handsome. His open shirt wavered in the wind showing off his chest made strong by hard labor. His eyes shined brightly against his dark caramel skin tone and his deep quiet voice sounded pure. "Hello," he greeted them. "How can I help you today?"

For a second, Deklan and Jeddah just stood there in front of this man with a blank stare. Jeddah then glanced at Deklan and then Deklan returned eye contact.

The man stood in the doorway and asked again, "can I help

the two of you?"

Deklan swallowed.

Could it be?

Deklan wasn't sure if this was his prince just yet. There were a lot of similarities from what he could remember, however a few nights have passed since the last time he saw his heart felt mate and the costume change made it difficult to tell.

Jeddah stepped forward first, eluding the discomfort of the unexpected encounter. Quickly thinking, he made up an introduction that sounded legitimate. "We have come in gracious greetings to thank you for your visit to the Royal's birthday celebration a few nights back. Did you enjoy yourself?"

Confused, the man answered, "I'm sorry, I didn't attend any event recently and neither did my brother. Are you sure you have the right house?"

Deklan's heart slowed as he observed the man's hands. They were quite swollen from being overworked and his knuckles were surly too large for any ring to comfortably slide over, unless it was a big one. The ring he carried with him on his finger, especially wouldn't fit. "We are terribly sorry to trouble you. We must have the wrong address. Our purpose was to pass on our personal thanks to those that did attend. Please excuse our intrusion."

The man remained cordial. "It made for a nice break in the day. Please let it be known that it was alright and no trouble at all."

"You say you have a brother?" Jeddah interrupted.

Just as Jeddah asked, a call echoed from inside the house and footsteps came with it. "Whose here?"

Before the man standing in the doorway could answer, the voice from behind him stepped into view. He stood beside his big brother looking just as handsome to Deklan. His heart began to race all over again.

Could this be who he was looking for?

Wind furrowed his brow as if some sort of magical sign just presented itself. Deklan noticed the boy's hands while watching him button up his linen shirt. They looked to be the right size, but trying the ring on would only tell. He blinked to pull himself out of the trance.

"Is there something we can do for you?" The younger man blinked back, pressing his hands down the front of his shirt, presumably ironing out the visible wrinkles.

In a nonthreatening manner, Jeddah moved his hands behind his back and linked them together. "We are looking to find the person who lost this ring at a recent event that took place a few nights back and would like to return it. It appears to hold some value and it would not be right if we didn't get it back to the rightful owner. Did either of you lose a ring recently?"

Deklan shakily held out his hand as Jeddah reached for it blindly.

The two men admired the glistening jewelry piece. As they did, Deklan twisted the ring from his finger and held out a hand for the younger man to take it. If the ring was going to fit either of the two chaps, it would be him.

"Go ahead." The older brother insisted, pushing his younger brother's hand toward Deklan's. "It looks like yours," he lied.

The younger brother hesitated just as the older brother grabbed the ring and forced it on his smallest finger. Even pushing with extreme force, it didn't fit the man's large hands. Besides, he admitted he wasn't at the Royal's party a few minutes before the cute younger brother showed up.

The younger chap held his hand out, fingernails up, motioning Deklan to place the ring on his finger. It was a longshot but he did it anyways.

Deklan noticed the man's hands were gentle to the touch and it brought back memories of the night he held Logan's in the garden. He hesitated at first, twisting the ring between his fingers as if not wanting to continue, but then placed it onto the young man's ring finger where he remembered it came from. It fit loosely and nearly fell off as he dropped his hand to his side.

The handsome young man lifted his hand back into view and switched the ring from the finger it was on to his thumb. "Perfect," he said. "You have found the owner."

Disappointed that these two good looking men could be so

dishonest had Deklan more than disturbed. He held out his hand to get the ring back. "I am sorry, but that is a promise ring and belongs on somebody else's ring finger. May I have it back please?"

The young man felt a bit ashamed at what he just tried to do, pulled the ring off and placed it gently back in Deklan's open palm. "Not mine," is all he said and then quietly turned away.

Before the older brother had a chance to close the door, Jeddah and Deklan moved away quickly as if they were two mice being stared at by a cat.

They continued the afternoon going from one home to another, hopeful to find the person they were looking for. The day was physically and mentally exhausting with no vision of finding Mr. Right. Nobody seemed to match or connect with Deklan's soul nor did the ring seem to fit any of the caramel colored men they visited. Or at least the ring didn't bring about the magic he was expecting when it was slipped on any of these men's fingers.

"After the next visit, let's call it a day. Please!" Jeddah begged.

Glowering, Deklan somewhat agreed. He was getting tired as well, so he figured it wasn't a bad idea to make the next stop the last.

The final visit of the day was high on a hilltop with a long drive lined with juniper trees. The pine sent was evident and filled the air all around them.

There was probably no need to knock on any doors this time because there were young children playing kick-the-ball along the front lane. All of them being fleshy white, which made both Jeddah and Deklan believe there was a slim chance the owner of the house was the skin tone they were looking for.

The children saw the carriage coming up the drive, consequently they all took off running to the front porch and then stood there staring. The smallest child, that looked to be less than thirty inches tall, ran in the house and slammed the door behind him.

Shortly after the door banged shut, a tall white man reopened it and stepped out onto the porch. Quite a change from what just ran through the doorway. Call it a magic trick. It sure seemed like one. Standing with his hands on his hips and the tiny kid wrapped around his leg, he waited for Jeddah and Deklan to get there.

"Should we just turn around and go?" Jeddah asked. "This doesn't look promising."

"Don't be silly, we are here now. Keep going," Deklan replied, scanning the place for any odd activity other than the rambunctious kids that raced around like wild animals.

"That man at the front door doesn't come close to matching your description of the fellow you met the other night. Look at him, he's huge." Jeddah pointed out. "This visit seems futile, and the seventy two children he has running around should tell you he prefers not to share his bed with another gent. Let's get out of here."

"We mustn't be rude." Even though good friends, Deklan was becoming distraught with Jeddah's nonsense. "Besides, if we turn around now, he will only think we are up to no good and will chase us down with blazing shotguns."

Jeddah pulled back and sat tight. "I'll stay here. You go." He flicked a pointy finger.

There was no need to get out of the carriage this time because as soon as they arrived at the front porch, the man that appeared to be towering seven feet tall marched up and leaned over the two of them like a full grown redwood. "What brings you here?" He growled with a big voice that sounded like timber cracking.

Covering his eyes to block the sun that placed a halo behind the great big guy, Deklan gave him the reason they were there.

The tall father of eight brought up that there was nobody that matched their description on the premises and then asked them to leave. Politely, but firm.

They took his advice and turned the carriage around to go back where they came from.

The night was closing in on them rather quickly, noticeable by the sun going down and the moon beginning to glow brighter above them.

The snap of the reign's told the horse to move faster so they could get back home before dark took complete hold of the night. It was important to return unnoticed before Deklan's father found out what they were up to all day and to keep his rage at a minimum roar.

As planned, they pulled into the Manor drive just as the sun bumped into the horizon.

Chapter 16

With arms entwined across his chest, Deklan's father was standing on the stairway landing evoking a temper that the two of them were trying to avoid.

Deklan stopped the carriage with a tug on the reigns and they both hopped out.

"I don't think this guy will ever be happy with me," Deklan mentioned to Jeddah.

"The man is only looking out for you. Give him time." Jeddah looked past Deklan with one eye trained on his father who was still standing at the top of the stairway.

Fury simmered when Dante discovered who was with Deklan. "Jeddah, Is that you?" He squinted and then straightened back up.

"It is, sir." Jeddah addressed him as if he were king. "How have you been?"

"Very well, thank you," he replied. "What brings you out to the manor?" Even though he had his suspicions about the two boys, he still welcomed Jeddah cordially.

"I heard there was a celebratory event for Deklan, which I

missed, but decided to keep my plans and still visit," Jeddah answered. "I'm glad I did. Deklan and I had a good time today."

"It's good to see you, Jeddah." Dante seemed to ignore Deklan and spoke directly to Jeddah the whole time. It seemed discourteous, but considering the current situation between him and Deklan, and that he had not seen Jeddah in quite a while made the interlude acceptable. "So, what have you two been up to?"

Deklan interjected, "We had a few hours to kill so we took the carriage around town. Played catch up on lost time. Met a few people. It was pleasant."

"Did you tell Jeddah about the wedding while you were out?" Speaking to Deklan, Dante made sure to mention it.

"Father!" Deklan raised his voice. "Please – Now is not the time."

"It's inevitable, Deklan." His father reprimanded. "Any time is a good time."

"Not now." Deklan bawled again, followed by an apology to Jeddah for the unnecessary outburst. At the same time he bantered back and forth with his father, he turned the horse and carriage toward the barn.

"There is no need to argue with me, Deklan. You know this will not end well for you." Sir Dante made certain Deklan heard him by reaching out and grabbing hold of his arm, like a mad man.

Deklan tugged back, trying to break free, but his father's grip was too strong. "Whatever you say, dad." He looked him in the eye and repeated what he mentioned before. "Remember how many lives you will ruin if you go through with this." He pulled his arm free at the moment he felt his father's grasp loosen.

At that moment, Deklan felt a downward spiral with his father's usually robust disposition. There was an instant of weakness that was evident in the hold he had on his arm.

Was the king crumbling by an intelligent statement by his young son? Was he realizing what he was doing was wrong?

The whole time Jeddah stood quiet, feeling a little uncomfortable and embarrassed. He didn't know if he should stick around or walk away so the two of them could resolve their own misunderstanding. He decided to walk around to the opposite side of the carriage in order to remove himself from firing range, but at this time, he'd already seen the bullets fly and it seemed as though the whole thing was coming to a close anyway.

Deklan's father suddenly stopped talking or arguing, or whatever it was called. The look on his face was one that could be sad realization of what he was putting his son through or discouragement of not being able to get through to him.

Why couldn't Dante understand like Jeddah could?

"I wish you good fortune, Jeddah." Dante then turned to walk up the stairway. Before he did, he walked back to his son, hugged him tightly and kissed him softly on the forehead. "You too, my son," he whispered, and then finished his ascension up the stairs.

The sentimental gesture concerned Deklan. His father never showed affection like he just did and for him to wish good fortune made Deklan think that he was being sent out to pasture for good. What did he mean by that? On the bright side, he didn't hear the door lock as his father entered the Manor. Was there real reason to worry?

"I am tired of fighting," Deklan confided to Jeddah. "Maybe I should just get married to a lassie like my parents want me to. It would certainly make this easier."

"Don't you dare." Jeddah spun Deklan around and made him look at him square in the eyes. "That will not make it easier or make it right and you know that."

"Is it better to have them hate me?"

"No, but it isn't good to live a lie all your life just to make them happy. What about you?"

Deklan dropped his head and led the horse to the barn. "I don't know. I'm tired. I just want this over with so I can move on."

"Getting married to a girl you don't love or even know is not going to bring this to a close in order for you to move on. It's only going to make matters worse. For you." Jeddah was right. He was thinking more clearly than Deklan was. "Let's get the horse put away and you can sleep on it. You will be wiser in the morning. It's been a long day."

"I suppose you're right." Lazily Deklan agreed.

"I know I am." Jeddah helped Deklan disconnect the harness from the carriage and then helped remove the bridle from the horses head. He hung the gear over the large hooks on the wall while Deklan walked the horse into his stall. A quick brush across his neck and back and the job was done.

"Are you able to go out with me again tomorrow?" Deklan asked, hoping he didn't have to continue alone.

Jeddah bowed his head. "Unfortunately not. I have to get back to the plantation as early as possible. I could only stay for the day."

Disappointed, Deklan slouched. "Well, thanks for going with me today. I'm not sure I could have done what we did alone. Having you with me was a big help."

Jeddah reached over and wrapped his arm across Deklan's shoulders. "Hey, you would have managed. I'm glad I helped you get started. I know you'll find him. You're on the right track."

"Yet so far," Deklan added. He looked up at the great big house he lived in and wondered if he should just stay outside in the barn with Chadwick. The tension on the inside seemed too great.

Jeddah squeezed his shoulder, transferring confidence over to his friend. "Come on, let's go inside."

Deklan tried the door. Thankfully his father didn't lock him out like he thought he would, but it seemed his dad was in a better place with him than he thought.

Deklan and Jeddah went straight to Deklan's bedroom without addressing his mother or speaking to his father again. He wanted to leave well enough alone and not start up any more arguments.

Closing the door behind them, Deklan fell backward on the bed with a huff, arms stretched high above his head while Jeddah dropped in a chair in front of the fireplace. His feet lifting from the floor and back down again. A puff came from him as well. They both reached their comfort zone and there they both wanted to stay. At least for the time being.

Even though it was a long drawn out and tiresome day, the two of them reminisced for hours before retiring for the night.

Chapter 17

Bright and early the next day, Deklan let his friend Jeddah go. He saw him off in the minicab carriage back to town before he himself went out on his own to search for his real true love. It was a repeat performance of the day before, only with different people and without the support of his good friend Jeddah. The day seemed longer than it did yesterday, which might be because he was on his own.

It was hard to believe that in this day and age people were deceitful in so many ways. Crafty even. Some lied about who they were, just so they could take possession of a ring that wasn't theirs. Others just simply tried to steal it. Sure it was only a ring, a white gold ring that most would let go of than to die for, but the particular jewelry piece Deklan had was more than special to him. It didn't belong to any thief, liar or swindling hooligan. It belonged to the man he was falling in love with who he met in the garden a few nights ago. Unexpectedly. He was not about to let go of it until he found that man. The one his heart had linked itself to. The one he really loved and desired to have back in his life.

Deklan moved on, continuing his search in and out of the city. With each rejection he received made him feel even lonelier than the one before. With the unsettling notion of being alone, only made him desire to locate the owner of the ring that much more. He pushed on, but his will to call it a night overpowered his determination to keep searching.

Before the sun began to set, he decided it was time to turn the carriage and head for home. It wasn't the way he hoped the search would end, but at least the ring was still circling his middle finger instead of in some stranger's hand. Neither the right feeling nor the perfect fit was found today.

~~~~ * ~~~~

Logan was returning home from his evening swim out back in the river, bare chested and a cotton towel only wrapped around his waist and the day had already changed from sunset to nightfall.

He didn't normally take to the open field half naked, but he was in an *'I don't care'* kind of mood. It was darker than usual, so aside from his caramel colored skin that seamlessly blended with the night, the only part of him that was visible were his piercing white eyes, pearly teeth and the bright ivory towel. His existence of wandering the woods was far from being invisible, which as a result, his earlier thought of blending in and being unseen was a total misconception. As it appeared, the cotton towel was floating in mid space because the moonlight made it glow while his deep colored flesh tone disappeared into the blackness around him.

The way he always did at night, Logan headed toward the lanterns that illuminated the manor and the window of his carriage house, but noticed there was a flicker of light stemming from the barn out back this time.

"Bollocks," he said while swiftly ducking out of sight behind the biggest maple tree he could find. Of all evenings he chose to walk home half naked, somebody had to be lagging out in the horse barn. He figured it was Deklan putting the horse and carriage away, the same as he did many nights before, but wasn't too sure about that. Logan stayed quiet, hiding, because he wasn't siding with being seen by anybody while running around outdoors in the nude.

Why was he hiding from him when he wanted him so badly?

One by one, each lantern in the barn went out, which made Logan believe that whomever it was closing the place down would be vacating it any minute.

"Oh, bollocks," Logan said again and took off running toward the carriage house, heading straight for the back corner to stay clear of any shining light. As he ran, he crouched forward as if it would help conceal his presence a little better, as well as make him move a little faster.

He finally made it to the carriage house, but by the time he did, all the lanterns in the barn had been shut down. He could only hope he made it safely and unseen by whomever was lingering out in the barn. Logan stood against the house with his backside pressed tightly against the clapboard wall and sidestepped with slow proficiency toward the front door. The only way in.

Logan breathed shallow and quietly crept along the wall in order to keep his footsteps as silent as he could. His grip was lost on the towel and it fell loosely to the ground at his feet. His favorite word of the night came out again, "Bollocks." He picked up the towel and covered up his private parts that swung so freely in front of him when he had nothing to hold all he had in place. Logan's bum was left exposed and he felt the rough woody surface of the carriage house scrape against his brown fleshy orbs. He winced a bit and mumbled, "Ouch." Not bollocks this time, but ouch.

He finally reached the door, naked and mostly uncovered, thankful that he made it unscathed. All the animals in the house met him the second he stepped inside, wanting food or at least a friendly pat on the head. He pushed them out of the way with his bare hip and a foot while softly groaning during his attempt at shutting the door.

"Move, move, move"—he begged and then said—"please." As if adding a word of pleasantry was a more persuasive way to get an animal that bleeps or clucks to do what was being asked of them.

Before Logan made it in and successfully got the lock bar latched, he heard a deep voice behind him. "Hello there, kind sir."

It sounded like him. Was it Deklan?

"Could this predicament get any better?" Logan sarcastically mumbled beneath his breath. He could feel his face heat up, but because his skin was dark, the blushing he was sure would go unnoticed.

He turned around smiling as if nothing odd or awkward was taking place. "Good evening," Logan shortly said, holding the towel in front of him while anchoring the door in place with his right foot. He struggled with everything at hand and prayed he didn't lose his grip and put all his private parts on display. Logan was no small guy in the lower regions, hence keeping his treasure in place behind the ivory cotton towel was a mighty chore if only using a single hand.

When Logan saw Deklan standing in his doorway, admit be articulated, his heart almost stopped. With a bang, his free hand hit his chest as if by doing so was a way to keep it beating. It seemed to work because the loud thump in his ears was similar to a wake up slap in the face.

"Oh. Well now. Hi there." Deklan backed up, staggered to see it was Logan and that he was standing freely without any clothes on. His forehead wrinkled. "What are you doing here?" A second night in a row he asked that same question to a black man who stood in an open doorway. First it was Jeddah and now Logan. He looked up, down and around the place to confirm he was standing in his own back fortress.

Logan stood stupidly, like a flamingo does on one leg, wobbling and on the verge of falling over. "I – Unh. Yes. It's true. I – yes. Um – I live here. I do – in this coop. With the animals – I unh, you see here." Wanting to be truthful with Deklan, several broken phrases that hardly made any sense escaped his tongue. He sounded uneducated while he fidgeted with the towel in front of him. He tried to save himself from humiliation, but as it turned out, he was tumbling downhill like a snowbound landslide. Quickly and all over the place.

With his forehead still wrinkled, Deklan started laughing. "Really? How long?" He looked down at Logan's hand while it scrabbled with the twisted towel and then laughed some more. Shifting his vision a little higher, he observed how fit Logan was. He lifted an eyebrow unconsciously that established his approval of what he was seeing for the second time.

Logan could tell by the way Deklan was looking at him that he liked what he saw. Again.

This could be good.

Logan went on, still sounding rash, "Unh – A while now. I work in the garden and part time in the kitchen when needed. Here." He pointed to the ground, but meant that he worked at the manor, not actually here in the coop.

"Wow," is all Deklan said while he rubbed his hair shadowed chin.

Logan wasn't sure if Deklan was upset with him for not being truthful a while ago or if he was happy to see his mostly naked body standing in front of him.

Logan only thought to ask, "would you like to come in?"

Deklan crossed his arms over his chest as if he were protecting himself from a mad man such as Logan. Not saying anything at first, but then eventually took the invitation. "Sure, why not. It might make the circumstance a bit less absurd."

On his comment Logan had to laugh. He opened the door wider to make it easier for Deklan to cross the threshold, but still kept his half-dressed body hidden behind the shadows of the door. A slight gust drifted into Deklan, opening the front of his shirt even wider than it already was. What Logan saw perked his temptation and his instincts were to reach forward and touch him, but the right time to be exploring with eager hands was not then. Instead he properly stood at ease and only transferred a reserved glance from Deklan's blue eyes to his well-groomed hairy chest. He plunged even deeper in love with him after what he saw hidden behind the placket of leather buttons.

Deklan looked around Logan's small living space. "Nice. Cozy." He nodded, dropping his arms at his sides. A sparkle ricocheted from his hand and poked Logan in the eye. He was wearing the ring.

Another 'Oh bollocks' echoed in Logan's head.

Logan turned away in private to rewrap the towel back around his waist. "Sorry about this." He looked back over his shoulder and saw Deklan staring at his cocoa rear-end. He spun back around, grinning. "I just returned from swimming in the river, so I wasn't expecting guests. Sorry for my unsightly appearance."

"Don't be silly. There is nothing unsightly about you. At least I don't think so. You look fine." Deklan bent over and wrangled the ears of a nearby goat, hopeful to create a distraction from what just came out of his mouth. It appeared that he was hoping Logan took his comments to heart and understood them as flirtatious, but he went nervous and didn't know what to do with himself other than pet the animal in front of him. The ring sparked again, this time catching his attention. He pulled back and stood up, looking at it for a moment. Time stalled for a few seconds and all sound went with it. Deklan sighed, holding wonder on his middle finger.

Logan turned back toward him, securing the folded knot he made at the front of his waist. The towel was short, which meant wearing it low on his hips necessary to prevent his oversized male extension from unexpectedly appearing below the trim line.

Is it a burden or a gift?

Logan's dark broad chest remained unprotected and he came to the conclusion that Deklan didn't mind. He caught Deklan looking a few times and acting like he was only moving his gaze from one part of the room to the other. Logan was actually enjoying his sneaky method of taking him in. It lifted his spirits as well as made him feel desirable to another attractive man.

Logan looked at the ring again and couldn't believe it had found a way back to him. The mirror man told him that the ring and the pendant would remain connected and so will the two people that wore them.

"Don't just stand there, come on in." Logan fanned the empty space between them with a come hither wave. "Have a seat at my table and don't pay any mind to the animals. They will relax in a few minutes as soon as they figure out who you are and why you are here."

Deklan took two steps to his right and snagged a chair from the crooked dining table, spinning it with some talent on one leg so it faced him. He dragged the chair with one hand across the floor, sat down in it and then scooted himself forward with his knees tucked neatly beneath the table. As he did, the ringed hand went into hiding in his lap, for the good reason that he was finished with thieves and scoundrels and wasn't too sure if Logan was one or the other.

Logan watched him intently.

"How come I haven't seen you around here before?" Deklan asked. "I thought I knew everybody at the manor. You are definitely a servant I would have noticed." He started sputtering, "I mean, not because your skin tone is lighter than most other servants. Or I mean – I'm sorry, I didn't mean that." His hand went to his forehead. "It's just that – I meant to say, you are a good looking gent that doesn't seem like he would be shoveling pig poop to survive." Another hand went to his forehead. The ring flashed. "Oh, Dagrats! – No, wait. I don't mean that ugly people should be doing the dirty work. Dagrats! What I wanted to say was — Oh forget it." He huffed and made it a point to stop speaking.

Logan held back laughter. Not because he was fumbling for a way to call him handsome, but because Logan saw him to be cuter than ever after making such a muddle of himself. Logan acted like he didn't hear a word Deklan said and made every effort to ignore what the poor lad was trying to say as Deklan looked up at him in a peculiar way. "I keep mostly to myself and the animals I live with. I don't really socialize with anybody, servants or the employer. I just do what needs to be done and then go home."

Logan turned the flame up on the lamp in the middle of the table before he moved it aside so it didn't block his straight on view of Deklan. He wanted to see his handsome face and he was pretty close to believing Deklan wanted to see his too.

"I was wondering?" Deklan shifted in his chair and brought his hands to the tabletop, unconsciously exposing the ring. "When I brought you home the other night, why didn't you want me to know you lived here?"

Logan glanced at the white-gold band that shimmered on his finger and then quickly looked away. Instead of answering, he stood up and mentioned that he should go get more clothes on.

He was feeling out of place and it wasn't just because of the question Deklan asked.

"No. Stay." Deklan hastily bayed. "I mean, you're fine the way you are. I don't mind." He sounded eager to keep him there without any additional covering.

Logan actually liked his response. It validated his attraction toward him in an obsessive sort of way.

That is what Logan wanted, wasn't it?

"I'll be right back." Logan sprinted upstairs and exchanged the towel for a light linen pant his mother made him. Even though they hung lower than the towel did and showed off every bit of what he had beneath them, he felt much more comfortable out of that cotton towel. He climbed back down to his tiny kitchen space to join Deklan and revisit their previous conversation.

When he got there, Deklan had snapped open the rest of the buttons on his shirt. The front panels dangled toward the floor at his sides. He leaned back in his chair, looked at me and smiled. "It's hot in here, don't you think?"

What was he up to?

Logan presumed it was his idea of making his circumstance a bit less uncomfortable. He didn't care, Deklan looked amazing to him. He actually became choked up at how much more gorgeous he was with his shirt nearly off. The dark hair neatly feathered across his chest played with his mind while other areas of his body were trying to bust loose. Deklan was beautiful and with an open shirt, he instantly gained Logan's undivided attention. If Logan said anything at that moment, it would come out more jumbled than the first time he spoke nonsense to Deklan earlier that day. He stayed quiet and just gawked. He could only imagine what presented itself at the end of the hairy trail running down the front of Deklan's abdomen. He quickly looked away to camouflage the rising affection he had for him.

Oh good bollocks, Logan loves this chap.

Evidence revealed to Logan while he stood in front of Deklan that he did too. He caught Deklan staring at the smooth dark muscles across his chest for a few seconds and then tracing his torso downward until his eyes met the hair that was sprouting above the linen hip hugging waistband.

Deklan cleared his throat and quickly looked away, afraid Logan would see him peeking. "So?" He repeated, "why the secret?"

"Secret?" Logan mimicked his word. "What secret?" He said it again, sitting back down in the chair across from Deklan and acting as though he didn't understand what Deklan meant by secret.

Deklan smirked. "How come you didn't want me to know you lived here?"

"Oh, that secret." Logan leaned back in the chair. "I'm not too sure. I guess I wanted to keep to myself. I don't know. I liked you the minute I met you and was thinking if you knew that I was a servant around here you would treat me differently or maybe conclude that the employer and the help should not mix."

"What? That's silly." Deklan looked him in the eyes. "I liked you just the same and with you living in this stable would not have changed what I thought of you."

"That's a relief." Logan stood up again and reached for a pear. "Would you like one?" He held up the biggest and shiniest fruit in the bowl and offered it to Deklan.

"I'd like that," Deklan replied, smiling and looking at Logan's strong brown chest again. He seemed to be hooked.

Logan felt his chest burn as Deklan's gaze fixed on it. He grinned as he turned to the cabinet where he stored the sharpest knives. He went back to the table with a cutting block and started slicing the pear into edible wedges.

Deklan shifted in his chair again and Logan noticed him watching his hands while he cut the pear into pieces.

"What's going on behind those blue eyes, Deklan?" Logan flirtatiously asked, catching him off guard.

Pulling himself out of wonderment, Deklan fought with his reply. He nervously twisted the ring on his finger and his hooded eyes turned soft. He stared at Logan for a long time and then shook his head to remove himself from the dreamy trance.

Logan's head dropped to the ring Deklan was spinning around and over his knuckle. He recognized it. It was his. Logan gently placed his open hand over Deklan's, letting him know it was alright to say whatever he was planning to say. The contrast of his dark hand over Deklan's was incredibly sensual. Logan knew what Deklan was trying to say so he was helping him speak by offering a gentle touch.

Deklan looked up at Logan and gave in to an oncoming smile. Slipping his hands from beneath Logan's, he removed the ring from his finger and softy whispered, "Let me have your hand."

Without reluctance, Logan placed his palm gracefully into Deklan's. The warmth he felt from him was beyond anything he could explain. He connected with Deklan even more as if a ghostly influence had passed between them.

Deklan looked deep into Logan's eyes and slipped the ring onto his finger. It sparked and sent rays of light around the room as if a force of magic was coming from inside. From above, there were additional beams of light shining down that appeared to be coming from the pendant on the bedside table upstairs. The pieces fit.

At that moment they both understood that it was the definitive connection between two people. The right two people. It was clear to them that their souls have finally met and secured their bond with the return of this very ring.

Logan did his best to hide his face from Deklan so he wasn't able to see a grown man weep. He was supposed to be strong as his mother once told him. His eyes welled up and when he blinked, tears tumbled from them and fell to the table in a motion so slow that time seemed to move backward and everything around him stopped. He was wondering at the same time if it had the same effect on Deklan. His tears hit the wooden surface the same way rain meets the earth, with a splash that then reaches back to the sky in pointy formations.

Logan felt his hands being squeezed by Deklan. "It is you?" Deklan spoke softly. "My striking prince I thought I'd lost. I've missed you, Logan."

Logan looked up at Deklan with a boyish smile that let Deklan know he was the one.

Without losing Logan's gaze or his grasp, Deklan stood, knocking the chair he was sitting on backward to the floor. It landed with a bang and a chicken balked and flapped away. Deklan stood majestically in front of Logan and asked, "Can I kiss you?"

Logan moved in close and their lips lightly touched. Deklan's kiss was warm and his touch felt strong.

Logan was in a place exactly where he wanted to be. The very place he was meant to be.

Deklan pulled Logan closer and the space between them was squeezed away. The hair on Deklan's chest comforted Logan when pressed up against him

"I've missed you so much, Logan." Deklan quietly whispered in Logan's ear and his warm breath made him crumble.

The back window was open, the moon was full and a cooling breeze coming in from the river out back softly circled them like a palm frond generates wind. They went on kissing and Deklan drew Logan even closer with clasped hands against his jaw. Deklan's tongue turned to fire and this time there was nothing hesitant about his enthusiastic quest to take what was his.

There was no holding back.

Logan gave in as Deklan pulled him closer. Both quickly went firm.

The anticipation of knowing Logan was now connected to him set Deklan's mind ablaze. He was addicted to Logan and wanted to share his personal essence with him.

Chapter 18

The morning came fast following the night of discovery Deklan and Logan had with each other. By far it was the best night of Logan's life and he wouldn't trade it for ownership of this great big world. Deklan and Logan were in and out of slumber making love every chance they could get. They occupied each other's private spaces many times from dusk to dawn. Even though Logan presented the grander organ between the two of them and it was expected that the bigger man take on the leading roll, he was most at peace with the man he loved taking charge while rhythm dancing on top of him.

Logan laid Deklan back a few times throughout the night and gave him the love he had as well. It seemed true that he give his essence to his prince, and Deklan's face shining up at him showed he wanted it. Logan's dimensions channeled deep and sent what he had far within him.

Deklan cherished it, Logan could tell. His pupils were blown the whole time he moved in and out of him, and when he proposed to vacate, Deklan gripped sturdy and held him in place.

"Don't leave me," Deklan begged. "Stay and give me more."

Lying together in passionate gridlock was well overdue for starters and if a count was being acknowledged for how many times their bodies fused, the guess of transferred love would be eight or more spells throughout the night.

As they found out, there was no denying that they linked together perfectly and as the night went on, Logan's body effortlessly drew in every ounce Deklan was willing to give. The bond he experienced when Deklan introduced himself to him for the first time border lined on a dream, but what he felt inside told him it was real.

Logan woke up before the rooster got to him first and found he was lying tightly on top of Deklan's left side. Logan's head lay comfortably on Deklan's warm hairy chest, his cocoa leg crisscrossing over Deklan's, and his hand tightly wrapped around Deklan's extended member that felt as though it was ready to unite with him again. Deklan's erection felt like solid slate in Logan's grasp as his fingers gripped the thickened base. His warm hairy body against Logan's smooth chocolate flesh felt natural and Logan valued the moments he was having with Deklan.

Logan left the idea of making love another time up to Deklan. He found out last night that Deklan was certainly more aggressive than he was when it came to love, but still, Logan didn't want to wear him down on their first night together.

Deklan groaned, stretched hard and thrust his strong rugged hips against Logan's hand that was straining to stay wrapped around his bursting erection. Deklan's eyes blinked and then looked out the open window beside him and discovered that the moon was still there. "Hello Lover." He kissed the top of Logan's head and then brushed his tangled hair flat with his scruffy cheek. "How does one more time sound before I have to run home?"

Logan didn't object. No way.

Logan kissed him on the lips as he rolled over on his back, taking Deklan with him until his magnificent body stopped over top of his. Logan's caramel legs locked tightly behind his waist as his hands found a place against his strong hairy chest. As Logan caressed and stroked him, the soft hair tickled his fingers.

They kissed with greeting tongues. Deklan rocked with

grace above Logan until he freely found himself inside. The same way as several times last night, Logan's breathing became short gasps as he sensed the man he loved slip deeper than he remembered him going before.

To Logan, his existence felt sensational.

Passionately and slowly they moved together until their mind blowing orgasms started to rumble. Logan gushed heavily across his chest at the same time Deklan sprayed more of his charming essence deep within him. Logan could feel him expand with every powerful injection. Logan savored his gift as it flooded him.

They finished making love in the early morning with a long bottomless kiss and Logan's sticky potion bonding the two of them together until it cooled and ran clear. Deklan rose above him and balanced himself on the heels of his hands. As he did, Logan's clearing discharge somersaulted down his hairy chest and sparkled like diamonds by the light from the moon. Beauty above Logan was all he could think of. He came back down and they went on kissing.

Throughout last night, they exchanged real love and kept it going well into the morning in a way that they only could. They gave each other a part of themselves that nobody else would be able to fathom but them. Their hearts and their souls collided exactly at the time they were supposed to. They offered their beings to one another with intimate love and by doing so a part from within them traded places with the other. It was meant to be and was their distinct way of joining their souls that were meant to be matched.

"As much as I regret leaving *you* behind, I better get home before the rooster announces the rising sun and my parents find out I made love to the servant boy in the barn all night long." Deklan chuckled at himself being witty, regretfully slipping free from Logan's exultant body.

The void Logan sensed at the very moment Deklan withdrew made him sad past comprehension and it literally made him feel empty inside. Something didn't feel right to him as he watched Deklan get dressed.

Deklan kissed Logan softly on the lips and whispered, "'til

the next moon rises, my love. Hold me dear and keep me close."

Logan went weak.

Deklan departed.

Chapter 19

"What are you doing in my room?" Deklan asked his father while breaking through the door at five in the morning.

"You don't question me? This is my house." His father reacted. "Where have you been all night? I know you weren't here where you belong." His fists tightened into hard balls. His breath leaked out like it was stuck there for a week.

"I was out," was all Deklan said.

"That is not answering my question." Dante moved closer to Deklan, his eyes pinched closer together into a tight knot.

"What more do you want to hear from me?" Deklan ticked.

"I want you to be honest with me."

"I am."

"You are not."

"I am too."

"You were short."

"What?" Deklan wondered.

"Yes – Short."

"I don't even know what that means?" Deklan huffed.

Exhausted and wearing out from all the bantering back and forth with his father. "I don't want to keep doing this, dad."

"Doing what?"

"Arguing." Deklan tossed his belt in the chair next to the fireplace and then dropped into the one next to it.

Moving in front of Deklan, blocking his view of the fireplace, Dante tried to reason with him. "You need to listen to me," he pleaded. "This world is not kind and everybody here will try to hurt you by what you are doing."

"They need to mind their own business." Deklan squeezed the arms of the chair, anger surfaced. "And I'm not doing anything wrong."

"But they won't mind their own business. Don't you understand that?" Dante stepped closer to Deklan, more concerned about him than Deklan thought.

"Well, it's time they did." Deklan leaned forward and dropped his head into his hands. "We of all people can change this."

"Is that what all this is about?" His father asked. "You trying to make a change?"

"No, dad." Deklan looked up. "I can't help the way I am or how I feel."

"This is preposterous." Sir Dante's fists returned to knots of steel. "You can't? It is not right."

"What do you mean it's not right?"

"This whole boy meets boy false impression." Dante waved a finger up and down at Deklan. "It isn't natural."

"It is to me." He turned away. "There isn't a spinner that I can just rotate that will change the way I am. You may not believe this, but I was born the way I am."

"There is no such spinner that needs to be turned." Dante appealed. "Because you are not supposed to like boys the way you do. I said it before, it isn't right."

"There's more to love than boy meets girl, dad." Deklan faced him, angrier than before.

"There's no getting through to you. The marriage is on as planned." As if he were a child, Sir Dante stomped across the floor, carrying out his tantrum for not getting his way at that moment.

Deklan stood up and blocked his father from walking out the door. "Let me ask you. Do you love mother?"

His father turned. "Of course I do. What kind of a senseless question is that?"

"Hear me, please. Stop, right now. Don't love or care for mom anymore as if she didn't exist and replace her with a man." Deklan pierced his father's eyes. "Could you do that?"

Sir Dante stammered, "It's not the same thing and you know it."

"Sure it is." Deklan pointed out. "It's exactly the same. You cannot change the way you feel any more than I can, because it is in your nature to love her and the way it's meant to be."

"You're right. That is the way it's meant to be. A man and a wife. You are wizening up. Good to know."

"You are missing the point, father." Deklan tried to reason, disturbance evident in his tone. "I am talking about souls. Two souls are meant to be together and you cannot fight that no matter how hard you try to separate them. Besides, God does not differentiate man from woman, you've told me yourself, so why should we? We are all equal souls to him with slight modifications to our bodies in order to progress with his plan to populate the planes. If I wasn't meant to be here as I am, he would have made me differently. I am exactly the way he wants me to be and I, nor you or anybody else is supposed to question or make any changes to his reason for doing it. I am perfect in his image and so are you."

Sir Dante didn't say a word, just stared, which gave Deklan the impression that he may have reached his father's sordid thinking regarding his ability to only be with a man and not able to be with lass. His mind and body didn't work any other way than how it was intended to function.

Deklan watched his father walk out of the room quietly. No word was spoken, not even a good bye. He wasn't quite sure what to think of that.

Should he be thankful or should he be worried?

Deklan's whole message to his dad was clear and made a lot of sense. He's in love with another gent and he will do anything at this point to keep from being separated or crucified.

Deklan thought about Logan the whole morning and couldn't wait to see him again.

~~~~ * ~~~~

Logan thought of nothing else but to have Deklan in his arms again, kissing and loving him the same way they did the night before. To have Deklan's warm hairy chest pressed against his was more comforting than he could explain and to be attached to each other in gridlock of love was a better idea yet. Logan was falling in love with Deklan, even more-so now that he was carrying a part of Deklan inside of him and that treasured piece of Deklan was joining his soul.

Chapter 20

The morning routine was almost over for Logan and surprisingly he had stumbled across Deklan in the kitchen for the first time ever since he had been working at the manor. It's only been a short time, but Deklan was as gorgeous as he remembered him being. Logan thought Deklan purposely planted himself there because he knew Logan would run into him.

When Logan spotted Deklan weirdly standing next to where he needed to pick up the sack of garbage, he looked Deklan in the eye and politely excused himself. Logan didn't like that he had to act as though he didn't know him in front of the others, but the fact was they weren't supposed to be friends or even pining lovers for that matter. If they only knew Logan had a part of Deklan living inside him, they'd find a way to stone the both of them on the spot. Truthfully, the whole time Logan looked at Deklan, all he wanted to do was to kiss those luscious lips. Taste him. Open himself up to him again. Let him in and accept his love.

Aside from trembling when he saw Deklan standing there, Logan purposely brushed his shoulder against Deklan's chest in order to absorb some of the newfound love he had stored away for him. Logan caught Deklan's smirk, which did nothing other than tell him Deklan enjoyed his touch as much as Logan did his.

Oh sweet surrender, Logan is in love with him.

Logan's heart burned just thinking about how truly far away from Deklan he was at that moment even though he was standing right next to him.

Logan left the kitchen as he usually did, but this time nobody tried to plunge a foot into his bottom end. He was quite sure it was because Deklan was there and nobody wanted to show that they misbehaved or did anything other than what they were supposed to be doing. Logan was thankful for that, but at the same time was repulsed by knowing these greasy mice only played when the pussy cat was away.

As Logan turned to close the door, he looked Deklan square in the eye and smiled. His eyes sparkled, but the starry flash went away the minute Deklan sweetly winked back at him.

Logan wasn't quite sure what was going to happen next, so he went back to his chicken coop and pretended everything was as it was a few days before he kissed Deklan on the mouth. Out of all the people Deklan could have, Logan thought it was crazy that he was the one person in the crowd of many Deklan chose to hold hands with. Logan was certainly blessed and anybody with half a mind would say the same.

The man was striking and Logan of all people had him securely in his grasp.

Could the day get any better?

While Logan hung out in dreamland, repulsively he sniffed the air around him. "Pee-yew" he bawled, kind of loud. Wanting to say it was the animals that were putting off such an offensive odor, but sadly it was himself who smelled bad and needed to take to the river and bathe.

Working in the morning sun ripened him beyond fruitful with an odor that resembled pig poop. He swears he didn't roll in the stuff, but the rancid air around him thundered otherwise.

Logan grabbed a cotton towel and a fragrant detergent bar and took to the river to rid himself of the animal stinking stench that was clinging to his being. He whistled happily all the way to a place that was more secluded than usual so he could swim naked without much worry that somebody was going to see him.

Instead of tossing his clothes in the tree where he usually did before his swim, he decided to wear them into the river with him. Untraditional he knew, but figured it would be easier to leave them on for an overall rinse than to remove them first and beat them senseless against a sun heated boulder. He lowered his entire body into a deep part of the water, scrubbed every part of himself with the detergent bar until a lather formed. Soon after absorbing the suds, he then bobbed up and down until the water ran clear. Following his bobber bobbing, he unfastened his clothes and added a couple hefty bangs against a rock to work away the soot and grime that may have remained trapped between the woven fibers.

The water felt cool at first but he quickly adjusted to it when his body temperature dropped to meet the chilling invader. As soon as he was finished washing the soot from his clothes and draping them over a nearby tree branch, he belly flopped back into a more shallow part of the river and swam like a frog until he came across a spot where he could comfortably roll face side up. It was rather bright outside due to the early afternoon sun, so anybody standing in a nearby bush could clearly see his well-developed privates. Part of him figured who cares, but his more modest conscience kept him alert.

As Logan recently discovered, Deklan loved every part of him and was especially thrilled with the bonus he came across between his legs. With a smile on his face and right before he choked on it, Deklan told Logan that he liked a great challenge. To be honest, Logan's manhood was bigger than the average chap to the point of looking freakish. His extreme overhang always left him feeling a bit conscious so he did everything he could to conceal it from curious gawkers.

Logan looked around to make sure he was alone while he floundered on his back with soapy hands running across his blocky chest, rock splitting abdomen and hairy crotch. He was wishing the whole time he had Deklan's help when it came time to run the detergent bar down between his legs. As it turned out, his thick oversized bulge was Deklan's favorite place to explore. Logan was stirred just thinking about him being there, that his thoughts triggered a rise in his virile extension. It lifted and then dropped heavily against the center of his abdomen and laid there like a large dark log. The definite thud it made scared a couple nearby water birds and they flew away in a harried panic. In sequence, they frightened him too and he sat up quickly, stabbing himself in the chest with his prominent erection. Another couple inches and it would have bruised his lip instead of his chest.

Logan quickly lathered his entire body and rinsed off before disturbing any other animal within ear shot. As he did this, small rippling waves carried the bubbles away. The lavender scent from the detergent bar transferred to him and he smelled so much better than before.

He finished fast and then crawled to the edge of the river on his hands and knees like he was a bear hunting for fish. He laid his head against the grassy bank while letting the rest of his naked body soak in the sinuous water. Logan was content from the lavender scent his flesh was giving off and he felt compelled to close his eyes and relax.

"Well hello, good looking." Deklan showed up.

Surprise.

Logan must have dozed off for a split second, or maybe longer. He shuttered and splashed to cover himself from his unknown visitor.

Who was that?

Logan blinked a few times to clear his vision and then finally smiled. How nice. His prince followed him to the woods and he hoped he came by to ravish him. "Hello." He turned to his knees and did the best he could to cover his flopping organ with both hands. Success was far from being reached as every bit of him was hanging out all over the place. It was inevitable given how much he had to deal with below the waist. He was huge. Freakishly huge.

"As you were, my dear." Deklan chuckled, covering his mouth to hide his striking smile while staring at Logan standing naked in the river.

This time it was less uncomfortable for Logan than the last. "Thank goodness it's you," he said, shifting his hands in front of his hairy groin, gathering as much of what he could into both hands. Even though Deklan had seen him without clothes on before, Logan still had half of mind to hide himself. Things looked differently in the daylight than they did at night time. "Why are you still laughing?"

"You're cute." Deklan dropped his hand from his mouth.

"Cute?" Logan tipped his head. "I look silly."

"No. You look cute."

"Hand me the towel or come join me." Logan reached a hand to Deklan anticipating the latter choice would be decided on.

"I could use a bath," Deklan said, and then began to unlace his boots.

Logan's private zone began to swell as he watched Deklan unbutton his shirt and remove it. His beauty was more than Logan could handle and there was no stopping his reaction that was becoming more and more evident as time passed. Logan's eyes were pinned to Deklan's strong square chest, fascinated all over again by the soft dark hair that lay across it like feathers. Logan followed the hairy trail down the center of Deklan's abdomen where it disappeared into the front of his trousers where sprouts of darker hair emerged each time he released a clasp that was blocking his privates. Finally the magic was revealed and Logan hardened even more. He was a close second to Logan's size and between the two of them the male extensions added up to a substantial length.

When Deklan stepped into the water, it sent a chill up his bones and caused his stunning chest to expand as he inhaled the warm air. His muscles swelled that revealed everything he had to Logan.

Logan reached for him with an open hand and he took it gracefully. They stood there in broad daylight, kissing. If anybody saw the two of them lip locked and naked, it didn't matter.

They embraced each other and as they did, any space between them was eliminated. Logan felt Deklan and he certainly felt all of Logan. Together their impressive erections were locked in battle and even though confined between them, put out a powerful fight to dominate the other.

"You smell good." Deklan broke away sniffing and looked

at Logan.

"Lavender." Logan pointed at the floating detergent bar at their knees.

Deklan reminded Logan of how good it felt being next to him when Deklan kissed him on his lips.

Logan said Deklan smelled good too and then walked him to the middle of the river where it was deeper. He kissed his man again before lathering his hairy chest with the same lavender scented soap that he just used. His fingers tingled when he touched him. He made small circles over his chest with his hands, forming soapy spirals of hair that resembled the eyes of hurricanes. Deklan watched him sculpt, letting Logan carry on as he pleased.

Taking the soap bar from Logan's hand, Deklan started scrubbing his hair and face with it. He then went below water to rinse away the suds and when he resurfaced, he was more attractive to Logan than before he went under.

For the love of this whole earth, Logan was love punch busted.

Dripping water ran down Deklan's face that made him sparkle in the afternoon sunlight. Dark strands of glossy hair came with it, crossing in front of his eyes that made them look bluer than Logan remembered them to be. The water trickled from his broad shoulders and down his chest, weaving in and out of the feathered wisps of hair. Logan gasped and then he swallowed.

For the love of this whole earth, Logan is truly in love.

As if this was the first time Logan saw such beauty, he lunged toward Deklan with intemperate desire. "Come with me." He grabbed Deklan's hand and dragged him to the opposite side of the river to a more secluded place.

Deklan couldn't hold back his emphatic grin. "But of course."

They added another long kiss while they gradually lowered themselves to the soft wet sand that lined the far side of the river. Water flowed by them as they began to bond. Delicately Deklan positioned himself inside of Logan until all the love he had was driven into him.

Chapter 21

Back at the plantation, Deklan sat across from his mother at the dinner table, which put him to the right of his father who sat at the head. Servers came and went, bringing in meal courses as well as kept the drinking glasses full.

At the beginning of dinner there wasn't much socializing. Nobody said more than a few words. The loudest sound heard was clinking of silver dinnerware against china dishes. It was almost ear piercing on the verge of tormenting Deklan's nerves.

The first to break silence was Deklan's father. "It's our pleasure having you at the dinner table with us, Gretchen. The wedding will be more than beautiful with you dressed in white." He raised a brow hopeful that the lassie they chose for their son was an intact virgin.

She giggled. "Thank you Mr. Royal." Gretchen glanced at her own father who was thoughtfully placed at the tables end opposite Dante and then she poked a glance over to her mother who was sitting directly across from her. Gretchen could hardly breathe in her tightly wound corset as she sat only a few inches beside Deklan, her groom to be.

Discomfort was surrounding Deklan because of the upcoming plans his parents made for him. The only person he was thinking of was the chap he made love to earlier that day in the river.

How was Deklan going to get through the unsettling arrangement? He didn't love this girl. He didn't even know who she was. His parents organized everything without his consent or his blessing. How could they make him go through with this wedding?

Deklan tried to be cordial to the girl and her family, but the situation he was in cut at his insides like a rusty wood saw. He stayed quiet the entire evening except for Hello, Yes, No, Thank you, and Good bye.

~~~~ * ~~~~

Earlier advised by Deklan, Logan knew what was going on in the Manor and was fighting the same aches and pains that he was. They were meant to be together, not him and that lass. Logan was starting to resent the girl sitting at the table with Deklan even though he had no idea who she was. It didn't really seem right that Logan hated *that girl* as much as he did, but the people he worked for put her in that situation as an effort to take away the love Deklan and Logan have for each other, so his loathing was well engaged.

Logan paced the floor in his coop and came up with the ridiculous idea to bust up the dinner party to claim his man, but of course that would be imprudent. He would only look foolish and borderline wild. He decided to keep his heroic rescue mission at bay and stay put.

~~~~ * ~~~~

It took about ten minutes after finishing dinner when Sir Dante escorted everybody to the parlor adjacent to the dining room. It was more comfortable there and a better place to deliberate about the wedding plans for Deklan and the new Mrs. Royal.

The two dads went off together in front of the fireplace and behind them, the mothers sat drinking tea in facing chairs, chit-chatting about their pretty jewelry.

Deklan and his new girl roamed the room in a purposeless manner, hardly speaking and looking at things placed here and there as if they were in a small town museum. It was a scratchy interlude for the both of them. Clearly this was not going well for Deklan, but the parents and the giddy girl seemed to think it was. They all smiled while he was drowning in anxiety.

Plans were made quickly for the wedding and it was agreed before the group broke up and went separate ways that it would be carried out over the weekend. That quick.

It was decided. No questions asked. Deklan was getting married. To a lass. In four days.

After everybody left, Deklan caught his parents in the second level hall. "Why are you doing this? Don't you know this isn't going to work out?"

"You don't seem to understand, Deklan." His father retorted, turning away.

Deklan followed. "Understand what? That you are doing this for your own benefit and not mine? I can't marry Gertrude, Greta, Grace or whatever her name is."

"It's Gretchen, dear," his mother clarified.

"And I can clearly see you don't understand." Sir Dante jumped back in. "This *is* for your benefit and you will need to follow my direction as planned."

"And then what?" Deklan fought back.

"And then you will live happily ever after. That's what." Sir Dante assured.

"You are confusing the message. This isn't a fairy tale. Neither Happy nor Ever After exists in this situation. They don't go together and shouldn't be used in the same sentence."

"It does for your mother and me." Father knew best.

"Are you sure about that?" Deklan turned his gaze to his mother's saddened face. It was not a happy expression, but more a look of concern. Mother was the one that knew best, and by her appearance, this was not a moment of happiness that said she was agreeing with any of it. She knew that this was not right for her child. He needed a boy as his companion, not a girl. She was aware of it and knew it long ago.

"Your mother is fine with this. I know her better than anyone." He put his arm over her shoulder like he would a chum, jostling her closer to him. Her tense body was a certain sign she was not content, but Dante was oblivious to it or didn't want to see it.

Deklan mumbled, looking to the floor, "You're wrong."

"What did you say?" His father tilted his head. "Be sure you are ready for the weekend. You're getting married to this lassie and that is final."

"Why are you treating me like I don't have a mind of my own," Deklan yelled.

Dante raised his voice above Deklan's. "What I am witnessing, I see you don't have a mind of your own. Somebody around here needs to do the thinking for you because you're not thinking wisely."

"Forget it." Deklan turned away and left. It was as if he was falling uphill, stumbling all over the place but not getting anywhere. "I need to go. I can't be here right now." He kissed his mother on the cheek and walked away.

"Don't you go out and muddle this up," His father hollered.

Chapter 22

A knock at the door woke Logan from the onset of his evening slumber. He jerked awake and hovered in a place that was a bit out of sync with the real world, pulled on his trousers he lifted from the floor beside his bed and answered the door shirtless. It was Deklan. The evening instantly became so much better.

"Run away with me," Deklan blurted, squeezed through the open crack in Logan's doorway and then kicked it closed with the heel of his foot. He kissed Logan as he passed by.

"What? – Now?" Logan asked, still kissing back.

He pulled both Logan's my hands into his. "Yes – Now. Run away with me. Tonight."

"I am happy to see you and would love nothing more than to take to the hills with you, but I have already made it to bed for the night. Besides you're supposed to be getting married in a few days. Shouldn't you be storing energy for the big night?"

"Then let me stay. Here, with you. I can't go back in that house." Deklan gripped harder. "They can't make me marry that lass. I don't even know her nor will I be able to share parts of me the same way I share them with you. You of all people know that."

Logan pulled away conflicted with emotions as to how he should be feeling. He was angry. Confused. Sad. In love with a man the world would not let him have. He wanted to run off with Deklan so that nobody else could have him, but it would only make matters worse, for him and for Deklan.

Deklan turned toward the door as if to leave. His face went long and gloomy.

Logan's heart rate sped up, beating hard and loud. "Wait," he hummed. "Don't go." He reached out and placed both hands on Deklan's shoulders, squeezed comfort into his tense muscles that formed at the base of his neck. His head dropped forward and Logan moved closer to hug him from behind. Deklan shuddered with sorrow the second Logan wrapped his arms around him and Logan could feel him sobbing. He couldn't let him go. Not like this.

Deklan reached up and gripped Logan's wrist. His touch felt shattered and Logan sensed a weakness that he had not felt in him before. The prince that was normally Logan's source of strength suddenly needed him to comfort and carry him. The home Deklan lived in tossed his real soul aside and by what they were doing told him they hated him the way he was.

Deklan spun around in Logan's arms and looked at him despairingly. Definite tears were streaming down his face. "I am so lost right now that I don't really know where I belong." He didn't care that Logan saw his sadness.

Logan wiped his face clean with the pads of his thumbs and brought him tighter to his chest. Their hearts were racing against each other as if attempting to trade places. Soon the comfort of holding one another brought Logan's and Deklan's heart to a steadier beat. Logan held Deklan's face in his hands, looked him in the eyes and kissed him. "You belong here with me. We both know that. You can stay as long as you want." He offered Deklan a place to stay as if the home was actually his.

With that being said, Deklan's blues began to dry and soon showed signs of a silly grin. He chuckled goofishly and then told Logan he loved him.

What did he just say?

Logan froze for a few seconds and waited for his blood to start flowing after it stopped from lack of a beating heart. He wasn't surprised to hear Deklan say those three words, but shocked that he said them so soon. Logan gushed from hearing him say it and was happy he said them to him. If Logan was going to die of heart failure, it would be at that moment and thankfully it was Deklan's arms that were holding him when he did.

Deklan smiled, kissed Logan one more time and then let him go. "Do you mind if I sleep here tonight?"

He didn't have to ask twice, or even finish his question for that matter. "Of course you can. I think that would be a very good idea." Logan disclosed.

Deklan concentrated on Logan as he ran his warm knuckles down his dark bare chest and then slipped both hands around his back where he locked his fingers to hold him close. "Thank you. I promise I won't be a bother."

Logan's head tilted to one side in a way that Deklan found endearing. "The real bother is that I don't have anything for you to wear to bed. You will have to either sleep in what you have on or take to the sheets in the nude like I do."

"I'm most comfortable sleeping with nothing on. Hope you won't mind if I choose that option."

"That suits me perfectly. I'll be doing the same," Logan keenly said.

"Settled then. Which side of the bed is mine?" Deklan asked.

"I'm a lefty, so that means you get the right side by the window. The bed is small, so we will have to sleep pretty close."

"That won't be a problem. Cuddling is good and we can share the warmth." Deklan started undressing.

Logan doused the lanterns around his tiny home except the one on the table next to the bed. It let off an easy yellow flicker that mixed with the silver-blue shimmer coming in the window from the moon outside. Logan liked the way it made Deklan's skin radiate blue-violet on one side and white-gold on the other as he lay nude above the covers in his bed. The hairy trail that marked the center of his abdomen acted as a division line between the two beautiful colors. Logan's caramel skin looked royal-blue next to his and the sharp contrast between the two of them was erotically exciting.

They lay side by side in bed for a while just listening to the other breathe. They soon started kissing the way new lovers do, which then led to a slow romantic session of sensual love.

The same as before, their time together was the finest and it was difficult to separate them once they bonded. They made love in Logan's bed a few times throughout the night, which made them more tired than usual in the morning due to the lack of sleep. They didn't care. They were in love and wanted to share as much of themselves with each other as they possibly could. Their male essence was transferred between them in a way that only two men can and not a bead of it saw the light of day.

Logan cherished the small bit of Deklan living inside him. It was as if Deklan was making Logan a part of him. His body craved Deklan's gift, naturally drawing it deep inside. Fulfillment overwhelmed Logan as Deklan's thick molten flowed toward his heart and settled in. Several times during the night Deklan mounted, covered and filled Logan with as much love as he could give. Binding him in a way that laid claim on his lover for life.

Was it possible for two people to fall in love so quickly?

Logan wasn't sure if it was because they were held so far apart by the human race that made them connect so remarkably well or if they were just true soul mates that were meant to be together. Whatever the case may be, they were linked. Together. And in love.

Sleep finally came thumping in the night and both Deklan and Logan drifted into a much needed slumber. Deklan's hairy chest tightly pressed against Logan's backside kept him warm and helped him sleep.

Logan was so in love with Deklan that it hurt.

Chapter 23

"Oh wounded hell!" Logan groaned, frantically rushing out of his sleepy slumber. He nudged Deklan a few times to get him to wake up. The weight of his body on top of Logan was pinning him in place and he could hardly move. Logan felt that his right arm was asleep. He twitched. "Deklan, Get up," Logan groaned.

"What the – ?" Deklan coyly slid off of Logan and sat up, rubbing his eyes like a little boy. The morning sun persistently mined for his soul. A sign it was morning and he needed to get up.

"Stay still. Sshhh!" Logan kicked the bedcovers from his feet. "Somebody's here." He gripped and held his heavy erection up against the center of his abdomen until the swelling went down and then he pulled his trousers on at the same time the second bang on the door reverberated around the room. At least Logan thought it was the second knock. They were so sound asleep, neither of them was really sure. It could have been the third, fourth or even knock five. Who knew?

"Who is it?" Deklan sleepily asked while holding one eye shut to block out the intrusive sunlight coming in from the window next to him.

"I'm late," Logan answered, tripping over his big feet as he made a crooked route for the door to see who was there. "It's probably the kitchen help here to fry me for not having their food additives on the counter in time. They get antsy if it's even a minute late."

Deklan dropped back. "Really?" He put his arm across his forehead. "They disturbed us for that?"

"Ssshhh!" Logan's hand flapped behind him, politely shushing Deklan. "Don't let them know you're here. I'm dead if these people knew I was sleeping with the boss's son."

"Forget them and come back to bed. I'm rock hard and you're the only one that can relieve me of this misery that is purely your doing. Get over here and take a seat." Deklan pulled the covers back and his full blown erection sprang forward, begging for Logan to hop on.

"I can't, I have a job to do." But Logan imagined another great ride.

An unfamiliar voice rang from beyond the door. "Deklan. Are you in there?"

"Holy cow patties piled higher today than yesterday." Deklan sprang out of bed, his huge erection arcing forward as it faded fast. It was as though he was never sleeping. Sober as ever.

"What the – ?" Startled, Logan mimicked one of Deklan's famous lines and backed away from the door as if it was on fire.

"My father," Deklan whispered. "It's him. He's out there. Looking for me. Oh, Fiery hell!"

"Oh bollocks." Logan panicked.

"Quiet." Deklan held two fingers over Logan's mouth. Any other time Logan would have taken them between his lips. This time, not a chance.

"I am dead," Logan squeaked. "Period."

"You're not dead." Deklan softly paced the floor, holding his linen shirt in front of his hairy privates. "I need to think. Sssshhh!" He pointed a finger to the ceiling in front of his face. "If he knew I was emptying my erection into the guy who serves his meals, I'm the dead one."

Like a child, Logan clamped both hands over his own

mouth and tiptoed backward away from the door.

"Just stay quiet." Deklan was not sure what to do. Should he act as if he weren't here or should he answer the door and act stupid?

He chose stupid.

Logan climbed the stairs and hid in the bed corner with Bettie Lu, holding her beak to keep her silent too.

"Dad?" Deklan opened the door. "What are you doing here?"

"I should be asking you the same thing. Get dressed." His father ordered. "You're coming with me." He tipped his head around Deklan, trying to get a good look at the inside. Maybe looking for Deklan's boy toy. Logan stayed quiet while Dante's eyes scanned the place. "Pee-yew." He sniffed. "Remind me to have this dump cleaned."

Deklan would have answered that he wanted to be alone, but because his father continued barking out orders, he kept his mouth shut. He turned around, pivoted his glance in Logan's direction as he spun, hoping he was hidden from sight. "I'll be right back," he told his father.

Deklan climbed the stairs to grab his trousers and boots. After dressing, he leaned in and kissed Logan. Whispering, "I gotta go. Love you Logan." He turned around and left.

Logan smiled and hid the onset of weeping, not sure if the reason for the tears was because he loved Deklan so much or because he may never have him in his bed again. Whispering alone, "Love you too, Dek." It was the first time Logan said those words and the first time he referred to him as Dek. It was a strong name and seemed to be his alone to call him.

Logan heard the door down stairs close, which gave him the okay to move.

It was sad to think that Deklan and Logan had to hide who they were because other people in the world didn't understand them.

Love is love and it does happen between two men. It always has and always will.

Deklan was gone and Logan wondered if he was ever going

to see him again, the way he did last night. As a loved one. As a companion. His heart tightened the moment when he heard Deklan leave. Sadly Logan sat on the edge of the bed and wept.

Chapter 24

Deklan was led like an untamed animal on a chain from Logan's domicile to the great room where the wedding was to take place. His father was a few paces ahead of him, pulling on the imaginary chain.

Wattsworth on the other hand was already there directing traffic and pointing out where he wanted tables and chairs to go, telling everybody what to do like a boss.

Laid out on a table closest to the door was a large parchment page showing the room's layout with how Wattsworth wanted things to be organized.

He sketched out the typical layout for a large wedding. Tables lined the front entrance in order to collect any gifts brought in for the bride and groom. It was tradition.

In the middle of the room was an unexpected set of aisles dividing the sea of chairs into three elongated V-shaped sections. The placement of chairs angled the two aisles at the outside rear corners and then came to a fine point at the front of the room where a platform was being built for the two lovebirds to wed. A new idea that is certain to catch on where the bride and groom enter the room from separate areas and then join one another at the location where Parson Brown will marry them. The room was based on a typical wedding chapel except the hall trickled with less than a religious atmosphere and leaked of a more glamorous showplace.

Deklan's stomach churned at the thought of this being his last happy day on earth. The marriage to a girl he didn't even know instead of the man he really loved was unsettling to him. He stood behind the table with his arms crossed, expecting his hands to start trembling and his jaw to grind, but they didn't. Odd.

His eyes reduced to small slits and he said nothing. There was no point in voicing his opinion because nobody was going to listen to him anyway. This was their wedding not his. He knew this very well.

Deklan looked around the great big room, totally uninterested in any of it. He started breathing heavily and then walked away, his head down and his feet shuffled across the floor. He unconsciously headed down the right side aisle toward the fabricated platform at the front of the room and stood there staring at what was in front of him for a while. 'Why can't all this be for Logan and me?' Resonated in his head. 'He's the one who has my heart.'

"Deklan!" His father hollered, voice echoed in the large hollow space. "How does everything look to you?"

One tear tried to break free and stream down Deklan's face and he wiped it quickly with his floppy sleeve. He sniffed and turned. "Unh – good." He honestly muttered, sniffing again to hide the fact that he was truly unhappier than ever. "Everything looks nice."

He didn't want to break his parents' heart so he went with their plan to get married to the unknown maiden. His wish however was for them to notice his heart breaking and not let the marriage go on as planned unless it was to Logan, his real true love and soul mate.

"It all looks good, dad." Deklan walked toward him and Wattsworth who were standing over the floor plan. "I wouldn't change a thing."

"How many times have I told you not to call me dad?" His

father pointed out again. "You know you are to address me as father or Mr. Royal when the help is present."

"Sorry, Mr. Royal." Deklan turned cold. "You are doing a good job organizing your wedding. Call me when it's my time to walk the aisle with whomever it is you choose for me to marry." He turned and left the great room and then headed outside.

Chapter 25

Watching from his window, Logan saw Deklan leave the house in a hurry. Logan had his morning work to do so he wasn't able to go after him like he would have liked to. Deklan's actions told Logan that he needed somebody on his side, but Logan had no choice other than to let him go on his own. It was killing him not to follow and rescue Deklan from whatever anguish his family inflicted on him.

Logan moved as fast as he could to get the eggs, veggies and grains to the kitchen and then ran out with the trash in his hand before anybody had a chance to push him out the door with a kick to the pants. He saw a few eyes glance over at him during his blurred race around the kitchen, so he had an inkling they knew something out of the ordinary was going on. To take their thoughts on a trip, Logan mumbled, "This wedding is going to be the death of me." It was successful because he noticed they all started working faster too.

If they only knew, Logan was speaking truthfully.

Logan was finding it difficult to imagine Deklan walking hand in hand down the aisle of marriage with someone other than himself. Deklan kissed him, not *that* girl. He held his hand, not hers. They even slept so close together that their bodies merged, exchanged a part of themselves with the other to have and to hold. They relate to the other so well that the seamless connection was effortless and natural.

Logan took off running around the back of the barn to pour a few buckets of water over the vegetables in the garden and then throw food at the animals. He was in such a hurry that he actually threw the food at them. They all looked at Logan like he was crazy because he normally sat with them for a few minutes to make sure everybody got their fair share. That time was different and they didn't seem to understand his crazy actions or why he wasn't taking a seat. The puzzled look in their eyes told him of the wonder they were unable to speak. If he had one minute to spare he would have taken it and sat there with them, but knowing Deklan was troubled by what occurred inside the manor, Logan had no time for socializing with a pig, a chicken or a goat. They had to do without him just this once.

Logan was overheating like deserts dirt, sweating like the downpour of a rainy day, so he quickly grabbed a change of clothing and took off to the river to rinse away the morning workout.

The water was cold, but ignoring the chill was essential in order to finish fast and go find the love of his life and heal Deklan's noticeable pain.

As he hurried out of the river, Logan fell to the ground while trying to stuff one foot into his pant leg, which instigated an urgent re-rinse to flush away the mud clinging to his knees.

It was an 'oh bollocks' moment for sure.

He was getting nervous, afraid that there were too many steps between him and his boyfriend, and because of that, he would miss catching Deklan wherever he ended up. Logan pictured him sitting under the pear tree they staked as their favorite, so his decision to go there first was made quickly. He'd be surprised if Deklan wasn't there.

While running, Logan's flimsy straw hat caught wind during his race through the clover field. He removed it from his head and held the grassy rag in his hand. It made no sense to fight that too as he was already arguing with time.

Logan stopped at the top of the hill and saw Chadwick grazing a few feet from the pear tree. His intellect told him Deklan was there too. Thank God he went to the right place.

Putting his hat back on his head where it belonged, Logan strolled down the hillside to meet Deklan. There were at least two things he needed to do; be sure Deklan was alright as well as console his breaking heart. It was Logan's desire and new obligation as Deklan's lover to take care of him. He was his soul mate even if others saw it differently.

Fate can't be interrupted no matter how hard yourself or anybody else tries to stop it.

So that no sudden noise was made or would startle Deklan away, Logan walked quietly up to him. With his hands in the usual place he always carried them, tucked behind his suspender straps and close to his waistline, he stood in front of Deklan and waited for him to look up.

It didn't take long for Deklan to respond. His eyes showed definite signs of being sad but quickly changed for the better as soon as he looked at Logan. "I'm glad you came." His hand reached up and he pulled Logan down to the ground next to him. In the other hand he held a half-eaten pear out in front of him.

Logan leaned in and kissed Deklan on the cheek and then took a small bite of the crunchy pear he was offering. It was instinct that the two of them were there to help the other survive. With nutrition and with love. Logan hugged Deklan and felt his heart begin to slow down to a more normal pace right after his comforting grip.

They broke apart but still held hands, both locked together over Logan's right knee as they leaned back against the tree.

Deklan started to say, softly at first and then strengthened his voice so Logan could hear him, "I'm not sure I can go through with this, Logan. They are going to make me marry that maiden. It just isn't right on many aspects. Why can't they see that people's lives are being destroyed for their own self-regarding reasons?"

Logan slid his hand on top of Deklan's and gripped it tighter, nudging his shoulder too. "I honestly believe the light will come on some day. It may not be straightaway, but it will illuminate."

"Huh?" Deklan was thinking so literally at the moment that Logan's outlandish analogy made no sense to him at all.

Logan said it in a simpler way. "What may seem like an event that doesn't align the way you think it should right now, will soon fall into place the way it's supposed to. Two souls that are meant to share a life together cannot be denied."

Deklan's forehead formed a knot between his eyes. "You lost me. What?"

"I mean to say that life is funny sometimes. We all climb different mountains, but will end up on the other side where we are supposed to be. This whole messed up situation will all work out as it should. We've gotta believe that." Logan said it a different way hoping he would understand.

What Deklan didn't know and what Logan recently found out himself, was that he had a mystical fairy as a friend guiding him through life. Everyone does, however Logan was fortunate enough to meet his face to face. At least he thought he met him.

Worry lines ornamented Deklan's forehead. "What's going to happen to us when I'm forced to share my bed with that lass?" He went white when he thought about the untidy parts a girl was made of versus the equipment on a chap that he was so familiar with, enjoyed and preferred. The thought of lady parts made him queasy to the point of vomiting and he fathomed going near what she had to offer.

Logan watched him worry, wince and turn a couple shades of green. It wasn't pleasant.

"Will I ever see you again?" Deklan asked.

Logan wasn't prepared for his question. "Of course you will. I'll be right outside your window slaving away."

Deklan's face went sour.

What Logan just said came out in a bad way. For one thing he didn't mean that he was headed back into slavery as it sounded, nor did he mean to make Deklan think that he would only see him from his bedroom window. "Wait. No. I didn't mean that," he shuddered.

Deklan huffed and sank into the tree, pressing his shoulder against Logan's.

Logan was thinking optimistically. "Somehow we will figure this out." He laid his hand over top of Deklan's that was already resting on Logan's knee and he gave it a squeeze. "We love each other, so there isn't any way that anybody will be able to keep us apart." He rotated Deklan's chin toward him and pressed their lips together. Holding their bond in place, Logan took Deklan's cool breath into his lungs as if it was his only source of survival.

Deklan took Logan's as he lightly exhaled. It instantly settled his restless thoughts. "Let's get Chadwick and go for a ride by the river. Maybe take a swim." Deklan stood first, tugging Logan with him.

Logan walked tightly against Deklan's side, holding his hand the entire time. He crossed his other in front of himself and gripped Deklan's upper arm just above the bend. It forced the two of them closer than before and they stepped in unison during their walk through the field.

They met up with Chadwick who was about a hundred feet away, still grazing like he hadn't eaten for weeks. No worry in the world except for making sure his stomach was full. Logan let go of Deklan's arm and then Deklan released his grip on Logan.

"I want you in the front this time." Deklan leaned into Chadwick and pulled at the reigns.

"Okay, fine with me." Logan didn't argue with that and thought it would feel good to have Deklan hold him from behind, give him a sense of security knowing that he's there.

Deklan turned Chadwick around and Logan got on first, scooting forward to leave enough space behind him for Deklan to sit comfortably. The saddle handle was positioned badly as the bulge between Logan's legs fought for the same space it was taking up. He grunted while sliding ahead, a little concerned about damage that could come of his delicate state.

Deklan channeled a toe into the fendered stirrups, grabbed the handle in front of Logan and swung himself up in the back of the saddle like a cowboy that's been riding horses his whole life. He squeezed in behind Logan and his chunky manhood pressed against his backside. Logan felt a slight erection as Deklan pushed into him harder.

Nice.

Logan was thankful he had that effect on him.

"You okay up there?" Deklan hummed in Logan's ear.

"Doing well," Logan replied.

Very well actually.

Logan found it comforting having Deklan positioned behind him, even though the strain on his front side was taking a beating that would normally cause a pitch change in his voice.

Deklan reached around Logan and cupped his gents the best he could with a single hand. "You sure about that?"

Deklan shimmied backward to relieve the pressure on Logan's groin, leaving his hand right where it was.

"Perfect," Logan said.

"I agree." Deklan gently squeezed.

Deklan wrapped his other hand around Logan's waist and tucked three fingers inside his shirt, holding him tight. "Now it's even more perfect," he said and then gave Chadwick a gentle squeeze to his ribcage with his heels. The signal for Chad to start walking. A snap of the reigns meant run.

While they rode together on horseback, feeling every footfall Chadwick made, Deklan rested his chin on Logan's shoulder and held his scruffy cheek against his ear. It tickled a little and Logan could feel him breathing as his chest rose and fell against his back. Logan tunneled three fingers into his shirt over Deklan's and held his hand.

A sense of spirited freedom whirled around Logan with the wind.

In a split second Logan felt afraid. A nauseous feeling came over him caused by ignorant people who were somehow able to take the love of his life away from him. He just finished lifting Deklan's hopes only to feel his own spiral downward. Logan turned his head and kissed Deklan, hopeful to make both their worries disappear.

At that moment, Logan went shockingly scared.

Deklan sensed his fear and pulled Logan tighter against his chest. "It'll be okay, Logan," he whispered.

Logan stayed quiet and let his handsome prince lead them

to a place where safety from the wicked would present itself.

Chapter 26

Instead of going to the river, Deklan led Chadwick to a secluded lake somewhere in the middle of the woods Logan never knew was there. Logan thought he was familiar with the lay of the land, but it appeared that he wasn't. They were so far away from everything that it seemed to be their very own private kingdom. A secret place only a moment or two from the sun and nobody else could touch it but them. Logan loved it.

His fairy godfather would be proud of him.

Deklan tugged the reigns and Chadwick stopped.

Logan looked everywhere while taking in the air around him that smelled of pine and cedar. "This is beautiful. I didn't know this was here."

With his cheek pressed to Logan's, Deklan hugged him securely around his chest with both arms. "I found this a while ago and knew someday I would share it with someone extraordinary. You are that someone, Logan. This can be the place we call our own. A secret hideaway where we can come to and be together whenever we want. Nobody else but us, Logan. What do you think?"

Logan was wordless. He could only stare straight ahead.

Deklan gripped Logan tighter and shook him. "What do you think, my love?" He asked again.

"Yes. Of course. Ours. Our place." Logan wanted it to be, but he didn't like the idea that they needed a hideaway to sneak off to so nobody would see them together. It wasn't right nor was it fair, but it was the way of the world. He loved Deklan and it was necessary for him to show him without anybody standing between them or the love they had for each other. They shouldn't have to hide in the shadows of a make believe marriage. Logan's mirror man told him the relationship was going to be a struggle and he was certainly correct about that. Logan was seeing that already and their union had been short so far. He broke out of his trance. "Sorry. I just find it so amazing. It's a great place to call our own."

Deklan tossed the reigns over Chadwick's head and they dangled to the ground in front of him. His muzzle went down with the straps and he started eating grass again.

Deklan shifted, threw his leg over the horse's rear end and jumped down. "Your next my handsome prince." He held both arms out as a way to lure Logan into them so that he could carry him away.

"You're going to catch me, right?" Logan lifted his leg up and over the horses' mane and found himself sitting sideways in the saddle, ready to fall into the arms of the man he loved.

Deklan reached up and placed his hands firmly to Logan's waist just as he slowly slid down the side of Chadwick and graced the front of Deklan until his feet reached the ground. Deklan leaned in and pinned Logan's back to the horse and feverishly kissed him with an open mouth.

Deklan hesitantly backed off and took a breath. "Omigawd, I love you, Logan." He went for another kiss with more passion than before and Logan closed his eyes and kissed him back. Their tongues greeted and his hands connected with Logan's chest, feeling his heart pound with rising heat.

Backing away without really wanting to, Deklan grabbed Logan by the hand and pulled him toward the water. "Let's forget about everything and go for a swim. Come, let's go."

Logan went with him, tripping over his own feet like a love punched schoolboy. They stopped beside a large pine tree where its root system gave way and the surviving trunk extended gracefully out over the lake. It was the perfect tree to hang their clothes on while they took to the lake and swam.

They took turns removing each other's clothing, starting with their shirts and working downward to their feet.

Logan unbuttoned Deklan's shirt slowly, exposing the hair that blocked his perfect chest. Logan's hands caressed his chest as he slowly worked the shirt over his shoulders. He tossed it in the wind and it slowly drifted like a kite over the leaning tree trunk.

"My turn," Deklan said while he slipped the suspenders over Logan's shoulders until they fell freely at his thighs. He pulled his shirt up and out of Logan's pants and strangely started unbuttoning it from the bottom to top.

Logan grinned at Deklan's quirky way of removing a shirt and then smiled when he gently ran his knuckles over Logan's dark smooth chest.

Deklan grabbed Logan's shoulders, pulled at him and kissed him again. The hair on Deklan's chest warmed Logan at the same time it scrubbed sparks of pleasure through his perked up core.

Logan felt swelling between his legs, brought on by Deklan's masculine touch.

Deklan reached for and unfastened the clasps that kept Logan's pants in place until his dark semi-hard sex organ flopped out and banged densely against his left thigh. "There's my boy — I mean my man." Deklan grinned as he took Logan into both hands because one was never enough.

Logan returned the favor and untied Deklan's fly. Like a restless bull, his thickened organ busted forward, flopped out of his pants and rested heavily to the right.

The few times Logan saw Deklan's erection, the thing always looked so white. Maybe because it was surrounded by dark hair or perhaps because Logan was used to his own which was so much darker than Deklan's?

To Logan, Deklan was hairy in all the right places and it

excited him to see Deklan shirtless. Logan loved everything he saw. Deklan's hair covered chest especially, which was slightly thicker than the rest of him, soft and velvety like puppy fur and always looked impeccably groomed as if he took a comb to it every second of the day.

Their drive for the other helped the both of them forget about the upcoming event that was trying to pry apart their longing to be together. Logan had to believe in fate and had to believe that the travesty in front of them would come to a close in their favor. The mirror man hinted that it would and he was going to hang on to that tidbit of hope and keep on believing.

They were both breathing hard and had to back away from the other in order to catch wind, otherwise one of them was going to pass out without a doubt.

Deklan observed every part of Logan's body and ended with a long hard stare at his square bulky chest before he moved his hands over it and caressed its blocky mass. "Omigawd you are beautiful." He kissed Logan quickly on the lips and then took off into the lake. "Let's swim, lover boy."

Logan followed him into the water with a good grip on his genitals so that it wouldn't flop all over the place like a wild animal. Deklan laughed at him while he watched Logan run, but he didn't care. Deep down he knew Deklan loved every part of him, so no offence was taken and Logan laughed right along with him.

They swam to a deeper part of the water where the surface rippled level with their chests. The tiny waves that pricked at them sounded like musical bells being tapped with a metal pick.

Logan and Deklan joined each other after a few quick dives and then floundered at the surface until they adjusted to the water temperature that first felt cold.

"Come here," Deklan ordered, pushing his hair back away from his face with wet hands.

Logan did what he was told by swimming up to Deklan.

Deklan reached for Logan and pulled him into his chest. Deklan's body was hard and it felt like a rock when Logan hit it. Deklan's hands moved to the sides of Logan's face and he held it firm to kiss him. "We need to figure a way to be together, Logan.

Not just here in hiding, but always."

Logan whispered, "We will, Dek. I promise." His body leaned into Deklan as if the water from behind had pushed him. Their chests pressed tightly against the other and the kiss went deeper this time.

They spun with passion a few times while kissing and the force of the turn lifted Logan higher above the water. Deklan's hands found his bottom and he squeezed it as if wringing water from a rag.

They slowed their spin and when Logan came back down, he was centered perfectly at the top of Deklan's rising erection.

The sensation was new. Cold and hot. It was amazing.

Deklan bit his bottom lip, pushed his hips forward with a grinding grunt and savored Logan's pleasured reaction as he started accepting him.

Logan shuddered with unrestrained enthusiasm as Deklan's growing organ forced its way in. They moved together until every inch of Deklan's erection was buried as far as he could make it go.

Staying connected, they clumsily relocated to shallower waters so they were able to lie down in a more comfortable position.

The best fit they recently discovered was that Deklan spent most of his time on top of Logan. An hour of making love in the water made for physical exertion and neither one of them noticed the strain on their body until it was over.

By the time they burst, the both of them were exhausted, collapsed on the river bank and gasped for air. Eventually their breathing evened out and a sleepy desire came over them.

They noticed only a few clouds in the sky while lying side by side in the grass looking up. Logan held Deklan's hand the entire time they lay silent on their backs and listened to the other breathe. A few birds chirped, disrupting the silence, but it was tranquil all the same.

Deklan rolled over on his side to face Logan. He used a gentle hand and started combing his fingers through the hair above Logan's softening organ. His voice went low, "I am so – so glad we met, Logan. I couldn't imagine what it would be like if we didn't." His finger ran up the hairy trail that diminished a few inches above Logan's navel. After tickling his abdomen with the back of his nails, Deklan rested his palm against Logan's rocky chest he liked so much.

"Me too," Logan answered, looking his way. His crooked arm propped behind his head, lifting it off the ground.

"If you hadn't come along when you did, I don't know how I would have survived. I'm in such a mess, Logan." Deklan rubbed the large mounds of Logan's smooth cocoa chest, his touch felt soothing. "You mean a lot to me, you know."

Deklan caught Logan smiling.

Deklan rolled on top of Logan, pushing all the air he had in his lungs out. He puffed and giggled a little, forced on by the pressure of Deklan's weight.

Deklan was solid muscle and always felt like a load of rocks bearing down on Logan when he was lying on top of him. Logan didn't care though, because with that came the security he always sensed, like a blanket, when he covered him. The closer they were, the better. The less space between them, better yet.

Even though it's been less than ten minutes since Logan ejaculated, his groin turned thick and rigid all over again just seconds after Deklan positioned himself on top of him. Deklan had that effect on Logan. He was beautiful and Logan was in love with him.

Deklan looked at Logan pensively. "I don't want to go, but I think I have to. My parents are going to start wondering where I'm at."

"I - suppose - your - right." Logan pumped the words out between gasps. The weight of Deklan's body on top of him still restricted the flow of air to his lungs.

"Leave your door open tonight, I'm sneaking back over." Deklan kissed and then lifted himself off of Logan.

Regretfully Logan let him go, but the full breath of air felt good to him. The beauty of Deklan standing in front of Logan with nothing on left him hard and wanting more. Logan was obsessed and the evidence stood out.

Noticing Logan's fixation, Deklan grinned and then

whistled for Chadwick to come get them.

Chapter 27

"Where have you been Deklan?" His father Dante asked. "You've been gone all day, without word as to where you were."

"I needed some space." Deklan said, shortly. His good time with Logan quickly vanquished by his father's storming voice.

"We all need space, but we don't always get what we want." Dante replied. "Your mother's been worried."

"I am trying to survive with what you are forcing me to do."

"You need to listen and know this is right for you."

"Really? Right for me?" Deklan hissed. Glowering.

Before Deklan's father had a chance to reply, butler Wattsworth walked in the room with a handful of parchment pages that outlined his busy to-do list. Following him was Mother.

Deklan looked across the room and saw his mother leaning against the doorframe with her tiny hands clasped together in front of her waist. She seemed okay, but there was a certain sign of concern in her eyes. She didn't want this marriage to proceed any more than Deklan did, but father seemed to know best as the man clearly put it more than once.

Wattsworth seemed frazzled, parchment crinkled in his

nervous hands. There was only one full day left to get the place ready for the family wedding and looking around him at an unfinished chapel was triggering assured anxiety.

As it stood now, the grand hall looked nice. It was smothered in white and shimmering gray, the typical wedding hue in the day. Any light coming in from the windows were reflecting luminescent diamond sparks all over the place. It appeared magical. Perfect for a new beginning between two people that didn't really know each other.

The layout was clever. The Seats was arranged to welcome about one hundred guests. There were two aisles running in a V-formation that will take the couple from the far back corners of the room to the same spotlight point up front.

Draping every chair were silken white fabric covers held in place by a large wide gleaming gray ribbon and bow securely tied across the back.

To create a wall of burning light along the back section of the marriage platform, there were at least fifty wax candles on tall silvery sticks. It resembled a mountain peak by the way it crowned high in the center. Shorter pillar candles were plated and hung sporadically from the ceiling by what looked to be fish pole cord, giving the illusion that they were floating in mid space. Wattsworth's idea of bringing the outside stars to the inside.

Deklan and his father were blatant opposites, like night and day. His mother on the other hand was very similar to himself and that was why the feelings they both had about the wedding was quite the same.

Hearing his father carry on about how perfect everything was going to be, Deklan forced himself to ignore what he was saying and treaded foot on the first step of the alter so he could place distance between the two of them. His mother followed and stood beside him. He looked her in the eye. She was devastated and so was he.

She reached down and took his hand. "Deklan, I can hear your thoughts."

"Then why are you letting this go on?" He looked to the floor and took another step onto the platform.

Priscilla went with him and they both stopped in front of

the wall of candles. "This is beautiful." She looked up at the highest one. "I just wish it was for you and somebody you really wanted to be up here with."

"It isn't too late, mother." Deklan turned to her. "You can help me stop this. I can't do it alone. Father is too pig headed in his ways."

"I wish it were that simple, Deklan." Priscilla dropped her head to one side as if giving up. A sigh was expelled as she did. "Your father has a will that is firm, and when he has an idea, he always finds a way to make it happen. Look at the business he built. Just one example of his great achievements."

"Talk to him," He begged.

"I tried talking to him, but he will not listen. You know that."

"But this is major. It's not as if he's bidding on a horse at auction. This is my life we are talking about." Deklan's eyes were beginning to burn. Tears were surfacing at the same time his body started shaking. It was a tangled emotion. One knotted with fear and anger.

They both turned and faced the exit.

At the same table in the back where they left them, Wattsworth and Dante were still standing, pointing around the room and suggesting changes. Outside in the yard, the crew assigned was probably doing the same.

Deklan and his mother left the platform and headed to the back of the hall where Dante and Wattsworth were at. They stopped when they got there and listened to what they were saying.

Dante placed a strong grip to the back of Deklan's neck. "It's perfect isn't it, son?"

Deklan almost lost his balance when his father shook him. "No Dad, it isn't."

Dante's big hand spun Deklan around so he could speak to him face to face. "Now you listen to me. You will not disgrace this family any further than you already have by acting out your foolish fantasies. It just ain't right. You can't be showing a sweet liking to boys the way you've been?"

Like a strong soldier, Deklan gripped his father's arm and yanked it from his neck. He backed away and put his hands to his temples and pressed. "Stop it. Just stop it," he yelled. Squeezing his eyes closed to block out everything around him.

His father stood taller. His face tightened with anger.

Beside Deklan stood his mother who instantly placed both hands over her mouth and started to cry.

"Stop – Stop – Stop!" Deklan swayed as if honing in on a mental breakdown. "Stop everything." He fumed, bringing his hands to his sides. "You may not like this father but your son is a homosexual. Yes Dad, I like lads. There, I've said it." His arms went wide and he backed up a few more steps. "You've known this for a while now and you need to stop denying it. I am what I am and no marriage to a girl is going to change how I feel toward other chaps."

"This cannot be. It's not possible." Dante lowered his voice and corralled Deklan to a more secluded corner of the room. His mother followed closely behind, still crying.

"It is possible because here I am. Right in front of you is your homosexual son. The new word for who I am is gay. So I've heard."

"Don't say that. You are destroying a perfectly good word."

"The word is gay, dad. You need to say it."

"I won't say it. It doesn't make any sense. The word means happy and you cannot be happy like this."

"You're right dad, I'm not happy." Deklan bit his lower lip and turned away.

"Then marry this pretty damsel and you will be happy."

"No dad. That is why I'm not happy. I don't like the maidens the way you think I should. I'd rather be with the boy next door."

"No you wouldn't."

"Yes I would."

"No – You – Wouldn't"

"Yes – I Would. Why are you arguing about something that cannot be changed?" Deklan fought back.

"There is nothing to change."

"I'm glad you agree." Deklan's fists loosened a little.

"That is not what I meant and you know it."

"Dad, I don't have the answer or the solution you are looking for, but I do know that I was created this way for a reason. Call it Gods way of slowing production of life. I don't know?" Deklan went serious. "All I know for sure is that I cannot change no matter how hard you or anybody else try's to make me change. I also know that you cannot force what isn't supposed to be."

Deklan's father pursed his lips. He had nothing to say after that statement from his son. His eyes went dark. He looked from Deklan to Priscilla and back to Deklan again. "Be here tomorrow for this wedding or don't come home at all."

As his father turned and left like a retracting lightning bolt, Deklan bowed his head and huffed. He shook his head with total disappointment at the same time his mother grabbed his arm and squeezed it.

Deklan's hands went back to his temples and his fingertips tried circling the tension away. There wasn't much more to say and it was apparent that at this time tomorrow he was going to be married to some damsel his parents handpicked off the street the same way they select fruit at the market.

Without saying anything more, Deklan kissed his mother on the forehead and walked away. As the doors closed behind him, he caught a glimpse of his mother still standing there with the crumpled handkerchief in her fragile grasp. It was tarnished with tears brought on by a vile display between Dante and her son. She took a deep breath, glanced around the beautiful silver room and quietly crept out the door behind Deklan.

Chapter 28

Logan felt a void with Deklan not being with him and his heart cracked when he heard Deklan was still going through with the wedding to this mystery girl. It didn't come as too much of a shock because Deklan's father had such a strong grip on him and was able to nearly dictate every move he made.

It was either do as father said or you have no place to call home.

How incredibly unfair was that?

Sometimes it takes longer for certain people to realize that paired souls cannot be separated. In their case, Deklan's father was one of them. The degree of acceptance was higher when the issue hit home instead of somebody else's. There's more to think about when it comes knocking on your own front door.

Logan was sitting quietly on the wooden bench outside his front door when he spotted Deklan walking the drive and kicking stones. Small dust storms twisted off the ground like tiny tornadoes each time a pebble hit the dirt. He was boyish and cute even though sad and terrified. Logan's heart sank at what he saw, but instantly perked up at the first sign of him heading his way.

Logan sat up tall and put on a courageous smile. He had to, for his own sake and for Deklan's.

Deklan stood in front of Logan, casting a shadow that blocked the sun. His hair was a mess from what Logan could see in front of Deklan's cast silhouette.

Deklan sat down without a word and sneakily slipped his hand beneath Logan's thigh. His touch as usual settled Logan's nerves and Logan's connection did the same to his.

Logan leaned back against the coops siding with Deklan and listened to the birds chirp their springtime songs. It was nice considering the circumstances before them were far from being the best of times.

Logan dropped his hand to his side and it landed on top of Deklan's. Logan's grip tightened while looking around to make sure nobody was watching them hold hands in broad daylight. It was absurd to think that they had to stop, look and take notice before showing respectful affection for each other in a public place, but it was what it was.

They sat together in tranquil silence and watched two roosters in the distance walking side by side as if they were best friends. Deklan and Logan glanced at each other and grinned, delighted that a sign such as that was being presented to them in such a mysterious way. They were meant to be together as much as those silly birds did and were being told that very moment. It was clear that the two rosters weren't up to tagging a hen any more than Deklan and Logan were wanting or able to pin a maiden. It just wasn't natural for them and by the looks of it, for the two roosters either.

Deklan and Logan sat on the wooden bench observing the two roosters as they ignored all the hens that were trying to get their attention by fluffing their wings and shaking their tail feathers. It was comical to watch the roosters caringly interact with each other and at the same time not wanting anything to do with the lady birds. The roosters were obviously homobirduals.

Go figure.

Without question Deklan and Logan knew exactly what the birds were thinking.

It wasn't long after the roosters ran away when Deklan

asked if Logan wanted to follow him to the barn and visit with Chadwick.

Ludicrous it would have been to say no. Logan stood up first to let Deklan know he accepted his invitation and then they took off running for the barn like lovesick schoolboys, Deklan chasing after the lad his heart was crushing on.

Logan was happy to see him laughing.

Chadwick was standing majestically in the stall when they got there, but his tranquility changed quickly. His nose started bobbing up and down with excitement the minute he saw them turn the corner and then he hastily pranced in circles that were complemented by whinnies of contentment.

That horse loved Deklan the same way Logan did. He could see that by Chadwick's reaction toward him.

Logan brushed Chadwick's mane while Deklan scraped mud and soot from the underside of his hooves.

Before long, Deklan sought out a wash brush and a bucket filled with cleansing water. It wasn't big enough for him to get into and take a bath, so Logan figured he was planning to spot wash Chadwick.

Sure enough, Deklan started with his rump, moved down around his knees and legs before telling Logan that he may want to look away for what was about to take place next.

What could be so bad that it was necessary for him to step outside?

And then it happened. Oh sweet surrender.

Logan's jaw immediately dropped when he witnessed what Deklan did. "Holy bollocks," was all he could muster. The poor horse, he thought. It looked more than painful. It was a horrific deep cleaning from what Logan was seeing and he knew for sure he would not want it done to himself.

"What?" Deklan said, not expecting an answer. "It needs to be done to prevent buildup of dirt. It can get infected if not kept clean and then there will be a bigger issue in hand." Deklan extended the horse's genitals to its fullest length and started scrubbing it with the soapy brush.

No way in hell.

Logan couldn't stop staring at the size of this horse's genitalia. It was huge. No, it was enormous. The thing couldn't have been a fraction less than eighteen or twenty inches long. It looked massive in Deklan's soapy hand. It was offensive really, but Logan couldn't seem to look away. His own genitals started to hurt from watching that bristly brush being scrubbed up and down the poor horse's private parts. Logan crossed his legs as a way of soothing his imaginary pain. "Holy bollocks!" He squeaked again.

Deklan laughed at him and then let go of Chadwick's great big reproductive organ. It hung like a rope for a second and then quickly retracted into hiding like something scared it away.

Deklan was finished there but then moved behind Chadwick to flush his tail with the remaining water in the bucket. A clean hind end keeps the flies at bay. As dreadful as this bath was, the added laughter helped lift the dark cloud that was hovering so sinisterly above them, unfortunately at the horse's expense.

After that, Chadwick seemed energized. He perked up and started dancing.

"Are you done yet?" Logan said as if he was begging.

"Yep, that's it. We're finished." Deklan tossed the dripping scrub brush into a bin on the wall that was about twenty feet away while he heaved the large bucket upside down over the stalls post so it could simply drip dry.

To Logan's surprise, everything landed where it was supposed to. Deklan's done this many times before he could tell.

Deklan dried his hands on his pant legs, stepped up to Logan and kissed him on the lips. "There we go. Chadwick is squeaky clean."

Logan's reaction to Deklan's kiss was a bit stiff and he felt it. "Sorry, I'm still in shock over what I just witnessed. I had no idea Chadwick was such a big boy. Omigawd that was awful. You need to wash your hands."

Deklan kissed Logan again and started to laugh. "You'll get used to it." He tapped Logan on the nose with his finger, his horse cocked finger.

Logan screamed.

Deklan laughed harder.

"That isn't funny. GO wash your hands." Logan pushed him away and pointed to the water well outside.

"Yes mom." Deklan smartly obeyed.

Logan sweetly spanked Deklan's hind-end as he turned away and then followed him back to the water pump. Deklan held his hands out beneath the spout while Logan gripped the handle and started pumping the cold water up from deep in the ground. It took a few seconds for the water to surface, but when it did, it came out like the grand rapid falls.

Deklan scrubbed his hands and up his arms past his elbows. He made a mess of everything around him. He got wet and so did Logan.

Deklan shook his arms out in the open sun to promote the drying time to quicken. "Let's sneak in the house and grab us a change of clothes."

The look on Logan's face should have told Deklan it wasn't a good idea for him to be making an appearance inside the manor. "But what if they see me with you?"

"They won't. The house is large. They're all too busy to notice if somebody is out of place anyways." Deklan's arms were dry but his hands still looked wet. He shook them again, flicking droplets of water around both their feet.

"Are you sure about that?" Logan asked.

"No, but who cares. They are bound to meet my true love someday anyways." He wiped his hands on his pants to speed up the drying time.

"Aren't they about to set fire to any boy you bring home that will get in the way of your marriage to that girl person?" Logan mentioned her as if she was an unwanted object.

"Don't be silly. They may have their issues, but nobody is going to get injured or killed over this. Now come on," Deklan asked again.

"I've never been beyond the kitchen before, so don't be alarmed if I appear a bit out of place while visiting your bedroom."

"You're going to fit in fine. I know this. Now let's go." Deklan took Logan's hand and led the way.

"I feel sick." Logan held his stomach.

Deklan snickered. "My place is yours. I have forced my way into your sweet entrance, comfortably through the back, so now it's your turn to make your way inside mine."

"Did you hear what you just said?" Logan's mind wandered to an erotic place. He liked it.

"I know what I said. Glad you were paying attention and understood what I was referring to. Follow close behind me and keep your eyes on the prize."

Chapter 29

They were only a few steps from the front stairway when the door opened up and Deklan's father stepped out on the stoop yelling at somebody inside the manor.

It wasn't clear to them what he was hollering about and it didn't matter, but they thought it best to dodge the bullet this time and get out of his way.

Thinking fast, Deklan pushed Logan aside and he tumbled into the bushes at the base of the stairs. It wasn't a pleasant place as Logan found out on the way in. A few rose stems pricked his leg and he started leaking blood. Logan applied pressure to the wound with his finger and it stopped oozing in seconds.

Deklan quickly sat on the first step to make believe he had been there alone the whole time. His leg bounced nervously as his father approached from behind.

His father's mannerism was a bit more pleasant toward Deklan than the last time they were face to face. "It's nice to see you, Deklan. You might want to get out of the sun before you burn up. It's a hot one today." Dante looked to the sky.

Deklan stood. "I suppose your right. Thanks, Dad."

Logan heard every word they said as he hung out with his back pressed against the Iron staircase. The large shadow cast by the stairs made it a bit easier for his dark skin to blend in.

Logan thought it was nice to hear Deklan and his Father speaking in a civilized manner and it made their previous engagements seem less fierce.

For the first time Deklan felt a sincere connection with his father. It didn't happen too often and hearing his gentle voice today was far from what Deklan had expected. "Dad?"

"Yes Deklan?" Dante ground his heels in the gravel and turned back around toward his son.

Logan sank deeper into the shadow and stayed quiet.

"No matter what happens, please know that I love you and will respect your choices. I may not agree with all of them, but know that I won't let that get in the way of how I really feel about you and mom."

Dante didn't say anything at first, but reached for Deklan and hugged him. Hugged him hard. Then in a voice softer than before, he whispered, "I just can't bear to see people hurting you. You are my child for God sake and it is my job to take care of you and protect you."

"Thanks, Dad." Deklan grunted. "Thanks for looking out for me."

Dante kissed the side of Deklan's head as if he was still a young boy and he was sending him off to grade-school. He let him go and then turned to walk away.

Logan quietly rose from the bush, crying like a little girl and it wasn't because he was pricked by a rose, but because of what he just heard. That callous man really loved his kid and it seemed that he was only trying to look out for him the best way he knew how. Logan was dying on the inside and couldn't imagine how Deklan must have been feeling. "Are you alright?" He sobbed.

Deklan's voice cracked too. "I'm fine. Let's get inside."

They climbed the same stairway together that Logan had once before climbed alone. He knew what was on the other side, however the fear Logan felt this time was different.

"Why are you trembling?" Deklan asked.

"I'm trembling?" Logan asked. "I didn't notice." he fibbed.

"It'll be alright. My father is out."

They both took each step together as if they were trained for a march. The landing past the doors overlooked the grand hall just the way Logan remembered it from before, only this time it was lined with seating instead of obtainable virgins slinging cake.

Deklan led Logan down a short corridor to the left and then they walked a long hallway to the right that was lined with doors on both sides. It reminded Logan of an elegant hotel but without the noisy lovers on the other side of each door trying to bring more babies into a cruel, cruel world. When they made it to the end, Logan knew they reached Deklan's bedroom by the way they stopped and Deklan pointed him toward the door. Logan's anxiety perked up the instant he passed through the doorway of Deklan's magnificent chamber.

Deklan closed the door behind them and Logan heard the lock click into place.

Logan's heart raced with excitement and nervousness consumed him.

Even though Deklan and Logan had been together before, this was nothing like any other time. His room was like the space Logan only imagined for a prince and it made him anxious to think he was the one to lie with Deklan in his bed.

Inside the room was the way Logan expected it to be. There were a lot of dark colors. Rusty brown tones, some greens and light shades of walnut. It was nice and felt cozy the way a bedroom should feel. The fireplace along the wall to the left was mammoth. He could actually stand in it if he wanted to, but seeing the blaze burning inside it gave him the good mind to stay clear of the fiery well and not test his theory on measure. That wouldn't be wise.

The crackling fire called to Logan, so he went over and stood next to the open flame and let it dry the moisture from his damp clothing. Deklan followed him over and kissed him on the cheek. It was a sweet kiss and Logan liked it very much.

Deklan turned around and stood at Logan's side. "This is it. My sleeping quarters. Around the corner over there is the water closet and sink basin."

"Nice," is all Logan said, nodding his head and scanning the handsome room that was decorated for a chap.

"The wardrobe is over there." Deklan pointed. "So whatever you would like to wear is inside. Take your pick of anything."

Logan favorably smiled and again stupidly nodded as if he was just an invited guest that was being given a handout instead of a boyfriend being offered sanctuary. He liked the sound of that, 'his boyfriend'. It had a nice ring to it and it fit him perfectly. Logan could get used to being a Royal rather quickly.

Deklan and Logan were pretty close to the same size except Deklan was about two or even three inches taller. With that, the pant length might be an issue for Logan, but the top would work out just fine. Logan was looking forward to wearing Deklan's clothing to support the claim he had on him.

"How about we change real quick so we can relax and enjoy the rest of the evening together." Deklan opened up the wardrobe and took out a pair of gray woven pants that were trimmed just below the knee.

"Are those for me?" Logan asked, thinking the shorter style would fit best.

Deklan pushed the hanger toward Logan. "If you like them, they're yours."

Logan took the britches and then Deklan grabbed another pair that were pretty close to being the same as what he just handed Logan, only his were brown.

Deklan disrobed completely and then only slipped on the trousers, leaving his gorgeous chest exposed. Logan liked him that way, so he paid no mind to Deklan being shirtless at all.

Logan on the other hand put on a button down shirt. He rolled the sleeves back until they locked above his elbows and left several of the top buttons undone so he could keep cool next to the open flame.

Logan went to the window and looked out of it so he could place where Deklan's bedroom was located inside the great big house. Much to Logan's surprise, his room wasn't too far away from the kitchen and just a few paces to where he stayed every night. It was hard to imagine that Deklan wasn't aware of who

Logan was or had any idea he was ever down in that small carriage house. Logan has seen Deklan in the window before, but never associated it with the place he slept.

"It's funny isn't it?" Deklan crept up behind him, pressing his body against Logan's.

"What is?" Logan leaned back into him, wishing the shirt wasn't in the way of the two of them getting even closer.

"That you have been living right outside my window this whole time and I never even noticed you."

"Well that tells me a lot about my character."

"I mean, I knew that somebody was there, just never took notice that it was someone I would be so attracted to."

"Now that makes it much better."

"No, wait," Deklan choked. "I didn't mean that either. What I meant to say was that I just never paid attention to who was out there."

"I see." Logan grinned because he knew Deklan was trying to be sincere and the way he was obliterating himself so cutely made Logan want to kiss him.

"Forget it. I love you and you know it. You want some wine?" Deklan slyly changed the subject, hugging him from behind.

Spinning around, Logan gave Deklan the kiss he needed and then shimmied around his side to reach for the two metal goblets he saw sitting on the table in front of the fireplace. "Would love some," Logan said.

Deklan followed Logan and pulled the cork from the glass bottle. He made it a point to pour Logan's first and then his own. He's so thoughtful and sweet. It was red. Logan's wine flavor of choice. "I know it's predictable, but we can't drink our first bottle of wine together without making some kind of good cheer," Deklan said.

"Of course not," Logan agreed. He couldn't help blush over Deklan's shirtless chest. The perfectly groomed hair always got his attention.

"As ridiculous as it is, let's toast to everlasting love between you and me." Deklan made the typical motion of raising his metal goblet.

Logan lifted his and tapped it against the rim of Deklan's. The clink was magical, like the sound glitter would make if its decent made any noise. It was a beautiful chime that lingered a few seconds after their goblets touched.

As soon as the chiming ended, they sipped. It was so good. Warm, fruitful and delicious.

Logan didn't want to come across as being a wine drinking lush so he always waited for Deklan to sip from his goblet first before he made a swan dive into his own. Logan enjoyed wine and didn't have it at his disposal that often so when he did, he border lined on indulgence.

It was funny. Logan caught Deklan tipping the bottle over his goblet at every chance he could get. If Logan wasn't crazy, he was sure Deklan was trying to get him tipsy. Logan didn't mind though, the wine helped him relax and if Deklan was planning to ask him to share his bed, it also made it easier for him to say yes.

"I'm a little hungry. Are you?" Deklan asked.

Logan never ate in front of Deklan before except for maybe a pear or a cracker flake, so this would be one of the first times they both would enjoy a small meal together.

"Let's sneak out to see if we can raid the kitchen without getting caught." Deklan was acting like he was a young teenager on a sole mission to rob the place. "There should be plenty of food in there tonight."

"No way. Somebody in the kitchen will recognize me." Logan stood stiff. His eyes glowing.

"It'll be fun, like we're on a secret mission." Deklan grabbed Logan's hand and started walking like a crouched tiger before they even left the room.

Prowling already? What was that about?

Even though they were both in their mid-twenties and should be acting like adults, they felt like children and loved it. Logan especially did with Deklan holding his hand.

They crept through the hallway like burglars, tiptoeing most of the way until they came to a wall of bookshelves and stopped. Deklan reached for a lever that was tucked away behind a book and pulled on it. The entire wall opened up like a door. They squeezed through the small opening where Deklan took Logan down a back stairway that seemed like a secret passage only the owners knew of. It was very dark and narrow, used for escape purposes mainly and whomever used it had to move along in single file, making their way through the tunnel by touch alone.

Deklan stopped abruptly with a childlike giggle and Logan tripped down to the same step he was standing on. Turning in the tight spot, Deklan kissed Logan hard. Their tongues played while Deklan purred that he loved him. Logan felt Deklan's hands run up his sides until they reached his chest where they stopped. He massaged and caressed Logan before moving them down where he gripped the bulge in Logan's pants.

Deklan grumbled something that sounded like, "I want you."

It went unnoticed in the dark that Logan was blushing and that Deklan's touch sparked an erection. Even though their tongues were tied, Logan was still able to fluently return his testament and tell him he loved him too. They separated with puffs of air and Deklan patted Logan on the bottom before he gave it a friendly squeeze.

Deklan whispered, "Ready? Let's move."

Before Logan knew it, their mission was on again.

Reaching the bottom of the stairs, Deklan pressed his hands and ear against the door as if he was trying to detect if anybody was on the other side. Toward the top, a little higher than eye level was a small peep hole, figured to spy on whoever was on the other side before bursting in on them with an unexpected entry.

Even though Deklan was an inch or two over six feet tall, he still had to stand on the tip of his toes to place an eye over the secret spy hole. So he didn't trip back and fall, Logan held him in place with my hand to his back.

"I don't see anyone." Deklan whispered, turned back and kissed Logan again. It was so dark, his lips caught Logan's eye.

Deklan clicked the latch and slowly opened the door, peeked around the corner as if it would have made a difference to anybody on the other side and then slinked through the small opening.

After Logan meekly followed in his shadow, Deklan reached for a sack of potatoes and leaned it against the casing to hold the door open. When Logan turned to watch him work, he saw that the door they came through was disguised as a unit of shelves, similar to the one they entered through upstairs. It was even complete with a few mismatched items, presumably being used by the staff.

Logan turned back around and saw that they were standing in a small closet that looked to be the pantry or a storage room of some kind. The outside walls were lined with shelves and baskets that were stocked with odds and ends, pots, pans, utensils, nonperishable foods, books and many other items that would be used for serving meals. Despite the fact he has been in the kitchen countless times before, he never knew the room was there.

Deklan grabbed Logan's hand and led him across the room to the real door that would open up into the real kitchen. "You ready to invade?"

"Unh – I guess so," Logan murmured.

"Then let's do this." His grin went wide.

Deklan burst through the door like a barren soldier, ready to stab anybody that stood in the way of his only meal. He swiftly plucked a knife from the cutting block and stuffed it under the door as a prop for our quick getaway. He looked heroic in a dangerous sort of way.

Logan's blood pumped fast and he wanted Deklan badly after what he just witnessed.

They moved in like warriors of the wasteland. In and out. Fast and quick. Practically undetectable. A blink of an eye and they would be missed.

Logan figured the faster he moved the blurrier he'd be to whoever saw him snatch food from the cooling box or countertops. That way, his speed would make it less likely for anybody to know who he was. It was necessary for him to keep it on the down low. He couldn't risk being spotted by any of the kitchen staff.

Deklan took to the cupboards and Logan shot over to the cooler. They were sleek and feline fast.

The few people prepping food or whatever they were doing in the kitchen were probably more shaken by the sudden outburst to register that it was Deklan and Logan doing the stealing. Their startled faces from what could be seen were long and horse hung.

Like a whirlwind, they were in and out of there within seconds, including the doorstop that was pulled free by Deklan as they charged back through the pantry door and up the secret stairway. The doors closed behind them with a bang and they heard somebody in the kitchen squawk. It was a little late to be screaming, so it made both of them laugh.

Hallucinations or some sort of magic trick must have entered the kitchen staffs minds, because when the time came to cautiously take a peek in the pantry, they'd find no sign of prowlers, which meant they either disappeared or were never really there.

Ya gatta love these big houses with secret passages.

Logan was almost out of breath by the time they reached the second floor, but his will to make his boyfriend proud kept him going at full speed. Deklan could do it, then so could he. They were a team now. Lovers. No – they were boyfriends.

Deklan and Logan finally made it back to the bedroom where they could both catch a breath. Their full arms spilled food to the table near the wine and then Deklan ran back to lock the door.

"Omigawd, I was fitting out." Logan breathed heavily as he dropped to the floor and laid face up between the two chairs and the fireplace. From where he laid, the stone fiery structure looked bigger to him than before. It seemed to tower massively high as well as stretched wide.

Overhead Logan could see Deklan crawling toward him across the floor on all fours. From his position, Deklan looked like he was creeping along the ceiling, like an insect. When he reached Logan's head, he stopped and leaned down to kiss him from above. The sensation of being kissed upside down felt strange to Logan, but because it was Deklan who was kissing him, it didn't matter how he was getting the love. Deklan had been holding back for so long, it was coming at him one way or another.

"We did it," Deklan said, his lips still gracing Logan's.

"Let's eat." Logan rolled over onto his elbows to face the food on the table top and then sat up. He grinned and rubbed his hands together like a greedy banker does when they touch money. Not only was he beaming because he was hungry, but mostly because he wanted to elevate their spirits to a happier place.

Logan wanted that night, possibly their last together, to be special for the two of them, not wallow in despair and misery of what was ahead. He wanted Deklan to remember the finer times they had the past few days with them laughing, kissing, holding hands and making love. Like the time they met in the clover field unexpectedly and unaware they were a few days shy from falling in love. As well as the first time they shared a glance in the grand hall on Deklan's birthday, their turning point in life. Plus the moonlight kisses when he politely asked Logan if he could. Logan thought Deklan's kindness was cute so he had him then.

Logan wanted Deklan to remember their first dance in the Garden by the pool. The first time he entered his body and introduced him to his genetic matter that he so willingly took. The swim in the river where Deklan made love to Logan again. The shock and laughter Logan encountered the first time he saw a horse get a thorough bath. And their latest adventure, racing through the kitchen like banshees taking food that was meant for another occasion. Logan wanted to make another good memory as they sat together in front of the fire drinking wine and eating stolen snacks. It was working, Deklan was laughing.

After they gobbled up a portion of the next day's special dinner, Deklan and Logan went straight to bed without cleaning up. They carried on the way they always did when they slept together. In and out of slumber making love each time they woke. The most recent time they shared their bodies was about five in the morning and it was the most intimate time they'd ever had.

Logan was sure it had a lot to do with what day it was and the notion of it possibly being the last time they were ever going to bond in the comfort of each other's arms without a third party hovering someplace in their midst.

Deklan and Logan traded places a few times during their sessions of affection so that they both had the others genes swimming and making a home inside them. It was their gift to each other before they were forced to go separate ways.

Logan enjoyed the incredible sensation of having Deklan tightly wrapped around him as his dark erection ejaculated deep inside him.

Throughout the night Deklan made it a point to give as much of himself to Logan as he could, while making sure his boyfriend received and held on to every bit of his genetic matter. Deklan kept Logan's insides well soaked again and again as if it had to last him the rest of his life. After one final release from Deklan during the early morning hours, he remained submerged while holding Logan close from behind. They drifted off to sleep while their bodies remained snuggly connected.

Chapter 30

The infamous wedding day arrived for the Royal family. Their only son was getting married. To a girl.

How perfect for them.

Logan woke up with Deklan sitting on the side of the bed facing him with a hot cup of coffee, a stirring spoon coated in cocoa and a few fancy sprays of sliced strawberries.

Logan needed him as his wedded. Badly.

Logan blinked away the light and sat up, making more room for Deklan beside him. The blanket fell to Logan's lap and Deklan reached out and rubbed his dark chest with the back of his hand. His touch felt good to Logan.

"I brought this for you, my sweetheart." Deklan set the tray on the edge of the bed beside Logan. It made him nervous sitting there, but if Deklan was okay with it, so was Logan.

Logan was not much for putting his stomach through a workout so quickly after he woke, but he did like a good cup of coffee. Black. No added sugars, flavors or heavy creams. He didn't want to hurt Deklan's feelings, but it was necessary for him to be honest, so he told him that he would start with the coffee and then slowly make his way to the edibles. "I don't usually eat straight out of bed in the morning, but thank you for what you did though."

"We can share the strawberries later." Deklan pushed the coffee toward Logan and he took it.

"Very good," Logan purred as he sipped its goodness.

"I'd like to tell you how much I've enjoyed being with you these last few days." Deklan conveyed while he repositioned himself closer to Logan. The saucer of strawberries clattered on the tray as it rocked between the two of them.

"Same here, except I *loved* being with you." Logan sipped the hot coffee carefully, humming how good it was again.

They both knew what was taking place later that day and neither one of them liked it or wanted to even think about it. Logan set the cup back down on the tray and reached for Deklan's hand. They sat silent for a minute just looking at each other.

Logan thought it before and would think it again. 'omigawd he's gorgeously beautiful.'

They've only known each other for a very short time, but fused so strongly that they could practically read the others thoughts. With that in mind, Logan could tell Deklan's heart was tortured and knew he was conveying to Deklan that his was too. All the heartache because of what was to transpire later in the day.

Deklan was trying to be strong behind a smile, but Logan knew him well enough to know that he was crying on the inside. Logan was too for that matter and like Deklan he wasn't going to let it show. For sake almighty, Deklan had more to worry about than to console Logan, but he knew Deklan would try.

Deklan leaned in and gave Logan the biggest hug he'd ever received, nearly crushing him while he did. Even though Logan couldn't breathe at the moment, it was the greatest feeling he could experience and didn't want it to end. Logan could have died at that moment and it wouldn't have mattered, except for the fact that Deklan would really miss him.

Logan only had a few minutes left with Deklan before he had to go. Logan knew it and so did Deklan. That's why they clung to each other as long as they could and as comforting circumstances would have it, they couldn't let go.

Logan broke free and eased the situation by mentioning the coffee was going to spill if they kept crowding the breakfast tray as the two of them were. Deklan pulled away and sort of agreed.

Before too much time passed by, Logan pushed the covers down so he could swing his legs over the edge of the high bed and jump down. Deklan at the same time lifted the shaking breakfast tray from the mattress and carried it over to the table near the fireplace. A little coffee did spill, but didn't matter because there was a saucer and a tray to catch it.

Deklan turned back just as Logan was lifting his trousers from the floor where he left them last night. With one leg copying the other, he guided each foot into the pant pair.

"Let me help you with that." Deklan walked toward him with watery eyes.

Logan stopped midway and waited. All of him still hanging out on display.

They carried on with small chatter as if they just met each other for the very first time and Logan answered Deklan with what his plans were for the day. Feeding animals, watering the gardens, picking vegetables, gathering eggs and stocking the kitchen with whatever was missing. The usual routine. He wanted to stray as far away from wedding talk as possible, in fact, not mentioning it at all. Likewise for Deklan he was sure.

Deklan tried to lighten the mood by joking about how big and heavy Logan's sex organ was, even when it wasn't erect. He grunted while lifting it into his britches and nicely tucked it down against Logan's inner thigh. He buttoned him up and gave the monstrous member a gentle pat. "Where's your shirt?" Deklan smiled shakily and then kissed Logan short and sweet.

"Over there." Logan pointed to the chair by the fireplace.

Deklan went to get it and on his way back he held it over his mouth and inhaled deeply. His eyes closed as if embedding a memory.

Logan quietly told him to keep that one. "Give me one of yours to wear," he said.

"Good idea, Logan. I'd like that." Deklan put Logan's shirt

on and went to the wardrobe to get one of his own. He chose a good one that he figured to fit Logan well.

Logan put it on with his help. The scent of Deklan covered him and it helped ease the swelling in Logan's heart as well as his lonely soul. It was as if Deklan was wrapped around him.

Deklan buttoned Logan up in his quirky manner, from bottom to top, but stopped half way. He then laid his palms against Logan's chest and brushed the fabric flat. "Good as gold," he said.

Logan kissed Deklan with his mouth closed and held it for quite a while. Not moving or expanding his jaw to take him in. He just stood still and connected with Deklan, softly and quietly. Logan's eyes closed and a tear squeezed free. He couldn't stop it or hold it back any longer. He was weakening and about to burst if he didn't let his melancholy break free.

Once again Logan thought of how selfish Deklan's family was being and how they were supporting themselves instead of their son. It manifested and preserved anger within him.

Deklan moved his hands to Logan's shoulders, squeezed once and then wrapped his arms tightly around his neck. He hugged him even tighter than before, their scruffy cheeks engaged. "I will always love you," he said. "No one else."

With that, Logan broke down, hugging him harder as if he was trying to make the two of them into one person. Logan was angrier than he was before.

How could they take him away?

Chapter 31

Somberly, Deklan walked Logan out the front door and down the steps as if he didn't care that they were seen by anyone or not. Logan wasn't worried about it either. In fact it was a way for Logan to express his disappointment in the decision Deklan's family made, which would ruin a life that was sure to be a good one. Logan knew that it was childish for him to strike back like a brat, but it made him feel better doing it.

Logan walked to his small but cozy coop, turned back to look at Deklan so many times that he may have made the entire trip walking backwards. The appearance on Deklan's face showed Logan there was a hollow space left there. They separated from each other, which left a tremendous gap between them.

This was bad and it wasn't right.

Before Deklan had a chance to turn around and go back inside, horse drawn carriages with more favors meant to dress the wedding function rudely intruded the grounds in front of him and nearly ran him over.

Memories of Logan's mother returned and his blood started to boil hot. Deklan was Logan's beloved and when he hurt, Logan hurt. Deklan tripped backward, nearly falling into the thorny bushes Logan was hiding in yesterday.

Stinking carriages.

Alone, Logan sat on the wooden bench at his doorstep just watching. He didn't care if the manor got its food or if the fat cook was fed her grains. Logan wasn't feeling up to providing for the people that hated him and Deklan for who they were. Logan just sat still working up a plan to get his lover back.

Another carriage pulled up that looked more like a covered wagon.

What? More swans?

Logan presumed they were going into the pool out back. Maybe not, as they stayed parked at the front door.

All of a sudden, butler Wattsworth came running down the stairs, bumping into Deklan while hollering at the swan driver to take the birds out back. At the same time he circled a pointy finger above his head as a way of instructing the driver to turn the wagon around and go the other way.

In the mix of all the commotion, Deklan climbed a few steps, turned and looked at Logan before hanging his head low and ascending the rest of the way.

Before he disappeared through the massive doors, Logan took a good look at him and could see that there was an empty space inside him. Logan was missing from his life and the gaping hole it left was apparent in his saddened actions.

Logan stood a few minutes and then went inside, closed the door, crossly climbed the stairs and fell face down in his bed. All he could do was empty his eyes into the pillow beneath his head.

Logan's boyfriend was getting married, to a damsel, and there was nothing he could do about it.

'Sure there is.'

Logan heard a voice but thought it was in his head. He sat up and looked around the room and expected to see someone.

Was he going mad?

"Mirror man?" Logan called out. "Is that you?"

Chapter 32

Deklan passed by everybody running around like they were losing control of their heads as they tried to get everything done before the wedding guests arrived. There was eight hours left, but you'd think there were only two.

Deklan returned to his bedroom and locked the door behind him. He started breaking down the instant the latch clicked into place and then went over to the bed where Logan had slept the night before and fell forward against the pillow in the same spot that Logan had laid his head. He pressed his face deep into the pillow to muffle his sobbing from the outside world, pounding the poof several times with clenched fists to relieve his caged fury.

With all his sadness being released at once, in time his exhausted body went quiet and he fell asleep. Two hours passed before he escaped dreamland and woke up. Disbelief rattled him when he realized that nobody came looking for him to see if he was okay or even in his room. All in his favor actually, because he wasn't up to seeing anybody in the household anyways.

Deklan sluggishly came to life with the aid of cold water splashed against his face. It trickled down and sparkled behind the hair on his rising chest. While standing with is head tilted forward to let the water from his hair drip into the basin, he saw Logan's ring on the desk top next to the ewer.

Astounded that the ring was back again, he picked it up and spun it onto his middle finger. Smiling, he felt the comfort of Logan close to him again. He shook his head and looked up, seeing himself looking back.

After he observed his drying reflection in the looking glass for several minutes while he spun the ring around his finger, he peeled his shirt from his back and draped it over the one Logan wore the previous night during their great kitchen robbery. He buttoned Logan's over his with a delicate touch, secretly tucked the ring in the breast pocket and then safely hung the shirts on a hook in the back of the wardrobe where nobody would see them hanging together. Logan's holding his.

Another several minutes passed and with it came a tap on the door. The unexpected knock startled him, pulling him out of his distant thoughts. Deklan quickly closed the wardrobe door and answered with a single word, "Yes?" Bare chested he turned around, hands behind his back, pressing the wardrobe doors closed to hide what was in it.

"Deklan." It was his mother.

Thank God it wasn't his father. He wasn't ready for him. He snatched a nightshirt from the bed and quickly slipped it over his head. It dropped into place just as he unlocked and opened the door. "Hello mother."

She looked at Deklan, deep in his eyes. "Are you doing Okay?"

"As good as can, I guess." He closed the door and followed her to the chairs in front of the fireplace.

She sat down and Deklan did the same.

"I can see you're not doing so well." She knew him. She was his mom. "Why don't you tell me what's on your mind, Deklan?"

"I don't want to talk about it." He felt strange talking to his mother about what he was thinking. Love and sex with another man was not a topic he wanted to share with his mother.

"Deklan, whatever you have to say is not going to surprise me or make a difference as to how I feel about you." Both eyebrows lifted and got lost behind her strawberry blonde hair. "You met someone, didn't you?" She waited patiently for his answer, leaning forward.

"I would just like to be alone right now. You can understand that, can't you mother?"

"No you don't," she replied. "It's about a lad, isn't it?"

He looked down and then up again, giving a heavy eyed glance toward his mother. "Unh – It is – and I think I love him. No – actually I do love him."

His heart started beating hard while he waited for her to react. Deklan knew it wouldn't be the same way his father would respond, yelling, turning three shades of red and throwing things, but he prepared himself with an invisible shield in case it got ugly. He winced, pinched one eye tighter than the other and looked sideways at his mother.

She was calm and actually put on a smile. It was small and crooked, but the smile was there. Above her smile were the familiar green eyes that narrowed and showed a hint of concern and sympathy.

Deklan took her expression as a good sign and because she was so sweet about everything all the time, he gave in and leaked his secret.

He drew in a deep breath and then blew it out. "His name is Logan. The lad that showed up to my birthday party unexpectedly dressed in ivory and gold. I know in my heart he is who I am to spend my life with."

She studied him and he could tell she knew all along it was about the boy and not the girl. "I noticed you haven't been yourself since your birthday and I was certain it wasn't only because of the wedding that I would like to cancel."

"Then why don't we? It isn't right that I marry some girl I don't even know." Deklan included. "Mom, if I tell you something else, will you promise not to get upset at anybody else but me?"

His mother looked him over, more concerned about what he just said than anything else.

Deklan dragged in a ragged breath and then mumbled, "Logan is his name and he works here at the Manor. He is staying in the small feed barn out back by the kitchen and we have spent time together every chance we can get. Promise me, mom, please leave him alone."

Her face went blank. She normally knew everything, but this caught her off guard. "You mean Ms. Jennings' son? Little Junior? Why my stars - he is just a child."

Deklan corrected her. "Not anymore mom. He's my age. Twenty four."

His mother clasped the pearls around her neck and rattled them. "I never figured him to be" —she stopped, and then redirected what she almost said —"to be older than twelve or thirteen. My goodness how quickly time goes by."

He was glad she didn't faint to the floor or call the guards to have him escorted off the property.

Returning her hands to her lap, she wondered. "He looked so nice the other night. Very handsome and polished. Where did someone like him get clothing of such expense?"

"I know it seems strange the way he showed up to the party in such a costume, which I still have not asked about that yet, but if you are thinking it, he did not rob or steal them from anybody. He's not like that."

She froze. "I didn't mean to insinuate that, Deklan. Your father doesn't pay his employees well and to see a farmhand show up in dress-wear like he did, just made me wonder is all. I am sorry if I offended your judgment and your new friend."

Sulking, Deklan sank deeper into his chair. "I have such a good time when we are together and he makes me extremely happy when I am with him. He has only been away from me for a short time, this morning only to be exact, so when he isn't around I miss him like crazy and I hate this. It just doesn't seem fair."

His mother tilted her head and worry lines graced her forehead. Her eyelids lowered, shadowing her bright green eyes.

Deklan pressed the heels of his hands into his eyes as if they were going to stop him from weeping. He choked on his words as sadness swooped in and pecked at him. "When we're apart, I think about him every minute of the day, wondering what he's doing. Even right now I want to know. I wish he was here with me. Is this what heartbroken is?"

A tear found a way to squeeze beneath his hand and roll down his left cheek. He sniffed and held his sleeve beneath his nose. Fighting back the tears that were trying to rise from within him, he shook his head and realized he said more than he intended to. A part of him was disturbed that he spoke so freely, yet another part of him was glad to have his mother with him to share and help with his breaking heart. He swallowed his emotions that blocked his throat and he forced a smile to hopefully make everything alright.

To make Deklan feel better like she did when he was younger, his mother handed him a napkin from the table in front of her so he could blow and wipe his nose. "Life is strange, Deklan. It throws us curves that we are supposed to live through so we can discover the good things that will happen because of them. So perhaps your Father's marriage idea to this young girl helped facilitate your search to find your soul mate. Think about the event and how it led you to him. To your friend, Logan."

For a few seconds Deklan stared at his mother, totally shocked. "Do you think so? And, he is more than just a friend, mom."

"If this boy is your soul mate, *the one*, then you will eventually find your way back to each other."

She opened up to Deklan with an important story that led her to his father. Her soul mate. "I am going to tell you about your uncle Joseph."

"I had an uncle Joseph?" He never knew.

She scooted forward and balanced on the edge of her chair. "Joseph was your father's oldest brother. A handsome man, like you *and* like your father. They looked a lot alike. He was tall, but a bit shorter than your dad. Strong, inside and out. He worked hard you know." She added that last bit for some reason, her eyes looked dreamy.

Where was she going with this?

"Joseph and I were friends long before I really knew your father. We would still be friends today if Joseph was still around." She lowered her head, crossed herself and then dropped her delicate hands back into her lacey lap, crossing them on top of one another.

This did not seem to be going in a very positive direction by the look and tone of things.

She forced another smile. "That's how I met your father. Through Joseph, my friend."

"I never knew," Deklan's voice cracked.

"Well, this isn't something you normally share with your child. But you're an adult now, so it's okay that I tell you."

Did he really want to know?

"Your father and I met once during the latter days that Joseph and I were together – as friends. We were never coupled romantically and in a few minutes I will tell you why. In those days and at my age, I thought the relationship we had together was real love, but as I found out when I met your father that one fine day, how affection really felt. From that day, I've always known that there was a connection missing between your uncle Joseph and me and that I was tied more to your father somehow. At the time I wasn't sure what my feelings meant, but later on I did. It was a soul mate incident. I tried my best to keep my distance from your father because I thought that your uncle Joseph was supposed to be the love of my life. I tried many times to make your uncle show his affection toward me, but I quickly realized it was never going to happen. I could feel it."

"Ewe, Mom." Deklan winced.

"You see, your uncle Joseph was just like you, infatuated with another lad instead of me, and the funny thing was, the boy was a farmhand as well. Ironic don't you think?"

Deklan wanted to stop her. Afraid of what was next. He wasn't sure he was up to hearing any more of her story.

"I started spending more and more time with your father because it seemed more natural for me to be with him instead of Joseph. I eventually noticed Joseph becoming more and more distant and I first thought that it was because of your father, but as I suspected early on, it was because of the stable boy."

'Incredible.' Deklan thought.

"Your father and I were together on their ranch one afternoon and innocently stumbled upon Joseph when we were bringing lemonade drinks into the barn for him and the workers. When we arrived, we found your uncle Joseph and his gentleman friend locked in an embrace more intimate than we expected. I'm not too sure which one of us was more shocked, him or us. I remember we all stood there for a few minutes before Joseph took off running out the back of the barn. I will admit that I was hurt by what he did during the time that we were still together, but at the same time a little relieved that I was no longer trying to confirm what I had suspected all along. A woman knows these things." She looked at Deklan to see how he was reacting to all that was being said, making sure he wasn't in shock like his uncle was a few years back.

"The one thing through all this I know for sure and have always remembered was that your father was the one who picked me up and healed my injured heart. He always means well, you know. What I am trying to tell you Deklan, is that if two people are meant to be together, life will find a way. For example, your father and me. Even though it didn't seem right at the time, I was led to your father, my soul mate, in a way that was meant to be."

Deklan stopped her. "You said if Joseph *was* still around. What did you mean when you said that?"

Her eyes glistened as she remembered the past. "Your uncle denied who he really was for a very long time and in the end it hurt him deep inside. He couldn't live with himself the way he was so one afternoon in the middle of a thunderstorm he ended his own life in the attic of the barn. Your father found him. It was a bad day. Your uncle struggled too much with a lonely heart along with shame because he was always told there was something wrong with him. Back then two men in love was unheard of. People didn't understand it and understood it as a disease or some kind of mental illness. Some still do. Many men were imprisoned and even killed for being like Joseph."

Deklan was stunned. He couldn't believe what he was hearing from his mother.

She continued. "The reason your father didn't want you to know about all this is because he was afraid you might follow in your uncle's footsteps."

"What?" Deklan barked. "I guess it didn't work did it? I still turned out just the way he didn't want me to."

"No Deklan, not because you found affection for a lad, but because he was afraid you would hurt yourself like your uncle Joseph did or that somebody else would. All he's doing is trying to keep you from being hurt. He wants you safe."

"Well, he's hurting me in a completely different way," Deklan scowled.

"I am worried as well, but I will not stand in your way because I know what it's like to be separated from the one you love. I will protect you if I notice you're in any danger. It's just the way it is. I'm your mother."

Priscilla crossed over and sat on the arm of Deklan's chair. Suddenly he felt like a child again as she rubbed his back like a supportive mother does to make all her child's troubles disappear. "The two of you are bonded by a deep hearted connection and you will be together again. I promise."

A part of Deklan felt a little woozy when he heard his mother say he had a special bond with Logan. "I hope so," he said.

"There's plenty of room for hope." She stood up, rubbed his shoulders one last time and then walked to the door.

Chapter 33

Logan noticed it was getting late and his anxiety about Deklan's wedding was causing his heart to race. In fact he could feel it beating hard, plus the boom in his head was getting louder.

Knowing his soul mate was drifting further away, he was having a difficult time sitting still while watching the timepiece on the kitchen table tick. Logan was certain the hands were moving faster than normal, but the truth was it was ticking as it usually did and taking its sweet old time. Logan turned it over so he didn't have to look at the big hand jump to the next hash mark and the smaller hand creep close behind it.

Logan needed time to stop. Just for a while until he could figure out a solution to Deklan's and his situation.

While standing in the doorway looking down the drive at the activity starting to take place at the Manor, Logan could tell he was heading for a break down after seeing the first guest carriage pull up to the house. Following that one came another. Soon there were more lined up as though they all came in from town together. Like a train that had no caboose.

Logan never did see the bride-to-be arrive. He wasn't too

sure if she was already there and he missed her appearance or if she was ordered to show up at the moment the wedding bells chimed.

From what he knew about wedding guidelines, the bride dressed in her ceremonial gown was not to be seen by the groom until the chapel doors opened. He understood that it was bad luck for the groom to lay eyes on the virgin in white before it was time.

That gave Logan an idea, but it border lined on being evil.

Logan had no choice but to let the wedding go down as planned. But in his empty mind he was begging for the mirror man fairy person to show up and zap them all to their senses with a deluge of pixie dust. The ceremony needed to be stopped and fast. Logan was losing his man.

If there was a time when Logan needed a little fairy magic, it was then. He looked around his small room just in case the mirror man heard his silent plea. No such luck, the place was empty. Even the animals were outside enjoying life.

If it was up to Logan, He'd have the Manor set under fire so that it would smoke out the roaches and snakes that lived there. He figured the perfect time would be while everybody was still on their feet and in a position to run.

Out of curiosity he flipped the timepiece over to see how much time had passed.

"Holy bollocks." He just lost an hour. "Where did the time go?"

Logan heard footsteps creeping up from behind and it scared him. He turned and then screamed. "Holy bollocks," the words just fell from his mouth again.

Deklan was in his house. He gripped Logan's wrists and crashed their lips together in a tight bond.

"Wait – What? How did you get in here or – er what are you doing here?" Logan's words mashed together by the pressure of Deklan's mouth over his.

Deklan pulled back, his hands still gripping Logan's wrists. "I came in through the back window. You left it open."

"I did?" Logan knew he did. He usually left it open during the day to keep the place aired out. Helps keep it cool for the animals as well.

Deklan begged, "I've gotta have you, Logan. I need you right now. Make love to me. Please?"

Logan was not too stable at the moment and was teetering on the edge of gloom because the man he wanted to be with for the rest of his life was about to get married to somebody other than himself. Plus the strange and unnatural thing about it was that the somebody was a girl. "I don't know if your favorite parts will work the way you need them to. I'm a little blue at the moment, believe it or not."

"I am too, but we've gotta try. If I can't have you physically with me up on that platform tonight, then I need a piece of you alive inside me." Deklan opened his shirt so Logan could see his stunning chest, kissed him again while grabbing hold of Logan's soon to be stiffened erection. "Come on Logan, surge inside me. I need you so bad right now that it hurts."

That didn't take long. Logan was up and at it in no time.

Deklan walked Logan backward until his heels bumped against the first step leading up stairs to the bed where they've done it a few times before.

"Come. Let's have it on." After another quick peck to Logan's lips, Deklan took off up the stairway like a bolt of lightning. He was next to Logan one second and then gone the next.

Logan followed, unbuttoning his trousers as he climbed.

When Logan got there, Deklan was already undressed and looking exceptionally beautiful while on display across the bed with nothing on. Deklan laid himself out on his back and faced Logan with his legs wide open so Logan could easily find his way in and blurt his genetic energy where Deklan could carry it without anybody knowing. Logan's erection expanded just looking at him this way. His arresting hairy chest and stomach got Logan again. It never failed. The extension between his legs had him too. Logan couldn't resist that monster even on a really bad day. He was drawn to Deklan like a bug to a light.

Logan finished stripping and lay down beside him. He kissed Deklan passionately and rubbed his hands across his hairy chest. Logan's hand bumped the tip of Deklan's thickened erection as he moved it down his hairy stomach.

"Now," Deklan begged. "Do it now. I need this." Deklan made sure everything was slick with oil so Logan could ease in with no trouble at all.

Logan was just as enthused as Deklan was, but he battled strange feelings as if he was about to commit some type of crime. After all, he was headed for holy matrimony with someone else in a couple of hours, so Logan's arguments with his own feelings were well called for.

Looking down on Deklan, Logan positioned himself between his legs and gave his hips a little push. When he did, Deklan's body opened up and Logan took to hiding from the light outside. Logan hardened even more, pulled out and then pushed back in a little deeper than before. He gave Deklan a few more inches, letting him sense that he was going in. Deklan's face told Logan he was feeling it as his expanding organ dug deep. Deklan moaned and so did Logan.

"Shove it in, Logan. I need this," Deklan whined. "No need to be gentle." He looked Logan in the eyes more lustfully than he's ever looked him in the eyes before.

When Logan gave Deklan a few inches more, he noticed him breathing heavily as if trying to catch air.

Both of them knew it wasn't easy for someone like Logan to be gentle and his abnormal size would not allow him to just plow into his boyfriend without gut-wrenching results.

To make it easier for Logan's wide erection to bore into Deklan with less effort, he grabbed his ankles and spread his legs farther apart. Logan could see himself going in, yet there was still a long way to go. He hesitated, backed out and then gently sank in even further, letting Deklan get used to how several more of his thick chocolate inches felt.

"That's it. Go all the way," Deklan ordered.

As Logan did what he was told, Deklan threw his head back and started moaning to what almost sounded like weeping.

Logan pushed hard and went very deep, burrowing fast like Deklan wanted. The hair above his throbbing organ scrubbed against Deklan and it sounded like a crackling campfire. He groaned, loudly, but from complete pleasure as he tunneled deep inside Deklan, pressing hard against his secret niche that helped stir the great eruption. Logan moved inside him nice and slow, massaging that magic spot that made him squeal and squirm for more. Deklan's hips impatiently gyrated to help Logan along and he could actually feel Deklan pulling him in even deeper.

"I love you, Logan. I love you so much." Deklan moved his hands to the sides of Logan's face, looking him so deeply in the eyes that Logan though he could see right through him.

"Dek, I love you too." Logan dropped his chest against Deklan's, kissed him hard while he power ground his cocoa hips in and out of Deklan's white bottom.

They rhythmically rocked against each other for quite a while, going from hard thumps to slow sensual strokes. They both wanted their love making to last as long as possible, but at the same time were having a challenging time holding back their restless gifts to the other.

Suddenly it happened. Logan buried his face in the pocket of Deklan's neck and let go of a muffled roar. His passion was at its peak and he could no longer hold back his anxious release. Logan needed to let it loose and wanted it to find a place inside Deklan straightaway. He shuddered from the intense vibration that raced through his body, growled like a tiger and blasted everything he had into the man he loved. Logan's heart was pounding while his erection went on spitting hard and feverishly.

As Logan expelled, he could feel Deklan's warm clutch pulling him in as if his body was craving his essence. Deklan trembled and with a shaky voice, ordered Logan to keep moving in and out of him in the perfect way that he was.

Before Logan finished satisfying Deklan with his liquid pleasure, he saw Deklan's erection perk up and stiffen. His groaning went louder and his hair covered abdomen crunched inward and went firm. His body convulsed, which told Logan he was about to let what he had inside him go.

While Logan was still emptying his own love inside Deklan, he curled forward and took every bit of Deklan's expansive organ into his mouth. He went down the entire length until he felt him deep in his throat and the hair above his thick shaft tickle his nose.

Exhilaration swept over Logan as he took in the aroma that escaped his hairy groin. Logan held out a couple of seconds before retracing the same path he took going down and then gently toyed with his rock hard erection that was about to explode into his mouth. He couldn't wait. *Just* couldn't wait to taste Deklan.

The warmth of Logan's mouth that covered Deklan made his body shake. His hips rose to meet the back of Logan's throat again, making him quiver. "I'm close, Logan. Take me deep. Take it all." His body tensed and he jerked forward. "Swallow me, Logan. I need you to swallow me."

Not a second passed by and Logan accepted him whole.

A flare of heat shot through Deklan as he pumped his first spicy stream against the back side of Logan's throat. With each fruitful injection, Deklan's erect organ expanded and contracted across Logan's tongue, forcing his jaw to open wider than it already was. Logan backed off him for a split second so he could get a full breath of oxygen as well as squeeze out a much needed, "Omigawd!"

Logan quickly returned to where he left off as if the connection was never broken. The taste of Deklan's slick sweetness was pleasant as it gushed in thick spurts down his greedy throat. He swallowed everything Deklan parted with, refusing to let him go.

At the same time Logan's own charging essence went on saturating Deklan's insides, Logan took on and licked Deklan's enlarged member until it was clean.

Logan fell against Deklan, heaving, kissing him, and letting him taste the goodness of his own pleasing nectar that had coated his lips and tongue. As they kissed, their fingers entwined around each other's and Logan rotated them up and over Deklan's head. They stayed connected from top to bottom, quaking until the last drop of love was squeezed from Logan's erection and into Deklan.

"Don't leave me." Deklan tightened his grip, holding Logan in place.

Logan couldn't move. He just laid on top of Deklan, listening to the words being whispered in his ear.

Deklan's legs were locked around Logan's waist as a precautionary vice to keep him where he wanted him to be.

Sad but satisfied, Logan lifted himself above Deklan with most of his weight firmly balanced on the heels of my hands. He didn't move much while he remained deeply embedded up inside Deklan where he begged him to stay.

Logan looked down on Deklan who intently looked up at Logan.

The look of fear painted Deklan's face, which made Logan weaken fast.

Logan's shoulders shook and he started crying, not caring if Deklan saw him or not. He wasn't tough or strong when it came to this.

Deklan's face went even more dismal while struggling to pull air into his quivering lungs. His heart was so sore that his chest ached and his eyes welled up with vapor. When he blinked, there was a lonely tear that rolled down his temple and rested in the network of his lovesick ear.

Deklan gathered Logan in his arms and hugged him. "We will figure this out. I promise."

They lay fused for the longest time, feeling united as if they were one person that really shared a soul. As if Deklan's insides were starving for more, Logan could still feel Deklan's body stroking his relaxing erection.

Logan sniffled as he lay on top of Deklan. Loving his touch and missing it too.

Chapter 34

Pacing the floor just minutes before his arranged nuptial to a girl he didn't know, Deklan pulled the ring from Logan's shirt pocket that was still hanging over his and then tucked it in the breast pocket of the formal jacket he was wearing.

His eyes were puffy from overwhelmed sadness because he couldn't think of anybody else he would rather have at his side on the wedding platform other than Logan.

Deklan lifted his hand and it landed against his chest where he could sense the ring bonding with his heart and the pressure inside caused his heart to break all over again.

Aside from his watery eyes, Deklan was spot on dashing while dressed in crisp black and white.

~~~~ * ~~~~

Logan heard the bells chime in the distance like it was Christmas morning, and that told him it was time to make a dash for the door. He looked outside to see if the coast was clear and the time was right for him to head for the make believe wedding chapel. He grabbed the time piece from the table where he left it earlier and stuffed it in his shirt pocket. He didn't know why he needed it, but he felt he did. Call it a type of security. Like a blanket would be to a child.

He was getting anxious and his hands started to shake. He swallowed, still tasting Deklan's sweet essence on his tongue and in my throat. He cleared it with another swallow and then moved on.

Logan climbed the stairs to get the pendant from his bedside table and strung it around his neck. To keep it hidden, he dropped it behind his collar and let it rest against his bare chest. He flinched a little when it touched his skin. The chill of the cold metal startled him, but in time he quickly got used the cold.

He buttoned up his collar and put on an old brown and gray tweed jacket that used to belong to his father. It smelled a little dusty from hanging around unused for so long, but it was all he had and it would have to do. Logan didn't look too bad considering his best dressed consisted of an old coat, work trousers and a loose fitting linen shirt, that incidentally Deklan liked on him. He was dressed and ready to go see his lover get married to somebody else.

Oh how that hurt.

"Betty Lu, get back in the house," Logan yelled at the chicken as he was trying to get out the door. She had the big idea that she was going to the wedding too.

Silly bird.

The funny thing was, Betty Lu looked at him, turned around and walked back into the house as if she knew exactly what he was saying.

Maybe she was a brilliant bird, not a silly one.

Logan patted his tightly trimmed hair, pressed the shirt that was loosely hanging down his front side and pushed most of the fabric around to his back and tucked it in the waistband of his pants. He held his head up, tugged the lapels on his jacket and walked to the front of the Manor where he was going to quietly enter as a guest. If he ran into a problem at the door, his plan was to clear himself as the kitchen help and an acquaintance of the groom.

The homobirduals, Razzle and Dazzle as they were named,

scampered in front of Logan as if reminding him that it was okay for two chaps to be companions. It was comical to see the two roosters hanging out together and it made Logan laugh. He needed that.

Logan made it to the top of the stairs outside and then froze. *What was he doing? This is crazy.*

He stood outside for a couple of minutes trying to make up his mind as to if he should go inside or run back home. His head said run home, but his body was antsy to bust through the door and find a seat in the back of the home fabricated chapel.

Lucky for Logan there was nobody at the door when he opened it up. Logan stepped foot inside and immediately closed the doors behind him. He looked around the pretty room. Gleaming gray and white went on for days, scattered all over the place and dripped from every corner. Glitter and sparkle flashed around the room and bounced off every wall.

There was no way he was going to make it down the front stairs unseen, so he remembered the back stairway Deklan took him down that secretly led to the kitchen. The idea came to Logan that it was a better way to reach the main floor without anybody stopping him to ask questions or make him present an invitation that he never actually received.

Logan thought back to the kitchen raid and mapped the halls out in his head that Deklan took him down. It was easy to reimagine and thank God the second level so far was vacant. He crept along the wall to the left, and then made a right and tightly slithered along that wall too. Logan passed Deklan's room, fighting his urge to stop, kick the door in and take claim to his man. Soon he took another left until he reached the stairway behind the bogus bookshelf at the end of the hall.

Logan's escalated anxieties settled a little once he was safely behind closed doors. It was super dark in the tunnel as he remembered it to be, so the only way of finding the bottom was to feel each step cautiously with a tap of the toe while running his fingers along the walls. It felt like a long way down in the dark, but finally, low and behold he saw the light. The door crack down in front saved him from losing his mind and his way.

He stopped, looked back where Deklan and he once kissed

and then pressed his ear to the storage room door. Logan held it there for a minute or two, waiting to hear if there were any sounds coming from the other side. As a precautionary measure, he pressed an eyeball to the peep hole and looked through it.

Nobody was on the other side from what he could tell, but he still opened the door slowly in case he misjudged his feeling. Bravely he crept in like an unwanted burglar, taking the darkness in stride. Without Deklan holding his hand like he did the last time made the secret adventure within dark walls a little scarier.

Door number two was just ahead. Brighter light was spilling across the floor through the crack at the bottom and the small window in the center helped Logan see what was happening on the other side.

Strangely enough, Logan didn't see anybody through the little window.

His thoughts on that were perhaps everybody was outside setting up the dinner tables for the scheduled white wedding party.

He pushed the door open slowly.

"Bollocks!"

Logan heard somebody coming. He let the door close, ran to the back and hid behind a box of junk sitting in the corner. He hung out there for a little while until he felt comfortable that the coast was clear.

Logan went for the door again, gave it a slight push.

"Bollocks!" Not again.

Someone else came into the kitchen. This time Logan took off behind the bookshelf he came through. He felt safer there.

Logan peeked through the small hole in the door until he was at ease with coming out again.

He stood in the closet with a widened eye tucked in the lower corner of the small window like a stalker with a deviant mission, watching Wattsworth look around the room while counting on his fingers.

What was he doing?

The lanterns in the kitchen dimmed and Logan saw Wattsworth leave.

Logan gave the door another push, but saw light flickering outside the kitchens main entryway.

"Bollocks!"

What now? Who is it this time?

If Logan didn't get out of the closet soon, he was going to miss the sketchy nuptials. He let the door go and it bumped his toe with a thud. He winced. Not because it hurt, but because he was afraid somebody was going to hear the bang.

The light he saw from the incoming lantern wavered on the far wall and he spotted Wattsworth return to the kitchen. Logan stayed where he was, eyeball pressed to the windows corner and waited for him to leave.

Finally, Wattsworth was gone.

Solitude.

Logan grabbed a broomstick and a dust collector from the same closet he had been hanging out in for the last ten minutes, tiptoed quietly through the kitchen and then out into the hallway. His phony prop he carried helped make believe he was part of the cleaning crew and hoped it would fool everybody else that saw him too.

The layout of the hallway was the same as it was up stairs, which thankfully helped Logan keep his bearings while wandering around the big house he wasn't too familiar with. He noticed several doors running the inside wall and presumed they opened up to the grand room where the wedding was about to take place. At least he thought so because he heard voices on the other side.

Logan cracked the first door he came to and peeked in. He saw somebody lighting candles and also spotted the first few rows of chairs facing forward. That told him he was near the front and he needed to keep going.

Before he opened the door in the back of the room, he stuffed the broom and dust collector behind a drape in the hallway. Carrying it with him into the chapel would not be good if he was planning to blend in as a guest with everybody else.

Logan's nerves were a little rattled and the pang in his chest escalated as time ticked on.

After taking a deep breath, in he went. Noisy whispers were echoing everywhere. Everybody was trying to remain well-mannered while patiently waiting for the duo cord orchestra to start playing, which would be the cue that the wedding was about to begin.

As it was, everyone crowded the front rows, leaving the back mostly vacant. Logan chose a seat all to himself toward the back, yet close enough to others that he was still somewhat hidden.

He felt relaxed at that moment because he finally found his safe-spot after sneaking around inside walls like a dirty rat. His leg went crazy while he sat, bouncing up and down as if it wanted to get up and run away.

He clutched the pendant beneath his shirt and sat still like everybody else did and waited patiently.

The hum of the cellos started to play and the crowded room politely went silent. Other than the noise of rustling fabric as everybody shuffled to face the back doors, the place was eerily quiet.

Then Logan saw what he came to see. The vision he was eager to lay his eyes upon, but dreading all the same.

Deklan stood in the back doorway to Logan's right, the side he always occupied when they were together. He looked more gorgeous than ever in his white shirt, black and gray diagonally striped tie and a neatly pressed black against black pinstriped suit with a deep vee lapel. He was so crisp and clean that he appeared statuesque.

Logan held his breath, or more so, couldn't breathe. Deklan was so gorgeous to him. Inside and out.

Over to Logan's left, occupying the spot where he should be, stood the damsel in white. Her face was covered, as it should be, with a heavy lace veil so nobody could see her face. From what Logan understood, it was the traditional ritual not to unveil the virgin until she reached the pit of fire.

The two of them were separated by about twenty seats along the back and Logan wished it would stay that way forever and then some. She was honing in on his man and the way it looked, the permanent separation wasn't going to happen.

Logan went on holding his breath, choked back sadness and hid his tears behind a sniffle and a cough. He was the only one in the room who sat down before anything got started. It may have been a sign of disrespect, but he couldn't stand a minute longer and watch the insanity play out. Logan's legs gave in to weakness and his quivering chin made it impossible to keep his sadness locked up to himself. He was breaking apart and was near sure it was becoming visible to those around him.

Everybody in the place had their eyes on the bride except for one person a couple rows ahead of Logan who noticed he took a seat before he should have.

This person's concern meant well as he chose to make it his mission to stop Logan from crashing into a lonely pit of doom. It must have been Logan's facial expression that told the young chap his story.

It was Deklan's friend Jeddah who spotted Logan sitting alone a few rows back. He left his seat and went over to sit down beside him. "You're Logan, aren't you?" He said.

"How – how did you know? And you are?" Logan stammered.

Jeddah leaned into Logan, keeping his voice low and breathy. "I'm Jeddah. Deklan's friend. He told me about you. And from the look on your face and the way you have been observing him, I knew you were 'The' boyfriend."

Was he that obvious?

Logan cracked a slight smile at the way he said 'the boyfriend', but still kept his head lowered and only looked at Jeddah sideways beneath a heavy brow.

Logan was observing him so intently that his subconscious mind flashed an image of the mirror man as if he was sitting in place of Jeddah. At least Logan thought it was an illusion of his imagination. He blinked a few times to clear his head.

Was it a message in disguise telling Logan to go get his man back? He doubted himself and chose to sit tight and behave himself.

Instead of a hallucination, it was a voice this time. Another message came to him, ringing in his head, 'you must go get him'.

The mirror man spoke to Logan. He swore it was him. It was his voice. The Mirror Man.

As he turned his head toward Deklan and watched him, Logan rocked his bum in an awkward fashion that made Jeddah thing he was suffering from a nervous disorder.

"It'll be alright." Jeddah bumped his shoulder with Logan's.

Logan was glad to hear those words from Jeddah. A part of him needed assurance from somebody else. It somehow solidified the truth. Logan felt a little better but his heart was still aching as if there was a dagger being forced into it through his backside. It hurt like hell as it sank all the way through him, from back to front.

And then it went down and Logan's heart exploded and sank.

The progression of the nuptials started moving on both sides of the room. Deklan walked one side while the damsel in white toe tipped some strange skip and hop on the other.

'That should be me.' Logan Thought.

Logan watched his beloved closely. He couldn't take his eyes off of Deklan. He looked so elegant in his pressed suit and all Logan wanted to do at that very moment was scream with anger. Even cry. He was breaking.

Deklan unhappily walked toward the front of the room, and while he did, he brought his hand to his chest and laid it against the ring that was securely hidden in his inside breast pocket.

Logan gripped the pendant around his neck and felt it vibrate and lightly glow. At that moment, he returned his gaze back on Deklan and saw him glancing around the room.

Deklan knew Logan was someplace near because the ring inside his pocket was vibrating too.

Instantly, Logan saw his handsome prince fighting that crooked smile he knew and loved. Deklan's hand went tight and gripped the coat over top of where Logan's ring was tucked away.

Logan did the same to the pendant, crumpling his shirt with a knotted fist.

But then little by little, over the next few minutes, the hum, the glow and the link between the two metal pieces started to fade. The farther away from Logan Deklan marched, the fainter the connection became.

Was he losing him? Was this a sign?

Logan quickly removed his hand from the pendant in case his own flesh and bones were blocking the signal that tied the two pieces together. Not the case. The connection was still dying.

This can't be happening.

Logan's chest tightened as the evening's event began to unfold.

As Deklan walked away from him, the light between the necklace and the ring faded even more, and it seemed the damsel in white was winning the battle between good and evil.

Logan's chest went tighter as his thoughts returned to the man getting married. His man.

A few minutes later, a thought occurred to Logan. Somewhere in the middle of the vows there was that awkward pause where the minister asked if anybody objected to the two people getting married. That was going to be his last and only chance to put a stop to this ongoing nonsense. Even though they would be cast in the shadows by many of the people in the room for being in love, Logan decided to make that his time to speak out.

The only problem was how to pull off his approach without being stoned to death on the spot. How was he going to do it without embarrassing himself or Deklan? Plus he certainly didn't want to bring disgrace to Deklan's family by publicly pointing out that their only heir was in love with another man. That would be bad for everybody.

Time was ticking and that stubborn pause was soon to be mentioned where Logan was going to have to stand and speak his mind.

His hands were sweating and his bleeding heart was racing. "*Omigawd,*" Logan muttered for a different reason this time. His nerves were busted and his body felt like it was about to blow apart.

"It's okay," Jeddah said again. "It'll all work out."

Who was this guy?

In the back of Logan's mind he was near certain that Jeddah was another version of his fairy godfather. He looked much different to him from when he saw him last in the small coop of a home, but the words of confidence Logan heard were what would be spoken by the mirror man. He was sure of it.

Logan could see Deklan was completely distracted. He was on the platform with the bride-to-be and Parson Brown, but Logan could tell Deklan wasn't all there. He was quite sure Deklan's thoughts were on him.

The time came. 'Omigawd.' Logan was feeling sickly.

"Ladies and gentlemen." Parishioner Parson looked out among the crowd. "Does anybody have reason why these two should not be wed, if so, please stand or forever hold your thoughts."

Deklan turned his head, glanced around the room to see if anybody was going to stand. He stopped and stared at Logan.

Logan swallowed, taking the lump in his throat further down into my chest.

Deklan looked at his mother and then back at Logan, smiling at Jeddah as his gaze passed by him.

Logan started to stand, but before he made it too far, Deklan's hand gestured for him to stay seated. Jeddah at the same time tugged on Logan's coat tail, bringing him back to his chair.

Deklan's and Logan's thoughts must have collided somewhere along the way because it seemed that they both had the same idea as to how this wedding was going to be placed on hold. Logan was pleasantly rescued by the man he loved, which left him in the position where he didn't have to act on what he had planned. Deklan was going to stand up and cover him.

Deklan dragged his hands through his hair, stopped the wedding and attested to the marriage, insisting it should not continue. "I'm sorry. I'm sorry. I'm Sorry," He repeated several times. "We cannot go on with this wedding. It's just not a good idea to me."

Deklan's father rose from his chair in the front row, scowled at him and then looked back toward everybody seated, showing off a phony smile.

Logan was beaming and when he looked at Deklan's mother, she was smiling too.

Because it didn't matter anymore, Deklan lifted the lacey veil from in front of the brides face so that he could properly address her. She was a pretty little thing, but not the right type for Deklan as he and Logan both knew. He needed to explain to her and everybody else that he was in love with somebody else and it was not fair to her or him that the wedding go on as scheduled.

Deklan looked at the bride as if she was the only one in the whole place and that pleasant voice Logan has heard several times before softly spoke. "Gretchen," — he got her name correct — "you and I have known of each other for only a few days. I am not comfortable moving forward with this wedding and I can't imagine that you are content with it either."

She nodded as an unspoken gesture of agreeing with him completely.

He placed her hand in his. "It's important to me that I am truthful to myself and to you. I wish that I was strong enough to bring it up before now, but because I was afraid of hurting the people closest to me and not looking out for myself, I ended up letting it get this far. What I am trying to say is that I need to walk away from this wedding."

Gretchen's eyes went soft, almost appearing as if she was relieved. She whispered, "It's okay Mr. Deklan. I am glad you said something before the ring was on my finger."

Accepting her gratitude, Deklan smiled back at her. "You are a beautiful person from what little I know about you, but I have to be true to myself by following my heart and be with who I really love."

Gretchen's hand rested on Deklan's cheek before she turned to walk away.

Chapter 35

Deklan's Father stood with a glare in his eyes that could start a fire in a wet forest. His mind was booming, 'what have you done?' but his mouth stayed shut.

A good idea.

In the meantime, Gretchen's parents shuffled to the aisle and chased their child out the exit door.

On the other hand, Logan was happy to see her go. He didn't mean to be harsh, but it is what it is.

Logan sat quietly in his chair next to Jeddah, or the mirror man he thought, and waited for Deklan to make his next move.

Without further delay, Deklan turned toward all his parents' friends sitting in the chairs and said nothing. He just stared at everybody, almost looking through them. A low tortured sigh was his only message as he ascended from the platform and walked down the same aisle he came in on.

Logan stood up and Jeddah did too. They were the only two standing with the exception of Deklan's angry father who stood with fisted hands and what looked like flames shooting out of his ears. Everybody else sat stunned and gasped at what just took place.

When Deklan arrived at the row Logan and Jeddah were seated in, he stopped, waved a hand, wheedling for them to follow.

Excusing themselves as they squeezed by the people sitting in their way, Logan and Jeddah joined Deklan in the aisle and huddled next to him.

Logan felt like a spectacle at a show of freaks.

Still without speaking or giving up any sort of explanation to the people staring at them, Deklan grabbed Logan's hand and threw an arm over the back of Jeddah's shoulder.

They walked toward the door without looking back and Logan was sure the many faces watching them exhibited expressions of curiosity as to what was going on between the three of them.

Logan could have cared less.

Jeddah may have cared less.

And Deklan conveyed an 'I don't care what they think' look on his face.

Either way, they still walked fast.

Jeddah pushed Deklan and Logan out the door, "you two go on without me." He stood back and let the doors close in front of him while watching them skip down the steps two at a time.

The faster the better.

They left Jeddah behind closed doors and took off running hand in hand to the wedding carriage that was meant for Deklan and his brand new bride.

The funny thing was, Logan had dreamt the wedding carriage would be taking Deklan and him to paradise one day, but he hadn't imagined it to be like it was. It was thrilling in a nerve rattling sort of way, just like the night they hit the kitchen up for an evening snack. That required a quick getaway too and seemed to be the beginning of a regular event for them. Mad lovers on the run.

Deklan quickly pushed Logan in the seat first and then hopped in beside him. He kissed Logan fast and then snapped the reigns.

The horse stomped and took off running. Where to, who knew. Their only thought was to get away from the Manor as quickly as possible before somebody came up with the crazy idea of stopping them.

Dust lifted behind them as the carriage wheels spun over top of pebble and dirt. It was a bumpy ride for a few minutes until Deklan surprisingly tugged the reigns to the left and turned the horse toward the barn.

Logan looked at him with a genuine smile, knowing what he was thinking.

"Chadwick," was all Deklan said.

Logan was quick to respond to Deklan's thoughts and scooted closer to the carriage exit so he could quickly jump out and help Deklan round up his favorite Clydesdale.

Chadwick heard them coming and started prancing like a reindeer in the polar waiting for Santa Claus to arrive.

It was amazing how the horse was linked to Deklan. They were close to being best friends and could speak to one another by signals and grunts alone.

Before the carriage came to a stop, Logan pushed himself out and hit the ground with a choppy stumble. Like a choreographed dance, he graciously rose to his feet, ran to the barn door and lifted the crossbar from the cradle to relax the hinges so it would open.

Before they even entered, Chadwick was already up on his hind two, bobbing his excited nose and chopping empty space in front of him with his two front hoofs.

Logan grinned with astonishment that the big animal knew they were coming for him and that the two were in a desperate hurry. He was ready to bust the gate and get the hell out of there like Logan and Deklan were.

"Chad, Come." Logan heard Deklan holler. He rolled his hands over and over again against his chest.

Suddenly, as if it all happened in slow motion, Chadwick backed up, pawed the ground in front of him and then took a flying leap up and over the rail that was holding him captive. Beneath him Logan crouched out of his way, watched him fly above his head and land with grace only a few paces ahead of him.

Logan was stunned and it took him a minute to catch his breath.

While Deklan tossed the horse saddle into the back of the buggy, Chadwick trotted proudly, circled Deklan and nipped at locks of wavy hair on the top of Deklan's head.

How cute.

Deklan laughed as Chadwick tugged with affection in the only way he knew how.

"Let's go, Chad," Deklan said, patted him on the rubbery nose and then pointed toward the clover field the horse knew so well.

Chadwick bobbed his head and whinnied, cantered ahead of the carriage and then stopped to look back at Deklan as if thinking, 'are you two coming or what?'

They quickly climbed into the marriage carriage and Deklan snapped the reigns.

The lake. Their hideaway. They were headed for the lake.

As they passed by Chadwick, he squealed and then chased the carriage out of town.

The further away from the Manor they got, Deklan slowed the carriage. With his arm behind Logan's neck and draped over his shoulder, the ride became peaceful and the brisk bounce of the carriage relaxed him.

Logan leaned back against Deklan, reached up and held his hand while he gripped the reigns in the other.

Glancing to the right, Logan saw Chadwick walking beside the carriage as if he was tethered to it. The horse was keeping an eye on Deklan. He was so in love.

They arrived at their hideaway and stared out across the lake for a few minutes before getting out. It seemed peaceful.

They needed a moment. A quiet moment.

Their lake, as they called it, was tranquil at night and the stars above reflected off the surface like tiny sparks just begging for attention. It was magical and it was pretty.

Deklan jumped from his seat first and like a gentleman held

out a hand to help Logan down.

He's so sweet.

As if Chadwick had a plan, he head bumped Deklan from behind, getting his attention while he helped Logan out. Not expecting Chadwick to be playing matchmaker, Deklan tripped and fell against Logan.

Not a bad thing. Logan liked it.

Chadwick casually walked away and started drinking water from the lake as though what he just did never happened. It was always interesting how a horse could change its thoughts within seconds. One second the animal was frightened and the next it was content and eating straw.

Deklan pinned Logan against the carriage and peck kissed him twice. After the sweet kisses, he pulled back, whispered he loved Logan and then feverishly kissed him long and hard, chewing his cocoa mug with a rotating jaw. Deklan's cool breath filled Logan's lungs before he backed away, gently biting his bottom lip.

Whoa! Within a second Logan went hard.

Logan wasn't letting Deklan go so quickly. He tugged Deklan by the waist with both hands until he was back where he wanted him, pressed tightly chest to chest with their lips only a sand grain away from each other's. This time Logan pecked, whispered he loved him and then feverishly kissed him back.

Perfect. It worked. Deklan was rock hard.

Logan felt Deklan grin against his lips and he sensed his intrusion as their bodies wrangled from head to toe.

Chapter 36

They were alone together under a sky full of stars, well almost alone, other than Chadwick and the horse that brought them to the lake in the carriage, and they found a place on the ground under a tree to make fevered love.

The resources they had that would ease the link between the two of them were slim to nothing. Spit always worked in a bind even though a lot was needed to get Deklan inside and hitting the magic spot that always sent fireworks throughout Logan's body. Anything would have been considered just to feel Deklan moving inside him. Logan really needed Deklan to connect with him in order to put the dismay of what recently occurred to rest and to confirm Deklan was really his.

Logan lay back in the cool grass with Deklan comfortably on top of him, just the way he liked it and felt natural to both of them. They kissed at the same time they loosened their clothes, exposing the important parts first that would allow the much desired bond. Logan opened his legs and Deklan positioned himself between them for penetration.

Logan kissed him hard, taking possession of his tongue while Deklan aimed for his active entrance down below.

Tightening his abdomen, Deklan pushed and entered him. From there Logan lost his breath. Not from pain, but from thorough pleasure. Deklan's large erection felt amazing to Logan as it burrowed deep, filling him completely, opening him up until he could feel Deklan in his chest.

Deklan looked down on Logan, held still at first and then moved his oversized erection in and out of him with slow lasting strokes. The fiery sensation caused Logan's toes to curl and he felt every bit of Deklan as he ground against him. They delicately kissed each other, meeting in the middle with amazing sparks.

Deklan's hand ran under Logan's shirt where it found his expansive chest. Lightly he caressed him sending chills from top to bottom. Deklan's touch was gentle and his kiss was divine.

Rolling his hips into Logan, Deklan forced himself further. "I love you so much, Logan," he said to him.

Logan took every bit of Deklan deeper and the punishing pleasure made him gasp. "I love you too, Deklan." He couldn't hold back. He reached for Deklan's jaw and pulled him down. Their kiss went profound again as their tongues made contact.

Deklan's caresses and talented rhythm seized Logan with extreme pleasure, pushing his being to that desirable place of frenzy. Logan's entire body went tight and he ejaculated before he wanted to. Shuddering with pleasure, he squeezed streams of essence between their torsos.

Deklan felt the flood of Logan's eruption spread across his chest and the excitement of the warm sensation made him gush inside Logan. Deklan rumbled the whole time and then fell rigid against him, kissing Logan while his bounding body pumped everything he had from his insides out.

They held each other the way they always did after making love until the last drop was released from each other's fitful glands.

Logan felt Deklan's warm breath in his ear as he buried his chin in his neck.

Deklan huffed, "Oh sweet surrender I love you, Logan. Your touch and your grasp feel so incredible."

Logan hugged Deklan tightly and kissed his lobe. With his

soft tone, Logan whispered, "I love you too, Deklan. Will you marry me?"

Deklan lifted his head from Logan's ear, held the sides of his head with his hands and looked down on him as if he was trying to grip his thoughts. A kiss to Logan's lips was surrendered and then Deklan smiled. "Yes, my beautiful prince, I will marry you."

Deklan removed the ring from his jacket pocket and slipped it on Logan's finger where it belonged. "With this ring and in front of God above, I wed Thee. I love you, Logan."

Logan took the ring on his finger and hugged the man he loved so much.

It was official and between them it was real.

Still connected deep inside Logan, Deklan kissed him without end.

~~~~ * ~~~~

The seat cushions in the carriage were not fastened permanently, which gave Logan and Deklan the idea to use them as padding over the ground to sleep on for the night. The clothes they had on were all that covered them, but enough being that they held each other throughout the night when they slept anyways.

Their trousers were left off so Deklan could stay inside Logan all night long if he wanted to. Deklan liked it that way and Logan most certainly did too. They lay snuggling on their sides, Deklan tightly pinned to Logan's backside.

There was no going back now. Not back to the way things were. Deklan's father would have to accept that his son was sharing a bed with and making love to the lad next door. If Dante wasn't willing to adjust his way of life for Deklan, then Logan and Deklan would find no harm in making a life of their own on the outside of the Manor's walls. Jeddah lived off the land so why couldn't they?

Logan was formally Deklan's family and was probably the only one he had outside of Jeddah and maybe his mother. Their genes were mixed by the love they made, which solidified their family bond.

From the first time Deklan and Logan exchanged and absorbed each other's living genes, Logan was near certain he would start looking like the love of his life soon, as well as being certain Deklan's skin pigment would take on a more caramel color.

"Stay." Logan backed tighter against Deklan, feeling him.

"I'm still here." Deklan rolled his hips and he went deeper.

Deklan hugged Logan tight from behind and Logan felt warm knowing the chap he loved so much was as close to him as he will ever be. Inside and out. Deeply breached and reaching his heart.

Chapter 37

The sun seemed to be taking its sweet time coming up, but from what Logan could see through weary eyes, it was about to break horizon. He started to come to, still feeling Deklan tucked tightly behind his backside with his arms pinned across his dark chest.

Logan felt soft hair from between Deklan's legs scrub against his bottom, but wasn't too sure if they were still connected. To find out if they were, he adjusted himself to rouse Deklan into moving.

It worked.

Deklan groaned, stretched his relaxed muscles with a quiver that forced his expansive erection further inside Logan. The internal pressure against Logan's magic spot caused him to ooze clear crystal from his own raging organ without any stimulation being applied.

Deklan was talented that way or they just flat out worked perfectly together. Logan's guess was that it had much to do with both. Deklan's effortless talent and the seamless connection of their two souls.

Logan tightened the grip he had on Deklan at the same time Deklan pushed into him. Because of the way Deklan moved, Logan grew harder.

Deklan held Logan from behind as he started to shudder. "Oh sweet Logan, are you ready for me again?"

Logan lifted one leg and pushed back against Deklan with an uncontrolled growl. He knew what was happening by the way Deklan expanded and contracted inside him. If there was a word that Logan could describe how he was feeling, it would have bellowed from his soul. All that came out of Logan was, "Ohmigawd."

While Deklan blew more of his essence inside Logan for the fifth or sixth time that night, Logan propelled numerous streams of his own ejaculate clear across the grassy lawn. It felt reckless to release themselves without first tenderly making love to each other before the big explosions were expelled from within them. It was exciting for them to just wake up and immediately go at it like they did. There was a thrill to it, even if it was a quick and fevered ejaculation.

Regretfully, it was time to face the events that took place the previous day and bring themselves back to reality. With that awful thought, Deklan snaked himself out of Logan and they both took to the lake to clean themselves up. The water was cool, but they quickly got used to it. Deklan washed Logan with eager hands and then Logan scrubbed Deklan. They had fun while it lasted and it made both of them think how nice it would be to live day to day as they did throughout the night and into the morning. Going to bed and waking up exhausted in each other's arms would be the perfect happily ever after.

They dressed and as far as Logan could tell, they were left undisturbed throughout the night. At least it appeared that way. It saddened him in a way that nobody even came looking for Deklan to be sure he was alright.

"Deklan?" Logan spoke while buttoning his shirt. "Are you going to be okay if we go back to the house?" He thought a part of Deklan was rubbing off on him already, because he caught himself fastening the buttons on his shirt from bottom to top. The same way Deklan does that he thought was so cute and quirky.

Deklan's genes are inside him and he could already feel himself changing.

"I'm good, Logan. We can go back together and if the doors are locked, we have this place we can call home." Deklan whistled for Chadwick while he put on his boots.

Logan walked over to Deklan and fixed his jacket. Even though a little crumpled, Deklan still looked good to him. Logan brushed his hands down the front of Deklan's chest, flattening the lapels. "You look handsome," Logan told him before lightly kissing his lips.

Deklan looked Logan in the eyes after taking his kiss. "Thanks, Logan. And you do too." He took Logan's head in both hands and returned the kiss, giving it to Logan more passionately than he remembers kissing him before and the deepness of the kiss wrangled their souls.

Logan stepped back and turned toward the carriage, cleared his throat and took a breath.

Chapter 38

Dante stood in the gateway of Chadwick's empty stall and waited for Deklan, and who he knew as the stable boy to return from wherever they ran off to for the night.

Where they went didn't matter to him, as long as they both came home safe and without harm. That was all he wanted.

Dante saw them take off in the wedding carriage along with Chadwick the night before and figured they would be okay. They had to be. Letting them go to think about what they did was the only thing he could do for wise reasons.

It was unlike Dante to pick up a broom, but he reached for a weed claw anyway and started raking Chadwick's stall with it, piling up the old straw in the middle of the barn so one of the ranch hands could haul it away. He was no longer one to go at hard labor, but his mind needed a distraction from the horrifying thoughts that were tumbling around in it. Raking horse droppings and dirty hay was exactly what he needed.

While standing in the barn, older memories from when he was younger came rushing back to him. Sharing responsibilities of household chores with his late brother Joseph popped into his head. He shuddered and raked faster.

Dante was a strong man and would never let anybody see his weak side. He had one, but nobody ever saw it. He made sure of it. He was always harder than steel and made sure everybody around him knew it. Most people understood that he had been born without a heart. Nobody really knew, but it sure seemed that way at times. The only one that knew he had one and who ever saw it blossom was his elegant and beautiful wife, Priscilla.

As Dante pulled the trampled straw from Chadwick's stall to the pile in the middle of the barn, he visualized the day he walked in on his brother hanging by a cord from the rafters of his childhood barn.

That wasn't a good day, for anybody.

The picture in his head was as clear to him as the day it happened, and just then, his nerves started to spark and he thought of Deklan in place of Joseph. "Oh God, this can't happen again. Not twice. Not in my family."

He let the claw go and it dropped to the floor with a triple bounce. He nervously traipsed to the open door of the barn to look out, hopeful that the bright light from the sun would chase away the frightening image embedded in his head. He worked like mad to channel his thoughts to a better place while he prayed that Deklan was alright. His only son. The son he loved. "Please come home, Deklan. Please come home." He pleaded in silence, squinting away the sun.

His heart sped up the more he tried to get Joseph out of his mind and what he saw to be his son, Deklan. The strong man who built the plantation with his bare hands was trembling and for the first time was falling to his knees, repelled with himself for what he put his pure hearted son through recently. Again he bowed his head and pleaded, "Please come home, Deklan. Please come home."

As if the sun reached out and lifted his chin, Dante spotted a wavering speck with rising dust coming from it over the hilltop. It grew larger and to Dante it looked like Chadwick alongside the horse carriage he remembered taking off into the dusk with his son and the stable boy in it. As it made its way closer, he knew it was Deklan. Invisible to anyone, he crossed himself and clenched his hands together in a silent prayer. Another pleading prayer.

He stepped out from the barns shadows and shielded the bright sun with his arm above his brow. It was getting hotter by the minute and he couldn't wait to see his son.

Dante hated himself for what he put Deklan through and begged he would not allow their differences to come between them. He didn't fully understand it because he was not in Deklan's boots, but he had to leave be what was meant to be. The vision he was presented with in the barn that day was the message he needed to see. Like it was coming from above, telling him to leave a perfected creation the way it was supposed to be. Dante did as he was told and knew it wasn't worth losing his only son over.

~~~~ * ~~~~

Deklan and Logan looked at each other as they rode the carriage down the rocky hillside with the brilliant Chadwick leading them home. The horse knew where he was going as if there were a trail of carrots laid out that helped take him back to the place he started.

Logan could tell Deklan was getting anxious by the way he gripped the reigns. His knuckles went white as he squeezed the leather strips together in both hands. Somehow his father instilled an angry streak in him each time the two came within a few feet from one another. This time however was probably the worst.

"I'm not ready for this, Logan," Deklan said while he twisted the reigns together in his hands, grinding them as if trying to start a fire with two dry sticks.

There was no sense telling Deklan that everything was going to be fine, because honestly Logan had no clue that it was going to be. To Logan, Deklan's father didn't look too outraged and if he was correct, the man appeared to be concerned. Logan glanced over at Deklan and kept his mouth shut this time, only patted his knee and gave it a loving squeeze. Deklan needed to be touched by somebody that truly loved him. Logan knew this. Logan knew him.

Even though Logan knew his touch was cherished by Deklan, he felt no link coming from him. At that moment,

Deklan's reaction was triggered by the unbroken contact he had with his father. The connection left him tunnel locked as though he was trying to figure out what Dante was thinking before he got to him.

Deklan and Logan finally reached the barn where Dante was standing and by the way the air hung heavy around them, Logan sensed a bitter moment was ahead.

With a more cheerful voice than expected, Deklan asked Chadwick to go to his room. And without an argument or a stomping hoof, the horse did what he was told. Deklan then tugged on the carriage reigns and the horse that was pulling it stopped walking.

The clanging of the bridle sounded pretty and Logan was hoping it would lighten the mood.

"Father," was all Deklan said, as a formal way of saying hello. He tipped his head forward like a nod.

Dante walked around to where Deklan was sitting and rested a hand on the carriage wheel. As he did, it rocked a little at the same time Deklan and Logan hopped out.

Logan was a nervous wreckage during the frigid connection being made and he was pretty sure Deklan was too. Logan wasn't in the mood to speak, but from what he saw, Dante had changed overnight.

It was an incredible change and it was good.

"Where's Mom?" Deklan asked, working his hardest at breaking the ice between him and his father. The frozen wall was showing signs of melting, but needed some help to get it started.

For some reason Dante was not speaking. If love served its purpose, Logan would say the man was so happy to see his son, that if he spoke, he would turn into a weeping willow.

Could it be? A heart was making its appearance.

Dante's arms dropped to his sides. He stepped toward Deklan and took him in his arms. He hugged him with what looked to be an unconditional embrace.

At that point, Logan wasn't too sure where the display of affection was headed. It had him second guessing the intentions of Deklan's father as well as wondering what the outcome of the family hug was going to bring. Logan stood there halfway to crying because he saw a moment between a father and a son that was not heard of or seen very often or if ever.

Men don't hug or show affection. What would the world think?

Dante let go of Deklan and he finally spoke, "You look fine. Are you doing okay?"

Deklan backed away and looked stunned. "Yes father, I'm good."

"Are you and your friend hungry?" Dante asked, gripping Deklan's shoulders at arm's length, giving him a buddy like shake.

Wait. What?

Did Logan hear that correctly? Deklan's father was concerned for him as well? He didn't do much other than just stand on his own side of the carriage and stare. He couldn't move actually. He wanted to, but he couldn't.

Deklan looked over at his beautiful boyfriend and nodded, which meant Logan was supposed to go with the flow of things if he was hungry or not. "Yes, Dad, we could eat something."

Deklan's father smiled. "I like it when you call me dad."

Deklan grinned, thinking his father always hated it.

Logan let the two of them walk together while he lingered a few steps behind. He was planning to hold his pace at bay and let the two gentlemen bond the way they should have a while ago. It was important not to get in the way of the noticeable baby steps Deklan and his father were taking. Whatever happened during the night to Deklan's father ended up being a good thing. Logan was a little stunned, but really happy about that.

While they all walked, Logan overheard most of the conversation and felt at ease that it was okay for him to tag along too. No harm with him lingering in the back while he enjoyed what was being heard.

"Deklan?" Dante started.

"Yes, Fa—" —he clogged—"Dad." Deklan took off his jacket and flipped it over his shoulder.

"I love you, son. You do know that, right?" Dante stopped and turned Deklan toward him by the shoulders.

"Sure, Dad. Yeah."

"And I would do anything in the world to make sure you knew that, even if discovered later that a mistake was made."

"I know you would, Dad."

Logan claimed he had a bug in his eye, because he was starting to tear up.

Darn those nagging gnats.

"Deklan, please understand what I am going to tell you." Dante looked over at Logan while he rubbed his eyes. He nodded as if to say it was alright for him to overhear.

"No, I'm not crying. I have a bug in my eye." Logan purred.

Deklan's face went sour with an 'oh geeze, now what?' expression gracing it.

Logan just about did the same, but figured to be fair, he'd hear the man out first.

Shedding a little humor on the situation, which helped, Dante mentioned, "Your mother made me sleep on the floor last night. She said if I didn't come to my senses and put an end to all the hard headed nonsense I've put you through, then it would be a permanent place for me along with having to make my own meals if I wanted to eat."

Deklan laughed and so did Logan. They didn't mean to, but what Dante said was funny and he truly deserved it.

Moms know best and they are the real boss in a love-love relationship.

Dante broke the humor with a more serious tone. "Just know that parents do things for their child that they think is best. They may not always be good decisions, but we try. We make sacrifices so you don't have the same worries or problems that we do. Do you understand me?"

"Mm-Hmm." Deklan hummed.

"I was only trying to protect you from what is outside these walls. People don't take a shining to what you have with the stable boy." Dante pointed at Logan.

"Logan," Logan said. "My name is Logan." He waved, which made him look somewhat ridiculous.

A wave? Really?

Deklan grinned and the look in his eyes told Logan that he wanted to kiss him for being so cute and corny.

Logan wanted the same, but wanted to kiss Deklan badly. Very badly.

"Nice to meet you, Logan." Dante turned back to Deklan.

"Likewise, Sir," Logan answered, and waved again.

Apparently Logan didn't learn how senseless the wave was the first time.

Dante turned back toward Deklan and told him, "Your mother told me about the conversation you had with her the other day in your room and I don't want the same thing happening to you."

"You mean, Uncle Joseph?" Deklan clarified, raising a brow.

"Who?" Logan mumbled.

"Yes, Deklan. Your uncle Joseph. My brother," Dante confirmed. "I thought about it all night long so I spent the night out here in the barn to make sure there was no repeat performance of what happened to my brother years ago. I would die right along with you, Deklan."

"Dear lord, Father. I mean, dad. No, I'd never."

"What I want more than anything right now is for you to be safe and happy and I am sorry for getting in the way of that and making you feel as though I hated you for being the person you are supposed to be. I thought I knew best." The idea of Deklan getting injured by another hand or even meeting death because of who he was made Dante understand the treasure he would lose if such a thing happened.

They all finished walking into the house where Deklan's mother was preparing breakfast and the servants were cleaning up after the unsuccessful wedding.

The thought ran through Logan's mind that the white wedding should still go on, but instead, with Deklan and him standing face to face exchanging rings and blowing kisses. If only that could take place, but the truth of the matter was that it would never happen as they stand and breath and certainly not in their lifetime.

For now, Deklan and Logan would have to make up their

own private marriage and run off to their secret lakeside hideaway at every chance they could get.

After breakfast, and unknown to Deklan or probably anybody else, Dante pulled Logan aside and told him that there was a place for him under his roof if he wanted it. Dante said as long as Deklan continued to be as happy as he has been, Logan was part of the family until the end of time. In another breath, Dante let Logan know how good of a person Deklan was and that he was thankful his son was not in the least bit like himself.

That struck a chord with Logan and he had no idea how to respond to what he heard. He just listened and made sure he took in every word Dante said.

Logan saw a good side in Deklan's father that morning and was going to make sure to keep Deklan happy as long as he was alive. Logan wasn't sure Dante was ready for it when he said it, but Logan told him he'd never loved anyone like he loved Deklan.

Dante's face went warped when Logan mentioned the love he had for his son, but he wanted it declared and from what Logan witnessed, the man got over it quick enough.

After they helped Deklan's mother clear the table and stack dishes next to the water basin, they went outside together to visit with Chadwick. That smart horse knew they were coming and took to dancing around the stall like he always did when Deklan and now Logan showed up.

Chapter 39

Freedom was easing in on Deklan and Logan and it felt terrific but somewhat abnormal if that makes any sense. It was a different kind of feeling, but a desirable one.

Logan smiled, kissed the love of his life and then helped Deklan hoist the saddle onto Chadwick's back before they rode off together on horseback to their favorite place under the pear tree. Yes, that's right, the pear tree. It was the first place they met by accident. It was the place where Deklan and Logan sat during the more troublesome days. It was the same place they always seemed to run into each other whenever either of them were out and thinking they were alone. It was the place their souls actually collided one day and from then on it was meant that the two halves become one soul. It was in the plan from above.

As usual, Logan's prince climbed up on Chadwick first and then reached a heroic hand down to swing him in place at his backside. He was getting good at that and the weight Logan carried only seemed to make Deklan stronger every time he tossed him into the seat behind him. The horse was a big one, so it was a long way from the ground to the saddle on his back.

Deklan snapped the reigns and Chadwick took off running.

He mentioned the clover field to the horse and away he went. To Logan, he had never come across a horse that knew the English language like this one did, but harpin' horny toads that Clydesdale caught every word and knew what was being asked of him.

The wind Chadwick created while he ran felt good against their faces and the rolling gallop seemed much smoother than the buggy ride they took earlier. The way a horse runs feels as though his feet never hit the ground. The sensation of floating above the clouds always comes to mind when running the fields on horseback.

Deklan and Logan made it to the pear tree were they were finally all alone and their secret love for one another could get started.

Before getting down from Chadwick's saddle, Logan pressed his body against Deklan's back and gave him one of the biggest and tightest hugs he'd ever given him. His hand slipped under his shirt and he felt flesh and soft hair. It excited Logan and he pulled him closer.

Deklan turned his head back and nipped Logan lightly on the lips. "Omigawd, I Love you, Logan." His hand rested over Logan's and he gave it a gentle squeeze.

Deklan slid off Chadwick first the way he always did and then helped Logan down where he trapped him with his backside against the horse for that expected dismount kiss. If Logan wasn't crazy, he truly believed Chadwick was in on the ritual kiss and made sure not to move until Logan was touching ground and he was lip locked mouth to mouth with Deklan.

"Who do you love?" Deklan blurted out.

"You of course," Logan said.

When the kiss was over, Chadwick moved away.

Deklan grabbed Logan's hand and led him under the pear tree. On the way he plucked a pear from the closest branch, tossed it to Chadwick and then reached up for another one that both of them could share.

They sat under the tree in the shade while Chadwick munched on one of his favorite treats. Clovers.

Deklan and Logan shared the crunchy pear, kissing each other between bites. Sweet intoxicating love for sure, but it was the way they felt about each other and couldn't stop the feeling. One bite. One kiss. Another bite, another kiss.

Deklan took the last bite and then tossed the core someplace behind them. The same way he devoured the pear, Deklan went for Logan. One nip and one kiss at a time until it led them into something more. Soon after much petting and fevered kissing, both were lying nude beneath the pear tree.

Funny how that works.

Logan took to lying on his side and faced Deklan, completely in love with him without a doubt. Deklan's physical form was a true bonus and the fact that Deklan loved Logan's as much as he loved his, made the two of them insanely compatible.

Deklan ran his hand down Logan's chest. "I love your skin," he said. "It's like glistening brown silk and when I touch you I get chills." He continued down Logan's abdomen and then took his blossoming hardness into both hands.

After a brief moment of instant exhilaration, Logan smiled at Deklan and kissed his chest. Kissed his beautiful hairy chest that smelled like lavender oil and mixed spices. He then moved his kisses to Deklan's lips, pecking him lightly. "I have a thought," He mentioned, pulling his lips away slowly.

"What's that?" Deklan whispered and then he rolled on top of Logan.

Logan grunted from the weight of him, but wouldn't have wanted his pinned situation any differently. "I know it's light out and anybody passing by could see us, but let's be daring and make love, right here under this tree where we first met. It will complete the circle. Tie the knot."

"Let's do it." Deklan grinned wide and then dove for Logan's mouth to kiss him hard. His breathing went sharp and his hair fell down against Logan's face, gracing his cheeks as Deklan's head rotated to take Logan's tongue.

Logan's hands touched Deklan and the hair on his chest pleased Logan's fingers. The feel of Logan's hands against his chest only made Deklan grow harder. His extension was like a rock and it was getting bigger by the second.

A deep moan escaped Deklan as he sensed Logan's erection move side by side with his.

Deklan's hand found Logan's chest before moving it slowly across his torso until it gripped their erections together in his tightened fist.

Deklan rolled his hips and his expanding organ stroked Logan's. Between the friction and the anticipation of penetrating each other, clear essence leaked from them both.

Deklan felt warm, and Logan's body heated up from each kiss he gave his chest, his neck, his mouth and over his ear. As Deklan ran his wet tongue along Logan's jawline to get back to his mouth, the sensation of a climax seized Logan's body. He craved Deklan and needed him to enter his vacant body badly.

Logan was close to whining from the simple pleasure Deklan gave him and the thrust of his uncontrolled hip motion broke the fisted grip Deklan had on the two of them.

Logan was aching to feel Deklan connect with him, so he told Deklan he needed him straightaway.

To Logan's surprise, Deklan kissed him, broke their embrace and took out a small pat of butter from his shirt pocket that he sneakily stole from his mother's breakfast table.

Logan was proud of Deklan for thinking ahead and giggled a bit as well. He went even harder as he watched Deklan position himself between his open legs and coat his erection with the melted pat.

Deklan was stunning to Logan. He looked so masculine and powerful while he sat propped on his knees with his hand stroking himself. Logan shuddered when Deklan's oily hand brush up against his needy entrance.

Deklan didn't ask if Logan was ready for him, he just pushed his way in until every large inch was so far inside that Logan could feel him in his chest.

Deklan was gentle and powerful when he needed to be and after a few hard rolls of his hips that forced himself even deeper into Logan, Deklan then dropped down and passionately kissed him until tears greeted the corners of Logan's eyes.

Logan was so in love with Deklan that feeling their souls

join the way they did tipped his emotions to a level that made him weep. Every time Logan was with Deklan, it was incredible. Every time Deklan moved inside him, it was amazing. Logan really loved Deklan and his uncontrollable tears made it known.

Deklan groaned with desire for Logan as he felt his boyfriend take him in. It was peculiar in a perfect way how Logan's body craved him so much that it actually pulled Deklan deeper inside of him.

They moved together perfectly. Friction was building and massive explosions were about to be released.

Possessing Logan, kissing him with rising desire and need, Deklan hummed broken words in his ear as he lay tightly on top of him. "You're amazing, Logan." — he gasped — "are you - ready" — he huffed — "oh gawd" — he groaned — "for me - Logan." His face changed to a pleasured knot.

Deklan felt so good to Logan that he struggled with his answer. "Yes - Dek." He lost control of his orgasm and started spraying streams of hot essence between their chests.

The scent of Logan's release smothered Deklan and his entire body went hard and every muscle grew taught. An extraordinary buzz dominated him as he released a lively part of himself deep within Logan.

Logan went warm at the very second Deklan pumped his living essence inside him.

The orgasm was long and seemed to last forever. Deklan lay over top of Logan, sensitive and trembling as Logan did the same, but comfortably beneath him.

Their mouths met and they both inhaled each other's breath while convulsing until they settled. Slowly reaching their calm, they went on kissing as their passion turned from roaring lust to sensual and tender.

Halfway through cooling down from their rampant lust, Logan started laughing. He didn't mean to, but it just came out. He thought it was because he was happier than he ever was and he couldn't control his true emotions for the beautiful man on top of him.

"What?" Deklan laughed back, still moving his hips, but

slowing down as he did.

"I'm Sorry. I just love you so much and I can't believe this is happening." Logan squeezed him tighter, pulling him in. "I think after all this time, I am finally in a place I want to be and I feel relaxed enough to really enjoy my smile."

"That's a relief. I thought you had a change of heart as to how well I make you feel." Deklan came back down on Logan and they locked lips again.

"Never," Logan mumbled. He couldn't believe what they went through to get to where they were today.

To shut Logan up, Deklan pushed again, going deeper than he was before.

It worked. Logan's head spun and his eyes rolled back in his head. Deklan was surly talented and he did incredible things with his erection.

"Now let's trade places." Deklan's voice was deep and sexy, but a grunt followed it when he grabbed Logan's shoulders and rolled him over.

The ring was on Logan's finger and the necklace was still around his neck. "This belongs to you." He removed the neck piece and transferred it over Deklan's head. It looked good against his hairy chest and the glow the two trinkets made as they were separated let it be known that the two beautiful white gold pieces were married and shouldn't be placed apart.

Logan looked down into Deklan's eyes and every thought he had about him being exiled had vanished.

Deklan was free and so was Logan.

Logan loved Deklan and Deklan loved Logan.

Epilogue

A letter from Logan;

My time together with Deklan was marked as special. Very special, actually. It always was.

Our love affair on the great plantation started when my mirror man sent me on a secret mission to find my true love. He knew what he was doing and he picked the perfect time and day to do it. I never knew what happened to him after that night or if he even really existed. I understood my father had a hand in the great event and both also knew it was a chap I was looking for. I loved them for what they did for me and cherished their understanding more than they may know.

Deklan and I never really talked about that magical night, but I am sure in a crazy way that he wasn't dreaming either. Angel's and fairies quietly guide us in mysterious ways, I seem to think. Mine came to me in the form of a white image of myself and I seem to think Deklan's friend Jeddah was his Angel or Fairy as well. He also just disappeared after he closed and locked the door on that disastrous wedding day. We were two men in love and had help getting started by our guardians of mystery. However, we sadly had to keep our love for each other a secret from those who would rather see us hanged than watch us hold hands. This I do not understand and never will.

Our happily ever after started back then and when the piece I needed to make me a whole person was brought to me before midnight, I was happy that I could give Deklan the best birthday gift of his life. That precious gift was me and still is today.

Chadwick is still part of our lives and loves taking Deklan

and me everywhere we go, including that perfect pear tree that was and always will be our most memorable place. It still remains secluded in the middle of an overgrown field of tall grass and clovers and we still make love under that tree every time and again. I truly believe that some of our spilled essence just may be making that fruit tree grow into what it is today. It's one of the best trees in the field and not a single bad fruit piece comes off of it. I swear. Call it a fate of two souls that started and kept going with that flourishing tree.

As for the lake, Deklan and I have been slowly clearing a place for our new home. Chadwick has been a big help too when it comes to sowing the field. He's so smart that it makes me wonder if the mirror man found a place in him where he can keep an eye on both of us. I am still wondering about that to this day.

Anyway, back to the progression of our home on the lake. It's taking some time, but slowly and surely we will get there. My dream home with Deklan is a cozy little house, with a porch we can sit on with the dog and the cat while overlooking the lake out in front of us. The stacked stone fireplace on the inside will be a nice perk for when those cold winter nights creep up on us and cuddling with my handsome man needs just a little more heat.

Deklan's father is bequeathing the plantation to him and me, in which we will someday own and run, but truthfully the two of us would like to make a home of our own. So until that bequeathing day arrives, we are building the house of our dreams on the secret lake we call our hiding place while living together in a new wing at the Manor. Yes, I said together. We are a family now and I love that I can sleep with Deklan, share my body with Deklan and love Deklan every day and night under the same roof as his parents. Times are changing, but unfortunately not fast enough. We still have to kiss when nobody is looking. That part of our affair I don't like and find it strange that people see it as odd.

Here goes nothing. I would love to marry my man, my soul mate, my lover, my friend, but as I see it now, the written constitution will never be changed to allow it as long as President Chester A. Arthur remains commander-in-chief. Perhaps the next President will, or maybe the next. From what I can tell, neither I nor Deklan will ever see that day.

Today, Deklan and I still interrupt the others sleep during the night to make love and I don't see it coming to an end any time soon. Our new-lad love for the other just refuses to fade.

It's difficult for me to explain how much I love Deklan, but when he's away from me and out of my sight, my heart hurts and the ring on my finger hums. This proves to me the magic is still alive.

Until next time, Love from Logan.

THE END

ABOUT THE AUTHOR

Gregory Jonathan Scott was born and raised in Grand Rapids, Michigan where he met and shared a life with Scott that began just out of high school. Meeting by chance in Grand Rapids before relocating to South Florida where they live now with their lovable Shetland sheepdog and a sweet stray cat that showed up one day and decided to make their house a home.

As a child, Gregory was always told he had a creative imagination and the artistic ability to turn a blank canvas into an eye catching work of art. Shortly after high school graduation, and together with his true love Scott, discovered the thrill of pottery and ceramic art. Here is where the two of them opened a business for ceramists that quickly exploded before their eyes as the number one location for any hobbyist, storefront and scholastic industry looking for supplies related to ceramics and pottery. During this time, Gregory was approached by art magazines to write short articles and educational columns pertaining to the ceramic artistry. Captivating readers by his writing style grew fast, which ignited his desire to express himself further. From there, it began. Finding a love for writing, alongside his artistic hand, gave him inspiration to design and write this M/M romance Novel.

Gregory and Scott are still together and are currently enjoying home life in South Florida.

OTHER WORK BY
Gregory Jonathan Scott

HEARTBREAK BEAT

www.ingramcontent.com/pod-product-compliance
Lightning Source LLC
Chambersburg PA
CBHW030923120626
46554CB00001B/253